Lindsay Badenoch is an archaeolog
Anglo-Saxon period. Her interest   .... and
religious as well as the purely historical aspects of the past.
She lives in London and works for English Heritage editing
archaeological site reports for publication.

LINDSAY BADENOCH

THE DAUGHTER OF THE RUNES

A NOVEL

LONDON AND NEW YORK

First publised in 1988 by ARKANA Paperbacks
ARKANA Paperbacks is an imprint of
Routledge
11 New Fetter Lane, London EC4P 4EE

29 West 35th Street, New York NY 10001

© Lindsay Badenoch 1988
Printed in Great Britain
by The Guernsey Press Co. Ltd.

Library of Congress Cataloging in Publication Data

Badenoch, Lindsay.
The Daughter of the runes/Lindsay Badenoch
p.   cm.
Bibliography: p.
1. Great Britain—History—Anglo-Saxon period, 449–1066—Fiction.
I. Title
PR6052.A313C7 1988
823'.914—dc19   88–4265

British Library Cataloguing in Publication Data

Badenoch, Lindsay
The daughter of the runes.
I. Title
823'.914 [F]

ISBN 1–850–63114–X

AUTHOR'S NOTE

The novel is set in the 630s AD. Fryth, her village, and all who inhabit it, are my own invention, but I have tried to recreate as far as possible an authentic picture of life in an Anglo-Saxon village of the seventh century.

I have drawn extensively from the surviving record of Anglo-Saxon magic and medicine. All the charms, spells and riddles in the book, however corrupted by later generations of scholars (and my own attempts to make sense of sometimes very obscure passages), are the real voice of Anglo-Saxon sorcery. I have sometimes adapted, but I have made nothing up.

Students of Anglo-Saxon literature may be surprised to discover that Fryth was responsible for so many of the poems in the language. I hope they will excuse the liberty I have taken.

Some of the characters who appear in the book are historical personages. Peada, the son of King Penda of Mercia, was made king of Middle Anglia by his father. The City of Peterborough is named after him. He was murdered in 656. The Abbess Heiu was the first woman in Northumbria to become a nun. The monastery at Heruteu, modern Hartlepool, was founded by her, probably in the mid 640s, although I have set the date slightly earlier. Heiu was succeeded at Heruteu by Saint Hilda who went on to become the famous Abbess of Whitby. The only record we have of Hildigyth is her name on a tombstone found at Hartlepool. I have imagined her character and history.

Monasteries housing both men and women were not unusual in the seventh century. This is not the place for a discourse on distinction between the Celtic and Roman Church in the century before the Synod of Whitby, but undoubtedly there would have been Celtic influences at Heruteu, founded as it was under the direction of Saint Aidan. Aidan received his religious training in Ireland, as did my invention, the monk Cruithnechan.

For those interested in the history of the period, F. M. Stenton's *Anglo-Saxon England*, Oxford (3rd edition), 1971, is the major work of reference. For a more general introduction D. J. V. Fisher's *The Anglo-Saxon Age c.400–1042*, Longman, 1973, is very helpful. Both H. R. Loyn, *Anglo-Saxon England and the Norman Conquest*, Longman, 1962, and Christine Fell, *Women in Anglo-Saxon England*, British Museum Publications, 1984, illuminate Anglo-Saxon social and economic history.

There are fewer books for the general reader on the archaeology of the period. The best, though brief, is D. M. Wilson's *The Anglo-Saxons*, Penguin (re-issue), 1986. The more academic, *The Archaeology of Anglo-Saxon England*, edited by D. M. Wilson, Cambridge, 1981, gives a fuller picture and refers to the monastery at Hartlepool.

The following books were extremely useful in the researching of this novel. References found in them will guide readers who wish to know more about Anglo-Saxon religion and magic to further reading.

Branston, B. *The Lost Gods of England*, Thames and Hudson, 1957. (Reprinted 1974.)

Cockayne, T. O. *The Leechdoms, Wortcunning and Starcraft of Early England*, re-issue, Holland Press, 1961.

Davidson, H. R. E. *Gods and Myths of Northern Europe*, Penguin, 1964.

Elliot, R. V. W. *Runes, an Introduction*, Manchester University Press, 1959.

Mayr-Harting, H. *The Coming of Christianity to Anglo-Saxon England*, B. T. Batsford, 1972.

Meany, A. L. *Anglo-Saxon Amulets and Curing Stones*, British Archaeological Reports (British series), Oxford, 1981.

Owen, G. R. *The Rites and Religions of Anglo-Saxon England*, David and Charles, 1981.

Page, R. I.   *An Introduction to Anglo-Saxon Runes*, Methuen, 1973.

Storms, G.   *Anglo-Saxon Magic*, The Hague, Martinus Nijhoff, 1948.

I would also like to thank the author and publishers for permission to quote from 'Wolf and Eadwacer' from *The Battle of Maldon and other Old English Poems*, translated by Kevin Crossley-Holland and edited by Bruce Mitchell, published by Macmillan.

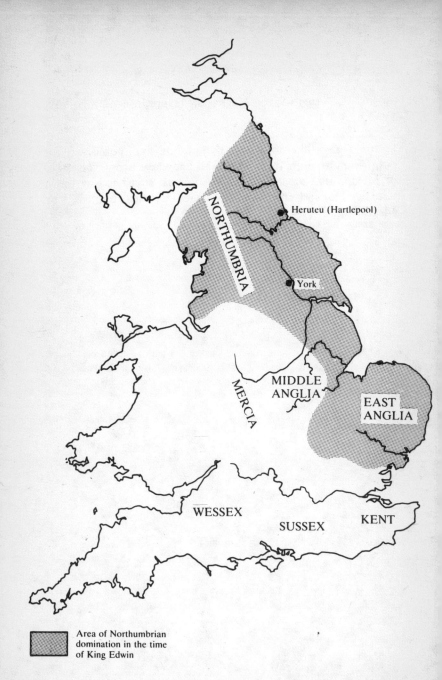

NORTHUMBRIA

Heruteu (Hartlepool)

York

MIDDLE
ANGLIA

MERCIA

EAST
ANGLIA

WESSEX

SUSSEX

KENT

Area of Northumbrian
domination in the time
of King Edwin

A shrill voice was calling. It grew ever more insistent as she struggled to ignore it. She was happy and at peace here in this cool, green shade. Whoever was summoning her wanted to drag her back, she knew, into a world of pain and suffering. The voice came from burning buildings, tortured bodies; it was a rising shriek of agony.

Her eyes snapped open onto dazzling sunlight. Its brightness seared her eyeballs, forcing her to clench her eyelids shut again. The shrieking continued, disembodied, closer now. She opened her eyes again, this time very slowly, becoming gradually accustomed to the light. She raised a hand to shield them and saw, before her face, long bony fingers whose joints stood out like pebbles in their wasted flesh. She let her hand fall back and felt her knuckles scrape on the rough wooden floor. She was lying on a thin mattress, scarcely higher than the floor itself. The floor looked pale and new and gave off a familiar smell. The smell meant something to her but she could not connect her mind with what it was. She groaned aloud, turned her face into the unyielding pillow, and fell at once into a profound sleep.

The sun was lower in the sky when she woke again, this time with no struggle. Her eyes opened easily and she slowly looked about her, taking in the room in which she lay. It was small and bare with a little window which, from where she lay, looked only onto sky. The floor was wooden planks, newly cut, with shaggy splinters. The walls were smooth and white, like chalk, like no walls she had seen before. A raw salty smell pervaded everything, prickling in her nostrils.

She was lying on her back with her arms down by her sides,

she raised her arms slowly, then caught her breath. The skin on her arms hung in loose folds. There was no flesh on them, or on her hands, or, she raised the coarse blanket covering her, on any of her body. She was a living skeleton,

Her head swam. Her eyes took in her wasted body and her white surroundings, but her brain could make no sense of what she saw. She had no idea what questions she should ask herself, she had no point of reference, nowhere to begin. She stared vacantly at the blue square of sky outside the window. A white bird sailed into it and hung there, almost stationary, barely moving its wings. Its yellow webbed feet hung down and it moved its head in quick jerks from side to side, eyeing her. Suddenly it gave a piercing shriek, shrugged its slow wings and disappeared from view.

Before the shriek had died away, echoing round the bare white room, everything came back to her. The full force of remembrance struck her like a blow, or like the flames of a burning building in the uprush of a draught. The white bird had called her back. It had seen her lying on this cheerless bed and called her from the spirit world. She clasped her bony hands together, feeling the loose dry skin. If it had not called her, she would never have returned. There would have been nothing left to come to.

Questions crowded into her brain. How long had she been lying here? Who had brought her here? Where *was* here? She tried to raise her voice and cry for help. Her voice astonished her. She mustered all the breath she had, but the smallest mouse would have made a louder noise than the frail squeaking coming from her lips. She tried again; this time it was weaker still. Thin tears filled her eyes. They came as tears of frustration, but soon that gave way to a real and dreadful sorrow.

She wept for all the past years; for all she'd lost. The anguish of her memories welled into her eyes and racked her shrivelled body with harsh sobs. But there was a pain even greater than this memory of loss. It was that she should have been brought back into the world to suffer it. She cursed the bird. For whose sake had it recalled her? Not for hers. She cursed a second time and, as she cursed, its pure white form sailed into the square patch of blue again. A little silver fish was dangling from its beak. The bird looked down at her, gave another shriek, and the fish fell twisting through the sky with the sunlight flashing on its scales.

Gradually her sobs subsided and she turned once more to sleep.

She woke at the light touch of a hand on her cheek. There was a rustling sound, then a whispered voice said excitedly,

'I think she's come back. Look, this isn't the way she normally lies!' There was a sharp intake of breath and then another whisper, this time a different voice.

'She seems to be sleeping. Properly I mean, real sleep.' Fryth stirred and turned her head. Two women were bending over her. When she moved they both started back, crossing themselves. They stared at her, then at each other, then at her again.

'Where am I?' she asked, as loudly as she could.

'Well!' One of them whispered on an outrush of breath, 'Who would have believed it!'

'Her eyes are open.' They were staring at each other again.

'It's a miracle, it must be!'

'Sorcery more like!'

'Whatever it is, it is truly a wonder!' Fryth's eyes had been moving from face to face during this whispered exchange. It seemed that in their excitement they had forgotten her.

'Where am I?' she said again.

'You see!' This was said triumphantly. 'She speaks!' Fryth was growing desperate.

'Please,' she repeated piteously, 'where am I? What am I doing here?' This time her voice checked the women's breathless rush. They paused and turned their eyes on Fryth again. One knelt down beside her bed. She looked straight at Fryth, as if seeing her for the first time.

'You're here, in Heruteu,' she said.

'Where's that?'

'Northumbria,' replied the other woman. 'By the sea.'

'Northumbria?'

'Yes, of course, where else?'

'I didn't know.' Fryth answered weakly. A wave of loneliness and isolation washed over her. In Heruteu, in Northumbria, by the sea . . . .

'So far from home!' She groaned aloud, 'Who brought me here?' She remembered the Northumbrian soldiers, and the fire-light leaping in her captor's eyes. The second woman knelt beside her too.

'Our Abbess Heiu.' The words came tumbling out. 'She was travelling in the south. She met some warriors at York, they were returning from a raid. They had you with them.'

'They found you among the Mercian pagans and idolators. They thought you were a Christian, and rescued you, and brought you safe to Northumbria.'

'But on the way they started to have doubts.' The women spoke as one, one taking up the story when the other paused for breath.

'You lay so still,' the second woman's eyes sparkled at the adventure she was recounting, 'and you scarcely breathed. You needed neither food nor water, but lay as if enchanted. They began to grow afraid.'

'Five days they carried you like that, but then they wanted to be rid of you.'

'They were decent men, but they had had enough. They planned to leave you there, beside the road if necessary. Heiu took pity on you. She offered to take care of you.'

'Those soldiers were only too pleased to have you taken off their hands.'

'And did your Ab.., Ab.., this Heiu, believe I was enchanted?' asked Fryth cautiously.

'Oh yes,' came back the definite reply. 'What other expla-nation is there? Do you know how long it's been? Two weeks! Two weeks without food or water, like a dormouse. What else could possibly account for it? We didn't think you would survive, you've lain there so long like a dead thing; and yet each day I'd hold my knife to your lips and each day your breath would cloud it.'

The second woman had left the room. Now she returned carrying a bowl of milk, and another filled with soup. The smell of food brought the saliva rushing painfully to Fryth's mouth. She had felt no pangs of hunger until then. The contents of both bowls were swallowed in an instant, and she asked for more.

'You'll soon get your strength up,' said one. The other shook her head wonderingly as she gathered up the pots,

'It *is* a miracle, wherever it has come from,' she said.

'We must leave you, it's time for Mass.'

'I expect the Abbess will visit you when Mass is over.'

Fryth's head sank back on the pillow. She felt extremely weak. She had not the energy to ask what Mass or Abbess meant, but she smiled a little to herself. These women knew she was enchanted and still had taken care of her, had taken her in. Her strategy had worked. It had carried her through the period of most danger. She was safe.

Her eyelids drooped. 'Like a dormouse.' The woman had spoken truer than she knew, for where had Fryth been but with the animal spirits, guarded by her fox?

PART I

THE PRIESTESS

The women left the village at dusk. The evening's occupations had begun; hearths were being stoked, pots stirred and looms pulled from corners. The quiet, familiar comforts of daily life were left behind as they crossed the open fields and entered the dense forest that lay beyond.

The path was narrow and overhung and the women followed the footsteps of their leader closely. They walked steadily and in silence, a silence which was broken only by the occasional cracking of a twig underfoot or the swishing of a branch swept aside. Their leader was the village priestess, and sorceress of all her tribe. She carried a small whimpering bundle, her baby daughter, whose complaints were the only human sounds in the forest. Tonight the new-born baby would be dedicated to her mother's calling.

The women emerged into a clearing and paused briefly, looking about them. Under the full moon the forest grove formed a bowl of white light carved out of the darkness of the trees. The clearing was wide; the large oaks which lined its edges made a natural apse. At the curve of the apse was a shallow bank. A small spring of clear bright water, gleaming now and then in the moonlight, flowed over the bank and into a huge urn at its foot. The urn, handmade, was decorated with an intricate design long since worn smooth and almost indecipherable by the continual overflow of water.

The women gathered round the spring. One drew a pitch-soaked torch from the folds of her cloak; another reached to her waist for the fire-steel that hung there. It struck flame with the first blow and the torch blazed out. The women were tall and fair. The torch light glittered on the massive gilded brooches that they all wore, and brought out softer gleams in their heavy swags of glass and amber beads.

The child was quieter now, her soft, unfocused eyes dazzled by the bright torch flame, but she let out a wail when her mother unwrapped the woollen swaddling. The small, protesting body was bathed in moonlight as the priestess raised it high in the air above her head. The priestess began a slow, rhythmic incantation and the torch was passed swiftly underneath the baby, so fast that not a flame could singe. The chanting swelled, its rhythm becoming more rapid and staccato. The women began to sway in time with the song, they rocked backwards and forwards, faster and faster, until, on one swift intake of breath, the child was plunged into the water in the urn, and out – as quickly – on the exhalation.

Crying now in earnest, the baby was warmly wrapped again and held closely to her mother's breast. The women drew into a tight circle round mother and child. They passed the torch three times round the pair, then dropped it hissing into the black water in the urn.

The moon had set.

CHAPTER 1

Fryth sat with her back against a tree. For once her small brother
had allowed himself to be distracted by the doll she had made
for him out of earth and spit. He was patting it about in the
dust a little way off from where she sat. The pigs, more torpid
than usual in the midday heat, flopped and dozed. Relieved of
her responsibilities for a short while, Fryth relaxed. She felt her
eyelids droop. The tree's rough bark was warm against her
shoulders; the sun filtered through its leaves casting a pleasant,
dappled shade. Just as she was slipping into a deep sleep Fryth
was roused by a slight tingling sensation at the back of her neck.
She opened her eyes. Something was wrong. She sat up straight
and stared about her. Nothing looked different. Guthlac had
squashed the doll and was happily smearing the remains over
his face. The pigs grunted and wallowed.

A sharp smell stung her nostrils. It was acrid and rank. She
stood up straight and shielded her eyes against the sun, squinting
down the track that led away from the village. She saw a faint
smudge in the air. A cloud of dust was hanging above the ridge
that separated this valley from the next. The cloud thickened
and gathered, the smell grew stronger and, cresting the ridge,
she saw a band of men. More than a band, as they came on
steadily up the path Fryth realized that a great troop of warriors
was marching towards the village, stinking in their sweaty gear.

Fryth snatched Guthlac up out of the dust. The pigs, startled
by her sudden movement, leaped to their feet squealing, and
scattered. Her first instinct was to chase after them, her second
to run as fast as she could and raise the alarm. She was hampered
by Guthlac, four years old and heavy for her slight frame. He

struggled and kicked, not understanding her desperation. Long before she reached the village the warriors caught up with her. Their leader, a young man with a thick red moustache, caught her by the arm, spinning her round. His eyes were full of laughter. He called to two of his men to round up the pigs.

'You'd make a better watchdog without these animals.' The young man laughed, indicating Guthlac who was trying to bite him, and the pigs squealing in a swirling mass between his men, who, with knees bent and arms outstretched, were by degrees assembling the little herd.

'There's no need to be frightened,' he said. His voice sounded odd and guttural, his vowels flat. 'We've not come to harm you. The elders of your village may even be expecting us. We'll follow you down.'

Fryth was reassured by his friendly smiling eyes, and more so when he unhitched the broad circular shield from his back, turned it upside down like a tray and sat Guthlac in it, then he hoisted the shield, child and all, onto his shoulder. Thus, led by Fryth, at the head of his troop he came down into the village.

Later that night Fryth's father came to her mother's house. Like all the warriors in the tribe Edward divided his time between his wife's house and the beer-hall. The men lived a communal life in the hall, drinking together at the tables that lined the walls and sleeping, if they chose to stay, on the benches or the rush-strewn floor. The men regularly feasted together, but many nights of the month Edward would eat at Eangyth's hearth and sleep in her bed. Tonight he was not expected.

A meeting was in progress in the beer-hall. Eangyth had been there earlier. She had poured her husband his first drink and stayed long enough to discover the errand of the visiting warriors. When she had learned all she needed to know she left the men. They were obviously set in for a long session. Maybe such an occasion would warrant several days' drinking.

Fryth was surprised, therefore, to see her father, obviously sober, and with a worried frown on his face.

'What is happening to us, Eangyth?' he said as he came in

through the door. Her mother turned from the fire. She had been preparing for bed. She looked at her husband, sighed, and kicked the fire back to life. Edward began to pace about the room. His face was alternately bathed in the firelight's red glow and clouded by deep shadows.

'To put ourselves under the overlordship of the Mercians. To give up our independence willingly, even cheerfully, for payment! How could Cerdic even consider it?'

Eangyth stood quite still, watching her husband's anxious movements thoughtfully.

'You knew this was coming,' she said. 'You knew it as well as Cerdic. You know we can't possibly withstand the strength of Mercia, or Northumbria for that matter, on our own. None of our tribe is Woden born. We're not rich, and we're not at all powerful.' Her husband frowned.

'Our warriors are brave and strong,' he said.

Eangyth took his arm, checking his restless pacing. She shook her head gently.

'Brave in the beer-hall, and strong at the plough. None of you are fighting men. We can't stand alone. If we fight for the Mercians against the Northumbrians they'll pay us well and give us weapons. . . .'

'We've got weapons. . . .'

'. . . to replace our rusty spears. If we refuse their offer they'll fight us sooner or later. And if they don't, the Northumbrians will. One way or the other we'll be defeated and enslaved.' She looked her husband in the eye. 'We've no choice, Edward.'

Fryth's father squatted down by the fire and held his head in his hands. Eangyth put a hand on his shoulder.

'This isn't a disgrace,' she said. 'There never was any disgrace in good sense. We keep our lands, we receive payment. . . .'

'Which we shall have to return as tribute.'

'Better that than slavery. Listen. Our ancestors settled here, not for the prospect of battle, whatever the men may boast in the beer-hall, but because the land was good, and easy under our ploughs. We worship Freya, the mother of the earth, not

14

the god of war. She has protected us. We've grown and flourished; our children are healthy, they live to take care of us when
we grow old. The Mercians are our brothers. There'll be no
shame in fighting beside them. Penda's a strong leader, a man
worthy to be followed. Surely you can see that it's better to be
a follower of a mighty war-lord, than a lordless slave?' Edward
grunted.

'The Northumbrians are our brothers, too.'

'One or other will have us,' said Eangyth wearily, 'nothing
can stop that now.'

'To think that it should come to this!'

'Cerdic's still our own war-leader, wherever we fight. Besides,
his thoughts are as slippery as eels. By tomorrow he'll be saying
that we've persuaded the Mercians to fight for us! Go and join
them Edward or they'll think you're the coward you think them.'

Edward sighed deeply and rose to his feet. He was a huge
man, a skilful farmer, famed for his singing in the hall. He had
once been a famous harpist too, but those days were over. Years
of hard physical labour had taken their toll and his fingers were
swollen with arthritis now. He looked across the room to where
their three boys were sleeping on mats on the floor; and then
to Eangyth's bed where Fryth, his eldest child lay. Although her
head was in the shadows, she quickly closed her eyes, pretending
to be asleep. Edward sighed again. Perhaps Eangyth was right,
Penda would certainly make a noble overlord. A man should be
proud to serve such a famous warrior. He spat into the fire and
went out to join the men.

Fryth, watching from the shadows, saw her mother shiver and
pull her soft woollen robe more closely round her. Eangyth
threw another log onto the fire. She reached into a box by her
stool and pulled a small leather bag from its depths. She took
a crystal ball the size of a pigeon's egg from the bag. She passed
the crystal three times through the flames and then squatted
down, staring at it in front of her, as still and quiet as a toad.

Fryth drifted to sleep. She woke in the pale dawn. Sounds of
drunken mirth floated over the village from the beer-hall. The

fire was out but Eangyth's body still held the same position. Fryth knew that her mother's soul was wandering in the spirit world, but where that world was, or how to enter it, Fryth did not know.

The English had been in the land for nearly two hundred years. They had come in small groups of people, little tribes pushing up the river valleys of the eastern seaboard in shallow-keeled, open boats. They cleared the forests with their finely balanced axes and cut deep furrows in the rich valley soils with their heavy ploughs.

They met with little resistance; most of the land they chose was uninhabited. Where they had fought, it was often against each other. Over the years, warriors stronger and braver than the rest, and more skilled in war, had carved large kingdoms for themselves out of the lesser tribes. These tribes were losing their identity, becoming, in the midlands, east and north, simply Mercians, East Anglians or Northumbrians.

Some small tribes had not yet been absorbed because their lands were either too poor or too remote to be worth the effort. But now, with the steady encroachment of the larger kingdoms over the whole country, the lands of even the smallest had taken on a strategic significance. Particularly where it happened that they lay between two warring powers.

Fryth's tribe had led a quiet existence since its arrival on the banks of a narrow, fast-flowing river in a remote part of the country known as Middle Anglia. They were skilled farmers and had done much with the fertile land. Their wheat fields were rich, their mares produced strong foals, their cattle gave plenty of milk and their sheep thick wool. They knew from songs that their ancestors in the old country had been warriors of renown, glorious in victory, falling to the last man in defeat. Every child was brought up on stories of the heroes, and there was much talk of deeds of heroism among the men; but only the very oldest of them had seen battle, and that had been nothing more than a local, inglorious skirmish from which, though this had somehow been forgotten, they had returned battered and defeated.

History, however, had caught up with them at last.

When the Mercian embassy had gone, Cerdic called on Eangyth. He stood outside the door and sent a page, his young son, into the low wooden building with its steep thatched roof. He himself would not step over the threshold. Magic concentrated round a powerful sorceress, and he preferred to meet her in the open air.

Eangyth came out. Both inclined their heads, each conscious of the status of the other. Cerdic cleared his throat.

'I've asked your husband for his advice,' he said. 'He believes I'm doing the right thing.'

'He thinks as you do, he understands you had no choice.'

'And you?' Cerdic searched her face anxiously. 'What do you think?'

Eangyth did not answer at once. Instead she looked up, squinting at the sky. A buzzard was wheeling over the forest beyond the clearing. It mewed once, a high-pitched mournful sound, and dipped out of sight. Cerdic, watching with Eangyth, gripped the handle of the knife at his belt.

'I have looked into the future as far as I can see,' said Eangyth slowly. Cerdic's knuckles whitened as he tightened his grip. 'I saw our fate threaded on the loom. It's always been one even colour, but now I see a skein of another colour waiting to be woven in. The colour is of blood.'

Cerdic let out a long breath. Then he drew himself up to his full height and squared his shoulders.

'This is no more than I already knew,' he said firmly. 'The weapons will be here soon. Meanwhile the men need training.'

Eangyth was sitting by the fire when her daughter came in from the evening's milking. Fryth went up to her quietly and sat down, leaning against her mother's knees. She loved to feel the softness of her woollen dress and to press her cheeks against the coolness of the metal keys hanging at her waist. They sat in companionable silence for a while.

Eangyth was the first to speak. 'You're growing, Fryth,' she said, stroking her daughter's hair. It was dark, a strange thing among all her fair children. Fryth was small and lightly built, her skin was pale and her eyes a bright restless blue. Eangyth remembered the child's frail body in the moonlight, the look of outrage on the tiny face, and her own pleased surprise that so puny a thing could take such treatment with no ill effect. Freya had marked her both in form and strength and soon Fryth would be given to her.

Eangyth gripped Fryth by the chin and turned her face up until she was looking her directly in the eyes. She smiled thoughtfully, and glancing down, touched the bunch of household keys hanging at her waist.

'You know what these are for, don't you, Fryth?'

'Of course, they lock your boxes.'

'And what about these?' She was touching another set of hangers, smaller than the iron keys. They were key-shaped in a way but were oddly flattened and lacked wards. Fryth caught her breath. She had always known that these hangers were connected with her mother's magic, but from an early age she had learned not to question Eangyth about her work; so had her brothers, and no one else would dare.

'Fryth?' said Eangyth, sensing the tension in her daughter, 'Did you hear me? I asked if you knew what these are for.'

'I know they have something to do with your work, at least I've always guessed they must, but I don't know what it is.' She paused then added bravely, 'Yet.'

Fryth was her mother's heir. The rôle of priestess passed from mother to daughter; it had done so for generations in the tribe. Fryth could just remember her own grandmother, who had been a famous magician in her day, recalling her as a hunched and frail old woman who sat mumbling by the fire. She remembered her toothless mouth and her peering rheumy eyes. It was difficult to imagine that she had once been held in awe, but Eangyth assured her that her grandmother's great powers had been feared and respected by the whole tribe. Eangyth had learned her arts from her mother and would one day pass them on to Fryth. Fryth had been brought up in the knowledge that a great inheritance was waiting for her, but Eangyth had always been reluctant to discuss it. Fryth had been told about the ceremony in the forest, how she had been shown to the spirits, how Freya had welcomed her and would recognize her when she came to be initiated; but when that initiation was to be, or what it was, Eangyth would not say. Whenever Fryth pressed her, Eangyth's response was the same, 'When the time is right.' But now she was, as it seemed, openly inviting Fryth to ask her about her priesthood. Fryth felt a shiver of excitement run down her spine.

'You know that the singers call the words we use our "word-hoard", Fryth?' Eangyth was saying. Fryth nodded.

'Well, a word-hoard has to be unlocked, but not, of course, with a key like this.' She touched one of her household keys again. 'The keys the singers use are music and inspiration.'

'And beer!' said Fryth. Her mother laughed.

'That's a man's key to most things. But I've another way to unlock my secrets.' She unhooked the girdle-hangers and put them into Fryth's hands. 'These keys show that I have the power to unlock the secrets of the spirit world. The power is in here,' she tapped her breast gently, 'not in the keys themselves, but I wear them to remind me of my great responsibility.' Fryth was stroking the polished bronze, rubbing the flat keys between thumb and forefinger. They were stamped with tiny crescent moons. She looked up at the word responsibility.

'To work with Freya *is* a responsibility, Fryth; to please her, to ensure that she looks favourably on us. Our lives depend on it.'

'I know that, mother,' Fryth said quietly. 'I know how important your work is.'

'But sometimes I think you see me as some kind of warrior, like Cerdic in the hall, looking for fame. It isn't like that, Fryth. It is hard and dangerous, but where a warrior must push himself forward to find glory, and bring honour and safety to the tribe, a priestess must lose herself, give in entirely to the goddess's will.'

Fryth scarcely dared to breathe. She drew a little away from her mother, watching her closely. She knew how even Cerdic, who feared nothing, was wary of Eangyth's powers. How only children and foolish old women were indifferent to the aura of danger that surrounded her. She gazed intently at Eangyth's face. It was calm and gentle, as it always was, but now Fryth was seeing her mother as a stranger might.

Eangyth's eyes were dark and penetrating. Fine lines radiated from them and dark rings circled them. Her face was drawn, but not with age. She was still a beautiful woman, but she had the look of one who had suffered a long fever and come through it stripped and refined, as if by fire. Fryth knew that her mother's face had been marked in the spirit world. Time and again she had faced its dangers and then returned to the world of men, burdened by the knowledge she had gained. Fryth looked into her mother's eyes and shivered. Eangyth leaned forward and took her hand.

'It's a responsibility you must be ready for, Fryth. It will take all your strength and courage to learn what I have to teach you. You are still very young, but it can't be long now before the time to begin.'

'How long?' cried Fryth. Suddenly filled with impatience she leaped to her feet. The flames darted in the fire, fanned by her skirts. 'When can I start?'

'When the time is right.' Eangyth stood up. 'This is your first lesson. It's a lesson in patience. You'll need more than you have of that.' This answer failed to discourage Fryth. She would have asked again, demanding to know more. She turned and held out her hands to her mother with an imploring look, but the moment was lost. Edward, her father, burst through the door with three small boys clinging to his arms. Shouting that he was hungry, he dropped the boys onto the hearth. Eangyth smiled, held

Fryth's wide open eyes in her own, then turned and reached for the cooking pots.

For many weeks after their talk had been interrupted Fryth waited for her mother to renew the subject. It had been the first time Eangyth had made any direct allusion to her sorcery, and for Fryth, that brief glimpse into the mysteries her mother commanded was a tantalizing glimpse into her own future. She took every opportunity chance afforded to be alone with her mother, haunting her like a shadow round the house, in the barn, at the hearth. But no more was said. In the mornings and evenings, when Eangyth went to the village shrine, she still expected Fryth to take charge of the household and the unruly boys. No invitation was made to join her.

Fryth was made to understand that she must learn her first lesson, and be patient.

CHAPTER 2

The long dry summer passed into abundant harvest-time. No one could remember when the fields had yielded so much wheat. All the able-bodied in the village turned out to bring it in. Fryth had been working in the fields from sunrise to dusk every day for a week. Her back ached, her skin burned from the sun and itched from the bites of harvest mites and the scratching of the chaff and straw which clung to her clothes and hair. Late one afternoon she was making her way down a row of corn in one of the last fields to be cut when she became aware of an additional discomfort, a nagging pain in the pit of her stomach. It increased in intensity, turning her back and legs to lead, until finally she was forced to abandon her work and seek the shade of a tree. She flung herself down groaning. The shade was already occupied by Gifu, a village girl who was not noted for her dedication to hard work.

'You look pale,' Gifu remarked. 'It's a pity I've just finished my water.' She turned her leather bottle upside-down as proof.

'I feel very bad, I've a pain in my belly. I've never had one like it.' Gifu's eyes narrowed.

'Probably not,' she said. 'Are you bleeding?' Fryth sat up. She looked earnestly at Gifu. Gifu was older than her, the women had received her last year.

'Is this what it's like?'

'Of course, go home, you'll see.' Fryth groaned again,

'Does it last?'

'They say your first child cures it. Find a husband quick is my advice!' Gifu dug Fryth in the ribs, her teeth were rotten and a waft of foul breath drifted from her as she laughed. Fryth's head swam.

'I *am* going home,' she said.

It was a long walk, and a slow one. The pain was almost unbearable. She found it difficult to think. She had been awaiting her first bleeding with mounting impatience. She knew it would mark a new departure in her life. It would mean that at last she could join the women, become an adult in the eyes of the tribe. That much she had learned at a very early age. No one, however, had told her that it also meant this pain. She did not have to think very far to know why she had been ignorant about details of what was now happening to her.

From her mother she had learned that a woman's monthly bleeding was a sign that Freya was working in her, giving her a part in the mysterious process of creation, it was a blessing and a privilege. Eangyth the priestess would not concern herself with whether or not the process hurt; and, as the daughter of the priestess, Fryth had always been set a little apart from other young girls, from whom she might have discovered the more basic facts. They tended to feel uneasy in her company. She had never been openly shunned, but neither had she shared the cosy intimacy, the whispers, the giggling, the exchange of gossip, and no doubt other information, that filled most of the spare time of the girls of her age.

Fryth's childhood had been different in many ways from that of other children. Fryth, being Eangyth's only daughter and natural heir, had to some extent been treated with the same careful respect as her mother. Even as a small child she discovered that she was not always welcome to join in the games, expeditions and adventures of the other children. Laughter would die away, and eyes would look down as she approached. Fryth did not have long to regret this since in her tribe the games of childhood did not last. Boys and girls became workers many years before they became men and women. But its legacy had had a deep effect on her. She was close to her father, they would sit together in the evenings, singing songs and telling stories; she was happy with her small brothers, and, most of all in her mother's company; but her isolation from her peers meant that very early on she had developed a strong and independent spirit. She was content to be alone.

The pain in her belly was intensifying and Fryth was forced to sit down again. She propped herself against another tree and drew her knees up, hugging them tightly to herself, rocking gently to and fro. By this time there was no doubt that Gifu's diagnosis had been correct; she had started bleeding. Fryth rested her cheek on her knee and moaned softly. It seemed hard that an event she had been looking forward to for so long should have this unforeseen and most unwelcome aspect to it. The reapers were beginning to leave the fields, Single, or in small groups, they passed by where she sat, hunched under the tree. No one paused to speak to her, or to wonder why she should be sitting there. There was nothing unusual in the sight of Fryth alone, apparently lost in thought.

She was often to be seen, a small intense figure, walking by herself; sitting in the corner of a field; staring at the swiftly flowing river; or leaning her forehead against the soft flanks of one of her mother's cows, deep in contemplation, the milking quite forgotten, until the beast, growing restless would stir, or knock the bucket, bringing her to her senses. Fryth was an outsider in the tribe, not part of the close-knit, comfortable world of friendship and exchanged experience; but the long hours she spent alone had brought her into close contact with the natural world, the world of the goddess Freya, whose priestess she would one day become.

Fryth learnt from observation that the spirit of the earth had immeasurably greater strength and power than the puny powers of men. The facts were obvious to her. The earth was the source of life. Mysteriously, unbidden and unheeding, it reproduced itself year by year. The sun and moon nourished it and measured out its seasons. Waters ran through it, learning its secrets. Rocks and stones heaved themselves up from its depths, containing its strength and its silence. Trees and plants rooted in it, feeding directly from it, budding and ripening, shedding and dying in an endless cycle. Only men and animals were separate, wanderers, free from the earth's firm grip, buffeted by its powerful forces, struggling continually with it, and with each other, for survival.

Fryth learned from her mother that the most important concern of human life was to establish and maintain its tenuous connection with Freya, the Mother of life, the goddess of the earth. She had been taught to venerate and propitiate her spirit in trees and rocks and water. She had been taught that animal spirits acted as her messengers and bringers of portents. She knew that Freya favoured particular places and that she was nearer and more approachable in her favourite haunts, a pool perhaps, or a particular tree, and never more so than in her special shrine where Eangyth her priestess made daily offerings to her.

Fryth looked out across the stubble fields. The moon had already risen, a cloudy disc in the dark blue summer sky. She knew that the blood that was flowing from her now was drawn from her by the moon. It was a blessing, her mother had said, and, painful or not, it had to be acknowledged. She scrambled to her feet, Eangyth must hear her news. Clutching her belly, she made her uncomfortable way home.

Eangyth received the news gravely. When Fryth had finished telling her, Eangyth shook her head.

'You are still very young Fryth,' she sighed, 'very young.'

Fryth, nearly doubled up with pain, was hardly listening. She groaned and Eangyth took her arm. After that her mother's response was entirely practical. She gave Fryth some of the absorbent sphagnum moss that all the women collected from the woods, and, since the pain would not relent, she lit a small brazier and scattered a few dried leaves of hemp on the coals. Fryth lay on the bed and inhaled the fumes. Her head felt strangely light, and her sensations weirdly intensified, but the pain eased. She fell asleep.

Eangyth woke Fryth early the next morning. The pain had gone. It was still dark and Eangyth had lit a lamp. Fryth sat up and looked round the one-roomed house. Her first thought was that in some way yesterday her life had changed, and yet nothing was different here; the mud-daubed walls, the split-log floorboards, and the rafters, hung with sides of ham, bunches of drying herbs, strings of onions, coils of rope and tools of every kind. Above the rafters was the smoke-blackened thatch. A thin plume of smoke was curling towards the small hole in the roof from the hearth, a raised mound of clay in the centre of the floor. Eangyth had not yet seen to the fire, the smoke was rising from last night's ash-covered embers. Round the hearth lay the familiar clutter of daily life: spindles, boxes, children's toys mingled with handmade cooking pots of all sizes. A tripod stood over the fire from which an iron kettle hung by two sharp triangular lugs, a precious possession that showed Eangyth's rank and wealth. Eangyth's loom leaned against the wall, its heavy clay weights dangling close to the floor. She was weaving a length of brightly coloured cloth. Fryth remembered collecting the lichens used to make the yellow dye.

Fryth would have protested at being woken so early, but she noticed that her mother was more alert and purposeful than usual.

'Get up Fryth,' she said, 'and try not to wake the boys, we've things to do before daylight.' Fryth, all her drowsiness gone, got ready as quickly as she could. Pulling her cloak round her against the cool morning air, she followed her mother out of the house.

The village was quiet, no one was about. A cock crowed from the midden in a neighbouring yard and a scrawny dog rose stiffly to its feet, a dark shape in the middle of the village street. It stretched slowly in two long diagonals, then shook itself with a clatter, sneezed and trotted off behind some sheds.

Eangyth said nothing as she led Fryth at a fast pace through the village. A faint light was gleaming in the eastern sky as they reached the shrine. It was built on open ground outside the village, on the opposite bank of the shallow river that ran through their valley.

Fryth had never set foot in the shrine. It was forbidden to children, and usually to adults except at special times. Only Eangyth was a regular visitor. Quite overawed, Fryth hesitated at the gate in the high stockade that surrounded its precinct. She knew that a ceremony would mark her entry into adulthood, but she had not expected this solitary visit with her mother to the shrine. Eangyth had still not said a word but, having entered the gateway, she turned and beckoned to Fryth to follow her. Fryth stepped inside.

The enclosure was small. In the pale dawn light Fryth could see that it was cultivated with plants in dense clumps, but she had no time to identify any of them; Eangyth had gone into the shrine. Fryth followed.

The building was low and dark, its walls had been thickly but roughly daubed with mud, giving the interior the feeling of a cave; an impression that was increased by the sound of trickling water. Fryth stood in the threshold, blocking almost all there was of the dim dawn light. Eangyth stooped down and lit a small lamp. Its thin flame gave just enough light faintly to illuminate the entire building before being swallowed in the shadowy rafters.

Fryth saw that the shrine had been built round a tiny spring. It welled up clear and bright through shining gravel from a shallow depression in the floor. The sides of the depression were packed with reddish clay and a clay-lined channel carried the stream across the floor, and out through the door where Fryth was standing. Fresh moss and autumn flowers edged the water course. Behind the little spring reared what Fryth, at first glance, took to be a central pillar. It was the rough, undressed trunk of a small tree, long since rubbed shiny, and gleaming with a greenish tinge. It was pierced with nails, mostly of iron, but some were bronze and a very few were silver. Offerings dangled from the nails: beads, little strips of cloth, dried flowers and wizened roots, sometimes even jewels. Eangyth had lit more lamps now and, as Fryth's eyes followed the central column up, she saw that it was not a pillar, but a full-grown tree, whose blackened lower branches spread out among the rafters, but whose top disappeared through the thatch.

To this moment Eangyth had not spoken one word, so her voice, breaking as it did into Fryth's silent wonderment, made her start and draw her breath in sharply. Eangyth was standing over the spring. Her cloak had dropped to the floor and she stood bare-armed in the lamplight. Round her neck she was wearing a striped badger skin; its grinning mask rose up behind her head. Her large cross-shaped brooches glittered on her breast. In one hand she held a small sharp knife, in the other, a round bronze box. The morning sun was now slanting in through the low door dimming the lamps. Black smoke spiralled from their flames.

'Erce, Erce, Erce!'

Eangyth's voice rang out, deep and sonorous, like the sound struck from a stone. She was calling on Freya, using the great invocation spoken by priests of the English people since the beginning of time.

'Erce, Erce, Erce!
Hear me Mother Earth.
Eastward I stand, favours I pray for.
May this girl be a field for you,
Let her grow and flourish, bring forth
Tall blades, bright fruit and brilliant corn,
All of earth's treasures.
Hail Earth! Mother of Life!
May this girl grow in your heart
Fill her with wisdom for the welfare of her people.'

A faint humming filled the air, like the sound of distant bees. The noise of running water intensified, and the branches above

Fryth's head shivered as if caught in a light breeze. Blood pounded in her ears and her breath came fast and shallow. The sunlight strengthened and Fryth saw that fine silver sand had been sprinkled in a wide circle on the hard, beaten floor behind the tree trunk. Eangyth turned and stepped into the circle, motioning to Fryth to join her. Light-headed and staggering slightly, Fryth followed her.

Eangyth handed her the knife and indicated with a gesture that she should cut a slice of bark from the tree. Fryth stretched out and prized a strip about two inches long from the knotted trunk. Eangyth took the wood and with the same knife cut a sign, unfamiliar to Fryth, into its surface. She stepped out of the circle leaving Fryth standing in it alone. She picked a small earthenware jar from several on a low bench against the wall, and dipped it in the spring, carefully filling it exactly half-full. Then she dropped the slip of wood into the water and sprinkled a fine powder into the jar from the small bronze box in her left hand. Her voice rang out again:

'Earth, strong Mother, overcoming all creatures
Mighty against malice, against those who forget her
    goodness.
May this health-giving water be protection and blessing
To the virgin girl who drinks it.'

Fryth took the jar and drank its contents in one draught, straining the wooden slip in her fingers as she swallowed. The water had a strong bitter taste. Before she had finished it her ears began to ring. Her head swam. She swayed and felt herself about to fall. Her eyes were growing dim. Half blind and in panic she groped wildly for support, staggering to and fro until, with tremendous relief, she encountered something firm. She grasped it and held on. It was her mother's arm. Eangyth held her in a strong embrace and they sank together to the floor. Eangyth settled Fryth's head against her shoulder, supporting the weight of her body against her own, and, rocking gently backwards and forwards, she began to sing.

Fryth heard her mother's voice as if from a great distance. It seemed to her to be both sound and light. It swelled and brightened and rose up through her spine, filling her body until she lost all sense of space and time, becoming one with the brilliant sound flooding her whole being. Suddenly, she was spiralling downwards into darkness. A sound of rushing water filled her ears and blotted out her mother's song. She was totally alone, drifting helplessly, unable through her own will to alter her direction, still less control her mind. A dreadful anguish overcame her, and with the anguish came despair.

Then, even as she gave way to despair she heard a sound. No more than the faintest echo, it seemed to come from a great way off. The weird, unearthly sound of an animal howling.

As abruptly as it had fallen, the darkness lifted. Fryth was in a familiar world again, lying on fresh sunlit grass. The air was filled with bird-song and the smell of flowers. From between two silvery aspen trees appeared a large brown-coated, light-footed, dog fox. He sniffed the air delicately and, unafraid, trotted up to where Fryth was lying. He stood still, eyeing her, then lifted up his left front paw. Where he had trodden three small strips of wood lay on the bright green grass. The fox barked three times and slipped away between the trees. Fryth picked up the little strips. Each one was marked with a strange symbol, etched in red.

Something was rubbing her cheek. Irritated, Fryth tried to brush it off. She wanted to roll over on the warm grass and go to sleep, but, whatever it was, it would not go away. She called out,

'Leave me alone, let me sleep!'

She intended to sound commanding, but her voice felt strangely thick and weak. She dragged her hand from the ground, and in doing so, she felt, not grass, but loose sharp sand. She reached up to brush her face again and met, and held onto, a familiar hand. She opened her eyes, looked straight into

Eangyth's face, and was at once awake. She struggled to sit upright in her mother's arms and groaned. Eangyth gently pressed her fingers to Fryth's lips. She rose stiffly to her feet and, making a pillow of her cloak, laid it under Fryth's head. She wrapped Fryth's own cloak closely round her.

'Sleep now,' she said. 'I'll leave you. If you wake before I return, wait here for me.'

And, immediately, Fryth fell into a deep and peaceful sleep.

She was still sleeping quietly when Eangyth returned at evening. Fryth woke at her mother's light touch. She felt refreshed and peaceful in a way that was new to her. Every moment of her vision was clear in her memory, more vivid than memories of yesterday. Eangyth held out another half-filled cup of spring water, this time pure and clear. Fryth drank thirstily. She caught her mother by the hands.

'Mother, I . . .'

'Hush,' Eangyth cautioned, 'don't tell me now, keep it in your heart until I ask.'

They walked together out of the little shrine. The evening sunlight slanted across the courtyard outside. The stream ran clear and bright between its built-up banks through clumps of herbs. Fryth recognized them all: mugwort, plantain, watercress growing in the stream, deadnettles, camomile, chervil, fennel, wormwood and here and there were graceful crab-apple trees, their arching branches laden with golden fruit. The sight of these small trees reminded her to look back at the shrine. Above it she saw what she had not noticed as she went in at dawn; a canopy of hawthorn leaves, contrasting brightly with the fresh gold thatch.

The sunlight was gilding the thatched roofs of the village houses, tingeing them a smokey pink as Fryth and Eangyth walked slowly home. The carved and painted lintels of their doorways glowed richly in the evening light; here a dragon's snout and there his wings, a serpent coiled sinuously round a doorpost, a boar arched his bristled back into the eaves. The smell of cooking wafted from a dozen roofs. Children were playing in the dusty street, and men and women, tired from working in the fields lounged in doorways, chatting softly. They passed the forge and heard the smith whistling above the rasp of his whetstone as he sharpened a sickle blade. From another workshop came the sound of hammering and the sweet smell of new wood shavings. A small, striped, ginger pig rootled in a pile of muck recently swept out of a back-yard gate.

It was all so ordinary, this world, that Fryth wondered for a moment if she had really been away. The moment passed as she sensed her mother intruding on her thoughts. She turned her head and looked with new eyes on Eangyth. For her, both worlds were ordinary. She passed as easily as a cloud from family and hearth to the secret, spirit world. Fryth's experience that day had only vividly confirmed a truth that she already knew; the spirit world was always only a breath away. Every day, sheltering from the rain, listening to the wind, gazing into the fire, she, and all her tribe, brushed against it. Today she had stepped inside. That was all. And she had returned.

It was not until the following day that Eangyth asked Fryth what she had seen. She was, as usual, quiet and self-possessed as she went through the morning routines, but when the small boys had been fed and their heads searched for lice, rather more cursorily than usual, she pushed them out of doors. They cleared a space by the hearth. Eangyth pulled a small chest to her feet and sat down on her stool. Fryth settled herself at her mother's feet, leaning against her knees. She looked up into Eangyth's face.

As she related her vision she could see that her mother was pleased. Eangyth nodded frequently, listening intently and occasionally asking for greater detail. Fryth came to the fox.

'Ahah!' cried Eangyth. 'This is what I had hoped for. You're blessed to have found your guide so soon.'

'My guide?' said Fryth.

'Yes, a sorceress must have a guide in the spirit world or she would lose her way.' Eangyth opened the chest at her feet. Folded at the bottom, underneath the crystal ball and several other mysterious objects, lay her grizzled badger skin. She lifted it out and shook it. The firelight danced on its silver hairs.

'You know that I wear this badger skin?' Eangyth continued. Fryth nodded. 'I wear it because the badger is my guide. We've worked together since I've been a priestess. He is slow but very strong and patient. He has been a good friend to me. And now the fox has come to you. I'm glad of that, you couldn't hope for a better guide.' Fryth looked questioningly at her mother.

'A fox is fierce and cunning, Fryth,' Eangyth explained, 'it glories in blood like a warrior. Also it's the swiftest of all earth-bound creatures, in body and mind. Our people are going to need a brave heart and quick intelligence above all. Freya has chosen well.'

Fryth nodded, glad that her mother was pleased for her. She glanced down and her eye was caught by the other objects in her mother's box.

'These are animals too.' she said, pointing to an eagle's feather, mounted in bronze, a beaver's tooth, also in a bronze mount, and the sinewy paw of a wolf. She had seen Eangyth wearing them on her belt when she visited the sick.

'Every sorceress has her own particular guide,' Eangyth said, 'but other animal spirits help us in our work'. Fryth fingered the amulets, and picked up the wolf's paw. 'The spirits of these creatures help us to drive away and kill demons.' Fryth held the wolf's paw to her cheek. She felt a shiver of energy run through her as the cold rough pad and thick black claws brushed her face.

'What about the strips of wood the fox showed me, mother?' she went on. 'They were like the slip I cut from the tree in the shrine, the one I drank. I think they were marked with runes.'

Fryth couldn't find the words to describe the symbols on the strips, so she scratched the signs clumsily in the ashes on the hearth. ⚡ ᚺ ∫

'Those *are* runes,' said Eangyth. 'Three runes. Let's see.' She bent down, peering closely at what Fryth had drawn. She became very still and quiet, concentrating intently on the curious figures on the hearth. Then she sat up straight and breathed out steadily.

'Runes are the most ancient treasure of our people, Fryth,' she said. 'All our wisdom is locked up in these signs. They're full of terrible power. The past, the future, even Fate itself is held in these small marks. One day I'll teach you all of them, but it's right to start with these, the ones that spell your own fate.'

She began, reading from right to left.

'This is the rune of the yew tree. There's a verse for each rune, poetry's always more easily remembered. This is the verse for the yew:

"A rough tree outside, inside steadfast,
Firm fire-guardian, fed by deep roots.
A joy to our native land." '

'The yew's a poisonous tree, mother.' Fryth was uneasy, she had waited so long to begin her apprenticeship but now the time had come she wondered if she was capable of the work, if she had the strength. Eangyth smiled, sensing her anxiety. She stroked her head.

'Just listen quietly, Fryth,' she said gently. 'You must be ready to understand. The only way to overcome fear is by under-standing. The yew is the rune that shapes your fate. What it predicts *is* dark and dangerous and rough.'

Fryth shuddered and grasped Eangyth's hand. She searched her mother's face for comfort but it had become distant and impassive.

'However,' Eangyth continued, 'this rune tells me that you'll always carry with you the power of the knowledge I shall teach you. It'll nourish and protect you so that come what may you'll remain firm and bright, like the bright golden wood of the yew tree. A yew can live a thousand years. It's a tree of steadfastness,

its leaves stay green in winter, they promise the return of spring.'
She shifted, as if to ease some tension in her body.

'Now, the second rune. It signifies hail.'

Fryth said nothing, her eyes remained fixed on her mother, almost as if Eangyth, not the strange symbols in the dust, were decreeing her fate. Eangyth continued,

"The whitest of wheat, whirls from the sky
Whipped by wild winds, turns into water."

This means change.' Eangyth's voice was slow and thoughtful.
'The yew told us that danger was facing you, and here it is. Hail
means cruelty and discomfort.' Her face darkened 'It's coming
to all our tribe Fryth, I've seen that myself, and you won't escape
it altogether. But these icy winds will carry you away.'

'What? Please don't go on!' cried Fryth. 'What do you mean?
I don't want to go away! I don't want to know my fate. How
will I live knowing this?' She had risen to her feet. She turned
her back on Eangyth and clenched her fists. She was afraid that
she might cry.

'Sit down, Fryth.' Her mother's voice was commanding, Fryth
had no choice but to obey.

'You are privileged to know your fate, you must prepare for
it. That's the task we face. Now. . . .'

Fryth composed herself by a great effort of will. Seeing it,
Eangyth permitted her daughter an encouraging smile.

'That's better,' she said gently. 'I know it's hard, but you *will*
learn to bear it. Besides the rest of what this rune has to say is
good. You are this white seed. You'll be set down by the wind
in some newly ploughed field, a new country. The hail melts
into water, the water swells the seed.'

'These runes are more like riddles mother,' Fryth said. 'Their
meanings are too complicated.'

'The truth is often hidden, it must be, it's dangerous.' Fryth
nodded ruefully. 'The freedom which the third rune predicts,'
went on Eangyth, 'has its beginning here in the second. You'll

find it in another country. We must all accept our fate, and yours will be very hard, but I can see it has a purpose and a guiding hand behind it. Look,' she said, pointing to the third rune. 'This is the rune that sets you free. It represents the sun.

"The sun on high, symbol of hope
To seafarers sailing the fishes' bath.
The horse of the sea, bears them to harbour."

So Fryth, you have the yew, a fire within, to shape you, and here, the fire of the sun to guide you to freedom. The sun will be important in your life. I think you're going to receive some kind of illumination, some new understanding.'

'The fox is a creature of the night,' said Fryth thoughtfully, 'and yet his coat shines like the sun.' Eangyth looked pleased. She smiled.

'You learn fast,' she said. 'Always try to see the hidden meaning. The signs will be there if you know where to look.'

Fryth sighed. Eangyth took her hand and squeezed it.

'You must be strong, Fryth,' she said. 'I've seen a great deal of sorrow coming to our people. Some new force is in the wind. Our alliance with the Mercians is the first sign of change, but they're just the instrument of Fate. We're already in the autumn of the old ways. Winter's coming on.' She looked down at the ashes. 'These runes signify a new life in some world I shall never see. You must learn all you can Fryth, everything I know. Whatever happens to us, our knowledge must survive to see another spring.'

CHAPTER 3

It was Holy Month. Harvest was over. The last sheaf had been
decorated with flowers and brought home, carried shoulder high
by cheerful villagers. Eangyth performed the welcoming
ceremony on the open space in front of the beer-hall, the gathering place of the tribe. The sheaf was set up on a high wooden
dais, for everyone to see and venerate, and two strong rams,
one black, one white, were sacrificed in thanksgiving. The
feasting and dancing of the harvest festival lasted well into the
next day.

The harvest had been so abundant that Eangyth decided to
record it in some special way. She consulted Cerdic and together
they planned a permanent memorial to Freya's bounty. The
tribe's sacred pillar had been standing outside the beer-hall for
generations. Like the tree round which the village shrine was
built, the pillar represented the world-tree which rooted in the
underworld, stretched up through middle-earth, the home of
men, and spread its topmost branches in the realm of the gods.
The pillar had become so weatherbeaten and worn with age
that no one could make out, still less remember, the carvings
that had once adorned it, and Cerdic and Eangyth decided that
a new one should be carved and set up in its place.

Eangyth took charge of the creation. The pillar would be over
thirty feet high. In Eangyth's design, the world serpent, source
of all created energy, lay coiled at the base of the pillar with
jaws agape. The rest of the column emerged from these wide-
spread jaws. Spiralling round the pillar were the sinuous branches of a vine, sprouting luxurious leaves. Among its branches
perched and peeped all kinds of animals and birds; wrens,

rabbits, ravens, wolves; fishes swam in the upper air and butter-flies drowned in flowers. Then there were creatures familiar to the inner eye; fiery beasts with heads of dogs and bodies of bulls or fish; masks of elves and demons with fierce rolling eyes and lolling tongues. And everywhere, caught up in the twisting branches, were seen the distorted bodies of men, engaged in a desperate and endless struggle to be free. It was a marvellous creation full of beauty, energy, danger and the ceaseless fret and motion of the world.

Eangyth supervised the drawing of the images on the long tree trunk, carefully chosen for its girth and straightness. She outlined some of them herself in thin red paint, explaining their significance to the workmen as the picture developed. Fryth loved to watch, and often accompanied her mother to the work-shop. She became so absorbed in the gradual transformation of the huge cylinder of wood, that she took to passing by the workshop even when Eangyth was not there, and pausing at the door to watch the men at work.

Eventually Eric, the head craftsman, called her in. He was a heavy-chested man with thick golden hair which he plaited into two fat pigtails that bounced on his shoulders as he worked.

'Come in, girl, don't be shy!' He boomed in a way that increased, rather than lessened the reserve Fryth habitually felt in the company of large and boisterous men; however curiosity overcame her timidity. Eric was working on a section of the vine, gently coaxing its smooth curves out of the straight grained wood. He was a master. There were men at work along the whole length of the tree trunk, chiselling and chipping and smoothing. They kept up a steady stream of chatter as they worked, interrupted by loud curses and yelps when a mallet or a chisel slipped. Fryth smiled, and as she smiled she saw, half-way along the trunk, a tall young man, pale faced with dark auburn hair. He had put down his thin chisel and was looking at her in a vague, abstracted way. He had noticed her smile and she broadened it to include him.

He was Wulf, the outcast, son of Ethelred. Wulf's father had been a farmer, a sober man who worked hard, gave intelligent advice in councils and was liked and respected by everyone. One black day, however, Ethelred's fate had taken an evil turn. It had been raining hard and the village tracks were deep in mud. He was driving his laden ox-waggon past the chieftain's yard. Cerdic's two young sons were playing by the wall. As Ethelred passed them a waggon trace broke and the heavy cart slewed round, catching the youngest boy between its great wheel and the wall. The boy was crushed to death in an instant.

Accident or not, the law was clear; the blood-price for a chieftain's son was far too high for Ethelred to find. To pay the debt he had sold himself into bondage, far from the scene of his downfall. His wife was left behind, his two children were suddenly fatherless outcasts. Unable to leave the land on which they depended, they were doomed to live in shame among the people whose chief their father had so badly wounded.

Wulf, as the only son, inherited in law and nature his father's blood-guilt. He was pitied and tolerated by the community, but he could never be accepted as one of them. He had no place in the beer-hall or the war-band. There was no feud between Cerdic and Wulf but there could be no friendship either. So, in all eyes, Wulf was only half a man.

He had, however, one great gift which the village did not choose to deny; from his boyhood days he could make magic with a knife in wood. He carved small toys for his sister: birds, animals, even bees, so delicate and lifelike that he seemed to have captured the very spirit of the beasts. Such a talent could not be wasted and, when he came to man's work, Wulf, despite his background, was taken on by Eric, the head wood-craftsman.

Pupil already outshone master and Wulf was set to the most demanding jobs. His most important piece of work so far had been some beautiful carvings on the door-posts of the beer-hall. They were the pride of the whole village and one of the chief glories of the tribe. Yet Wulf, whose hands had made them, was forbidden to enter the doorway. Few considered the resentment he might feel; but Fryth had felt for him, and she wondered now, watching Wulf teasing a wren out of a knot in the wood, how he would feel when the pillar was taken from the workshop and set up in front of that same hall.

She made her way round the crowded workshop until she stood beside him. He was working on a tiny feathered wing. Fryth watched him fascinated, holding her breath. One slip and the whole thing would be ruined; but the slip never came. Wulf worked with total absorption, his hands as steady and true as if it were a fence-post he were cutting, not this little creature. Wulf chipped, and Fryth watched, until the wren was sitting in full feather on the vine.

'One more chip,' thought Fryth, 'and it'll stretch its throat and sing.' She turned to Wulf, her face alight with pleasure, thinking he must have read her mind; only then did she notice that the workshop was empty and silent. She had been so taken up with watching Wulf that she had not noticed the men pack up and leave, their day's work done.

Wulf put down his chisel, stretched and smiled. His face in repose was usually tense and worried. Two small parallel furrows habitually creased the space between his brows, drawing them down into an anxious frown. Only two things smoothed them out, the quiet concentration of his work, and his smile.

'What do you think?' he said.

'I think it's going to sing when the pillar's set up and it feels the breeze on its feathers,' said Fryth. Wulf laughed.

'If you're right,' he said, 'it'll be the loudest creature on the pillar then, for all its size.'

'The king of birds.' she said, stroking the carving with her finger, 'and harm to those who harm the king.' They were the words of a children's song, but Wulf's smile vanished.

'When wasn't *that* a rule of life?' he said abruptly. He began stuffing his tools roughly into a bag on the bench. Then, straightening up, he caught the look of confusion on Fryth's face and his expression softened.

'Will you come tomorrow?' he said, 'I'm going to start on a boar. It'll be a fine specimen.'

Wulf walked part of the way home with Fryth, but he was anxious for her sake that she should not be seen with him, especially by her parents; he turned off before they reached the door of her mother's courtyard. Fryth was thoughtful as she walked the last few yards home. Everyone was ensnared by Fate, her mother had said, and powerless to act. It was certainly true of Wulf. She thought of her own fate as Eangyth had read it from the runes and shivered. Fate was certainly indifferent to the desires and fears of men, all she could do was try to be prepared to meet it.

Edward was sitting by the fire when Fryth walked in. Guthlac was on his knee and her other young brothers, Godwin and Athelmar, were gathered at his feet. Their eyes sparkled in the firelight.

'Go on, father, tell us!'

'No wait, let me think, wait father, I know!' Godwin loved riddles, his face was screwed up with the effort of solving this one.

'Do I know it?' called out Fryth, drawing near the fire. 'Tell it to me quick before Godwin works it out!' Edward held up his knotty hands to quieten the boys. He repeated the riddle.

' "A creature came shuffling to the hall
Where many wise men were meeting.
Two ears, one eye, two feet, one back
Twelve hundred heads for eating. . . ." '

'Ah, I've heard it before!' Fryth broke in. 'A one-eyed onion seller!'

'You shouldn't have said, you shouldn't have said!' chorused the boys.

'Well, I think it's feeble anyway,' said Godwin. 'I'd never have guessed. An onion seller couldn't carry twelve hundred onions. It's a stupid joke!'

'Oh, Godwin.' said his father, 'don't be so literal, you can exaggerate in poetry, it's for effect. We've enough real facts to be going on with, poetry has to be richer than life, or what's it for?'

'Father's right you know Godwin,' said Fryth, adding quickly before the mood changed, 'here's another one:

"On the way a wonder, water becomes bone!" '

'I know, I know!' chorused the little ones again, all uncomprehending.

'Ice!' said Godwin triumphantly.

'Right first time! You're a quick lad,' said Edward, rubbing his son's fair curls affectionately. Godwin was the oldest boy and would shortly take his place beside Edward in the beer-hall. Fryth often smiled at the thought of Godwin's youthful, rosy cheeks and silky hair among the tough work-hardened men.

Eangyth came in through the door and Edward stood up to greet her; Guthlac slid to the floor. Having lost Edward's attention, the boys drifted away to various occupations in the corners of the room. Fryth pulled her mother's stool to the fire and Eangyth sat down gratefully. She looked tired.

'Well, Edward?' Eangyth said. Fryth detected a hint of anxiety in her mother's voice. She shot her father a questioning look.

'A herald arrived from Mercia this afternoon, Fryth,' Edward explained. ' They're mustering an army and we've been called.'

'How soon?' asked Eangyth.

'Well, now the harvest's in, the fighting season begins. Within the next month perhaps, at any rate it won't be long. Cerdic's called a meeting in the hall tonight to make plans. We've been sharpening our spears for long enough!'

'How large a war-band do they want?'

'All those who are strong enough to carry a spear to the battlefield will go, it seems.'

'Godwin?' asked Eangyth. Fryth felt a sudden knot of fear in her stomach.

'No, not Godwin this time.' He put his hand over Eangyth's. 'The boy's too young yet. Things are not so desperate. Penda has plenty of arms and men. What he really needs from us is loyalty, not numbers.' Eangyth looked thoughtful. She prodded the fire with her foot.

'Two things must be finished before you leave,' she said decisively. 'No troop of ours can go to war until the new pillar has been set up. Freya must not be neglected. We must make arrangements for the ceremony.'

'There'll be time,' Edward replied. 'Cerdic knows we can't go until Freya has her due. The Mercians worship Thor and Tiw, but the war gods aren't our gods yet. Make your arrangements, Eangyth, Penda will have to fall in with them.'

'And then there's Fryth.' Eangyth looked down. Fryth was in her usual place at her mother's feet.

'She has come of age, Edward.' Eangyth smiled proudly.'We must prepare for her ceremony too.'

Edward gave a great shout of pleasure. It was the first time he had heard the news. The three boys playing in the shadows looked up, surprised. Not wishing to be left out of the celebrations, they came back to the fire.

'This is wonderful!' cried Edward, hugging Fryth to his side and kissing her cheek. He turned her face to his.

'My only daughter,' he said tenderly, 'you shall have the best of everything. Eangyth, we must send for the jeweller; he must bring his finest brooches!' Eangyth smiled.

'You're right.' she said. 'We'll ask Gadd to bring some samples of his work so that we can all decide; but don't forget, they must be suited to her calling. Fryth has begun to learn my craft.' She put a hand on Fryth's shoulder. 'She'll help me when the pillar is set up, it'll be her first act as my apprentice.'

'These things are not for me.' said Edward cautiously. 'But I'm pleased for you, Fryth.' He squeezed her hand. 'And now I must go, they'll be waiting for me in the hall.' He had an idea. 'Why don't you come with me, Fryth? Now that you're of age, come and pour my drinks for me.'

'It's too soon for that, Edward,' said Eangyth, smiling at his eagerness. 'Let it wait till after her ceremony, that must be arranged before you go away as well.' Edward acquiesced.

'But light me to the hall,' he asked Fryth. 'I'd like you to walk with me.' Fryth stuck a torch into the fire, and slipping her cloak round her, she followed her father into the night.

They walked together slowly to the centre of the village. Edward was excited by her news and was full of plans for the future.

'Of course you won't marry for a while,' he said, 'but when you do, make sure to find a good fellow, one you can be proud of.' Fryth smiled at her father.

'Like the one my mother found.'

'Well . . .' he began.

'Not many men would care to be married to a sorceress, perhaps she chose you for your bravery.'

Edward laughed. 'You'll have to find someone as brave as me then!'

Fryth laughed with him. 'Then I'll never marry!'

They were silent for a while, walking hand in hand. The beer-hall came in sight. Light was spilling through its open doors, and with it laughter and raised voices. Fryth could distinguish Cerdic's resonant tones rising occasionally above the general din.

'Father.' Fryth was reminded of something. 'I was watching Wulf, the outcast, in the workshop today.' Her voice was thoughtful. 'He has a real gift. Everyone values his skills. Surely if he can be accepted as a woodworker, he should be accepted as a warrior too. It seems so unfair to take from him, and give nothing in return.'

'We've plenty of warriors,' said Edward absently. His thoughts were elsewhere and he had not given the question his full attention.

'But, father . . .'

Edward saw that she was in earnest. 'Skills in carving such as Wulf's come once in several generations, Fryth,' he said. 'It would be offensive to the gods who gave him such a gift to deny him the use of it.' Then he added. 'Not to speak of the waste.'

Fryth sighed. 'It seems the law of outcasts can be cheated when it suits.' she said quietly.

'But not the law of Fate,' replied Edward firmly. 'And that boy is bad. It's not his fault, but there it is. Why do you ask me anyway?'

They reached the door of the beer-hall. There was excitement in the air. Men were hurrying in and someone caught Edward by the arm, greeting him with a cheerful shout. His question forgotten, Edward hugged his daughter and disappeared with his friends inside the hall.

'I don't know, father,' Fryth answered to the empty air.

Her mind was full, she needed solitude. Rather than return home she walked a little way out of the village, taking the path to the river. She was afraid. In her short life none of the men of the tribe had gone to battle. Her father was a farmer, not a warrior. So were they all. How would these gentle, inexperienced men perform when it came to war? She could feel the first touch of a chill wind blowing from the future.

The torch had burnt itself out, but the moon was a bright deep gold, almost copper-coloured; a harvest moon. By its light Fryth made her way to a small pool formed in a bend of the river. During the day women gathered here to wash clothes and children, and to gossip and exchange news. Now, deserted, it had that special air of loneliness that public places have when everyone goes home. The large stones round its margins were bleached white in the moonlight. Fryth settled herself on one of them and sat gazing at the stippled surface of the black, swiftly flowing river.

An owl hooted in the distance as it hunted over the stubble fields. It would be doing well, small creatures were newly vulnerable to its searching eye. Bats flickered above Fryth's head, swooping to and fro across the river, and, from deep inside the forest, came the sharp, high-pitched barking of a fox.

Sitting quietly, Fryth listened to the rhythm of the flowing water, until its steady beat became one with the beating of her heart. Once again she was caught up in a spiral current, but this time she felt herself lifted by it, high into the air above the night sky. The world beneath her was huge and still, and she could see a steady pulse beating in the heart of it, resonating calm and peace. Gradually, almost imperceptibly, Fryth felt herself being drawn into the beat until it seemed that she herself was the pulse and all that was was resonating from her heart. Then, by degrees she felt her own pulse beating quietly again and heard the rushing water. The rock was cold beneath her and the night was dark. She shivered and stood up.

She walked home slowly, filled with peace, and the certainty that, in the heart of things, deeper than the level at which Fate played with the lives of men, all was well.

The beer-hall was still lit up as she made her way back through the dark village streets. The men were singing now; loud, hearty, confident songs. They were beating time on the benches with the handles of their knives. She hurried by, but not so fast that she failed to see the figure of a man squatting near the open doorway, in the shadows beyond its shaft of light. His arms were locked round his drawn-up legs and his head was sunk down on his knees. It was Wulf, Fryth felt a stab of pity for him, hugging such despair. She would have stopped to comfort him, but they were set too far apart that night. She passed him by and carried on for home. Wulf did not raise his head.

Gadd the jewel-maker rode over two days later, bringing with him a selection of his best work. Huge, bowed, cross-shaped brooches cast in bronze. The decoration on them was extravagant, part of an ancient tradition that dated back to the days before the English crossed the sea. In remote tribes such as Fryth's the ornament still had meaning. It was becoming simply a matter of fashion where small tribes has been submerged, but here, among the Middle Angles the jeweller's art continued to be a living sacrament.

He captured the spirits of horses and eagles and other powerful beasts, transfixing them in molten bronze. The animal images the jeweller created protected the women who wore them with their strength and lent wisdom to their tribe. The images were always contorted, with twisted and disjointed limbs, but, though their proper forms were lost, the patterns retained all energy and vigour of the animals depicted in them. It took a practised eye to see the creature in the patterns, and Eangyth often picked out the separated elements of the eagles on her brooches for her children, pointing to their sharp talons, sparkling eyes and outstretched wings. All mothers did the same.

Gadd spread his merchandise out on a white linen cloth, which showed them to their best advantage. Edward and Eangyth picked them over.

'Fine work, Gadd!' said Edward, fingering a particularly ornate brooch whose beaded border had caught his eye. 'I'm sorry I've only one daughter!'

'And not too dear.' said Gadd reassuringly, 'a length of cloth, a pig, two sacks of meal. . . .' This was steep, but if Edward was taken aback at the price he did not show it. His hand reached for another set.

'Edward.' Eangyth caught his arm. She had picked up two bronze discs. 'These are the ones for Fryth.' She handed him the brooches. They had an open-work pattern and large, sprung, iron pins. In comparison with all the others on display, they looked positively dull.

'What!' exclaimed Edward, astonished by her choice.

'Those!' cried Gadd, seeing a handsome deal at risk. 'Dear lady forgive me. I hadn't intended to bring such humble objects, not to the house of Edward and our High Priestess! I don't know how they got into the box. They cannot do the daughter of such a house the honour due to her. But these,' he said, returning to the pair that Edward had picked out.'These are some of my finest pieces. Surely they're more fitting to your noble daughter?'

'Fryth's brooches must be suited to her work, Edward,'

Eangyth said firmly. She turned to Fryth who was sitting quietly, taking no part in the proceedings. She was content to let her mother choose.

'These,' Eangyth continued, holding them up to the light, 'are worked with the symbol of the sun. Look, here in the centre is its broken wheel, and here encircling it,' she ran a finger round the circumference, 'is the ring of heaven. The sun is Fryth's sign Edward, she must have these brooches.'

Gadd looked crestfallen and Edward amazed, but neither said a word.

'I'm sorry Gadd, the others are very beautiful,' said Eangyth. 'But I would like you to do a little more to these before we take them. Can you add a pattern?' She rubbed her thumbs over the smooth bronze surfaces of the brooches. 'I would like them to have a pattern of half-moon stamps, thirteen on each, one for each cycle of the moon,' she added, glancing at Fryth. 'Then the brooches will be complete.'

'Madam,' said Gadd sounding almost offended. 'Nothing could be easier.' 'Or less rewarding for an artist' was his heavy implication.

Eangyth left Edward to fix the price. He paid more than they were worth out of his embarrassment, but it was still far less than he had been willing to pay.

Gadd could not resist remarking sourly as he heaved himself into the saddle of his fat pack-horse.

'*I* am quite content that you have only one daughter.' He came back two days later with the brooches punched with crescent moons, and received a small yelling pig and a sack of meal for his pains.

Fryth's coming of age was celebrated a short while later. The night before the ceremony Edward took the three boys to sleep with him in the hall and all the male animals in the livestock were rounded up and taken to a neighbour's pens. Eangyth had swept out the courtyard and decorated the gateway with boughs of yew. Their red waxy berries glowed among the dark green foliage. Fryth slept alone in the large family bed.

At first light a deputation of women arrived at Eangyth's door. They carried garlands of flowers and jars containing honey, milk, blood and water. One had new clothes over her arm; another held the box containing Fryth's jewellery. Eangyth led Fryth, blinking in the light, out of the house to meet the women who were squatting in a circle in the yard. As she came out they began to sing a soft melodious song of welcome. Their voices rose and fell and the song was carried on the light breeze over the village so that everyone could hear that Fryth's ceremony had begun.

Eangyth led Fryth three times round the outside of the circle and then told her to step inside. The women motioned to her to sit down in the centre. One by one they hung the garlands round her hair and neck and waist. Four women made an inner circle round her, one at each point of the compass. They carried the brimming jars. One leaned forward and sprinkled her with water. Fryth felt it soaking through her thin night clothes as the woman began to chant.

'Water from the north,
Runs in secret through earth's veins;
Springing to life in the sunshine,
To feed her children, to purify their lives.
May it run through this woman, and bring her health.'

Hands reached out and clutched Fryth, she was turned to face the south, milk was poured into her cupped hands and tipped into her mouth.

'Milk from a cow of single colour,
Mother of all things, feeding her children,
Rearing them in strength, feed this woman,
Make her fertile.'

The woman with the jar of blood was sitting in the west. Fryth watched as she dipped a thick brush of hazel twigs into the pot. With elbow bent, she stirred it round three times then daubed Fryth on her hands, breasts and mouth, leaving dark smears on her pale skin and white shift.

'Life is within us, blood springs from us.
Herald of new life, strengthen this woman,
Guard her from demons and elves.'

Lastly, facing east, Fryth was given a spoonful of honey which she trickled over her tongue, savouring its warmth before swallowing it. All the women joined in the chant.

'We work and produce good things,
We cannot live without reward.
Bring her joy.'

The offerings in the ritual were homely familiar things; their significance was entirely plain. Fryth felt comforted and encouraged by the gentle ministrations of these women whom she had known all her life. She was grateful to them for their cheerful faces and their simple magic. They gave her the comforting feeling that she belonged in a sensible and friendly world. She wanted to respond and, as if in answer to her wish, words and music came to her. She rose to her feet in the centre of the circle. Clapping and swaying and beating her feet in time with the music, she sang the women a song of thanksgiving.

A response like this from a girl in the middle of her ceremony had never happened before. It was greeted with delight and the women swayed and clapped with Fryth as she sang. The song came to an end and left Fryth filled with light and happiness. She had never been moved to sing like this before. She had amazed even herself, and now she hesitated, faintly embarrassed by her abandonment. But she saw only wonder and delight on the faces of the women. It was as if they had been witnesses to a sort of miracle. Smiling she sat down again and the ceremony continued.

The large circle had reformed. The women sat in an expectant silence. Then one of them, an ancient crone, began to wail. It was a wail of mourning, a chilling eerie sound. She moaned and keened, working herself into a frenzy, beating her breasts and tearing her hair. Foam flecked the corners of her mouth. Alarmed, Fryth looked round her, but the circle was watchful and quiet. The old woman had risen; she began to dance, stamping her feet, swirling and dipping round Fryth in an ecstasy of woe. Then, abruptly, she stopped and her trance evaporated. Her eyes were clear and bright, like sunshine after a shower of rain. Her fists, however, had remained clenched and now she held them over Fryth's head. She opened her fists and salt poured over Fryth and trickled to the ground.

'Salt follows sweet, sweet follows salt,' she mumbled. 'Pain follows joy, joy follows pain. All women know this, and are wise.' The whole circle nodded in agreement.

The old woman rejoined the others and Fryth was alone in the centre once more. The ceremony was nearly over. The mystery of the private world of the women had been celebrated. All that was left was to prepare Fryth for the outside world.

The garlands were removed. Her old night clothes were stripped off and the women dressed her in an entirely new set of clothes; a white linen shift, long woollen dress of red and yellow checks, with silver fastenings at the wrists, and a dark blue woollen cloak. New calfskin shoes were laced onto her feet and a thin leather belt with fine bronze tips was tied round her waist.

When this was done the youngest of the women opened the wooden jewel box she was carrying. Inside it were the two disc brooches bought from Gadd. The bronze was brightly burnished and the half-moon stamps twinkled as the brooches were lifted from the box. The young woman pinned the brooches to Fryth's dress, one above each collar-bone. In the bottom of the box lay a shining coil of large brightly coloured beads; a huge variety, of all colours, shapes and sizes. Some were of glass in shades of deep blue or green, or multicoloured: yellow, red and black. Others were the colour of blood. There were also wedge-shaped beads of yellow amber, and some of shell and bone. The string was hung in deep swags from brooch to brooch and the unaccustomed weight of it dragged slightly at her head and neck.

All the women had taken part in dressing Fryth but the final touch was added by her mother. She produced a large sharp-toothed comb made of white bone. It had a high triangular back with scalloped edges and its teeth fitted neatly into a narrow case. Both comb and case were decorated with the same half-moon stamps, thirteen on each, that had been punched onto her brooches, and the ends of the case curled up into lively little horses' heads. It was a beautiful thing and Fryth was enchanted by it. She held the case, turning it over in her hands as Eangyth gently pulled the comb through her black hair.

When Fryth's hair had been untangled and combed straight the ritual was complete. One of the women slipped out of the gate to announce that she was ready to come out of her mother's house.

The gates of the courtyard opened onto the street and Fryth looked out over a sea of faces. All the women of the village were there to greet her. The men kept indoors or out of sight, but every female, from the youngest baby to the oldest crone, had turned out for her. They carried flowers and fruit and hung her with fresh garlands. Then, singing and dancing, they led her through the village streets, down to the river and over to the little shrine.

The atmosphere today was quite different from the secret, silent visit made by Eangyth and Fryth not so long before. The crowd led Fryth and her mother to the gate of the shrine's precinct and then parted to let them through. In the normal way Eangyth would have gone alone into the shrine to sacrifice in thanksgiving for the girl who had newly come of age, but she took Fryth with her through the gate.

For the second time Fryth walked through the massed herb

garden and in through the low door of the shrine. The almost overwhelming sense of awe that had come to her the first time returned, but tempered with a new feeling of security. This was her rightful place. It knew and welcomed her.

Inside the shrine a fire had been laid ready in a brazier. Through the gloom Fryth could see a small she-goat tethered to the tree. Eangyth removed the garlands from round Fryth's neck and hung the goat with them; it skittered and bleated at the end of its rope. Three jars, identical to those at the morning's ceremony, stood on the floor. There was an acrid smell of urine and animal fear inside the building.

Fryth watched her mother calmly anointing the goat between its horns with water, milk and honey. Its frantic bleats grew louder as Eangyth untied the rope and led the goat to the back of the shrine where a fresh circle of clean white sand had been spread. The sand shimmered softly in the shadows. Eangyth had lit no lamps.

Suddenly there was a flash of light. Eangyth had raised her knife. She held it, glinting above her head for a brief second, then, deftly, with one, long, practised sweep she slit the small brown throat. Blood gushed onto the white sand, rapidly spreading out in a deep red pool. The goat struggled feebly for a few moments and then quietly died.

Eangyth left it lying while she kindled the fire in the brazier. The flames leaped up, casting a ruddy glow over the blood-soaked sand and the twitching hairy corpse. She dipped a hazel brush into the blood and then into the pots containing the milk, blood and honey, mixing a little of the blood into each. Then with the same brush she fed the flames of fire with oil from a large jar standing near the hearth. She motioned to Fryth, who was quickly learning that silence was the language of the shrine, to pour the contents of each pot onto the crackling flames, finishing with the water which doused the fire.

That was all. Mother and daughter emerged from the shrine, Eangyth carrying the goat by its hind legs. A large crowd met them at the gate, this time both men and women, and the goat was swiftly taken from Eangyth as the crowd clustered round in a cheerful swaying mass.

Now it was the turn of the men to greet Fryth. She was hoisted into the air and carried shoulder high back into the village. On this short journey all the bearded boys were meant to try to pull her down; acting out a rough courtship. They leaped and shoved and tumbled round her and Fryth was in danger of being toppled the whole way. But she never was. The boys were reticent even in this playful game; Fryth, the daughter of their sorceress was too large a prize, too great an undertaking. Still, the laughter and the leaping went on until they reached the open space in front of the men's hall. Fryth was breathless and flushed when finally she was lowered to the ground. She had counted all the likely young warriors she knew in the jumping jostling crowd. They had come straight from the morning's training and were fit and strong and healthy. She looked round her at the throng of tall fair boys. There was nothing to distinguish one from another, all were large, boisterous and full of life. One or two she held in her deep gaze until they looked away uneasily; she knew they were afraid of her. A shadow crossed her face and the crowd fell silent.

In that moment she raised her eyes and saw the tall figure of Wulf. He was standing, as always, a little apart. He had not been in the jumping throng, but he must have left the workshop when he heard the shouting and the laughter. His face, with its customary frown, was thoughtful. She held his eyes in hers and he did not look away.

Feasting and dancing went on throughout the night. Part of the feast was the sacrificial goat, roasted, salted and sizzling from the spit. It made mouths water and bellies rumble and it was a long time before both were satisfied.

As the evening wore on the harp went round. All the famous singers had a turn that night. Edward sang several times. Godwin accompanied him on the harp. Then one of the women remembered the song that had come to Fryth in their circle.

There was a sudden clamour, they wanted to hear her song again.

Fryth was confused. She had learned to play the harp of course, all Edward's children could play well, but she had never sung in public. Besides, how had it gone? She took the harp and settled it on her knee. Everyone fell silent. Fryth breathed deeply, gazing up into the night sky as if for inspiration. Then, much to her surprise, the sense of exultation came again, bursting into music. Word for word, note for note, she repeated her song. Her audience was stirred and moved. Music and poetry were prized by them above all things. Everyone who heard her sing that night recognized that Fryth had received a special gift, the blessing of Freya.

She finished, and as the last note lingered in the air and died away, a great sigh went up from the company. They sat quite still. No one wished to be the first to break the silence. Then, from somewhere in the crowd, a pipe began to play a lively tune. The spell was broken, and the merriment started up again as dancers made a wild revolving circle. The mead at the feast was rich and powerful, stronger than their daily beer, and under its influence the young men grew braver. When dawn came there was not one of them who had not held Fryth's hand in the dance.

Only Wulf had stayed away. The outcast was debarred from joining in the celebrations.

CHAPTER 4

Fryth slept through most of the next day. She got up in the late afternoon and set about what was left of her daily tasks. Eangyth had spared her most of them but in the evening, as she often did, Fryth drove the family cows down to the village pond to water them and cool them off. Autumn lingered long this year and the day had been warm. The evening sunlight slanted across the grass and the bushes round the pond cast deep pools of shadow. Fryth was late, all the other cow-herds had gone home. Her cows had the pond to themselves. They wallowed in, sinking up to their hocks in its refreshing mud. Lowing softly, they stretched out their long necks to drink. Fryth watched them vacantly. Yesterday her mind had been too full; now she let it wander. Her eyes followed the slow ripples on the surface of the water as they spread quietly outwards from the animals to die away at the muddy margins of the pond.

She jumped at the light touch of a hand on her shoulder. She looked up quickly. Wulf was standing behind her. His hair was a wreath of red fire, his face dark against the the setting sun.

'You startled me!' She was annoyed.

'Sorry,' said Wulf cheerfully. Fryth resented his intrusion into the peaceful evening and wanted him to go away. She stared intently at her feet, ignoring him. But Wulf was unaccountably sociable. He flung himself down beside her.

'I saw you passing, just as I was packing up,' he said. Fryth said nothing. 'We finished the pillar today, you know. All that remains is to paint it, then it's done.' Still getting no response, he faltered, 'I thought you might be interested, you liked to watch me carve it, I thought you'd like to know we'd finished . . .

that's why I came.' His voice was losing its careless easy tone. Fryth looked up. She was touched, her resentment vanished.

'I *am* interested,' she said. 'Thank you for telling me.'

Wulf brightened. 'Eangyth will be coming to advise us on the painting,' he said. 'Why don't you come too?'

'If I have the time, I will, of course,' she said.

'Please make the time!' cried Wulf. Then, as if surprised by his own eagerness, he blushed slightly and fell silent. Fryth was silent too. There was a feeling of constraint between them. Fryth cast round for something to say to ease the awkwardness. She remembered catching his eye at the edge of the crowd the day before.

'I'm sorry you couldn't join my feast,' she said.

'Are you?' he said. He looked her in the eye and smiled, his tension melted. He rolled over on his back. 'Well I am too, I would have liked to hear you sing.'

'How did you know?'

'They talked about nothing else in the shop this morning. How our priestess's daughter would be even more gifted than her mighty mother.'

'You know,' said Fryth seriously, it seemed quite natural to talk about these things with Wulf, 'I didn't know I had the gift till yesterday. It felt entirely strange, as if it wasn't me. But then recently so many new things have happened to me. . . .' Here she did check herself. Her music was a public matter but some things should not be spoken of at all. After a pause she went on. 'You have a gift,' she said.

'Yes, but I've had mine since I could hold a knife. I can't remember when I couldn't carve. My gift is mine to use, at my will. How does yours come to you? Can you sing that song again, here, now, just like that?' Fryth thought for a moment and then answered,

'Yes, I think so.' She hesitated. 'But let me try another.' Wulf drew apart from her and sat cross-legged on the turf expectantly. It was growing dark. The cows came lumbering out of the water and set off home of their own accord. Fryth let them go. Godwin would see them in.

Wulf was waiting. Fryth let her mind float free. A skein of swans passed high overhead. From the beating of the wide outstretched wings came their weird, unmistakable, ringing sound. Words and music formed themselves in Fryth's mind with each beat.

'Without a sound   I step across the Earth,
Stay in my house,   or stir the still water.
At times in this   high tumult of air
My radiant robes   lift me over the lives of men.
The force of the clouds   carries me far
Over all people.   Then my pale pinions
Resonate loudly,   ring with a melody,
Sing out clearly   while sleepless I sail the sky
Or settle on grey waters.   A way-faring spirit.'

Fryth became aware of an intrusive sound that was not the swans' wings, or her own heart. It was Wulf clapping. He had leaped to his feet, his face shone.

'Beautiful! Oh, beautiful!' he cried. He reached out and caught Fryth by the shoulders. He was a head taller than her. Tipping her face up he kissed her. Fryth half pulled away, but his mouth on hers was insistent. She felt a strange sensation in her stomach, a falling away. She felt Wulf harden as he pressed against her. Decisively, she pulled him to her, one hand on either side of his face. They lay down together on the grass.

'I chose you yesterday, in the crowd,' she whispered, holding him closely to her. His hands were warm on her breasts and belly. He lifted his face from hers and looked at her. Then he rolled over, pinning her beneath him on the harsh close-cropped grass.

Suddenly Wulf shuddered and lay still. She could feel the blood beating in the veins of his neck. He lay with his head on her breast. It rose and fell with her hard breathing.

'So many new things,' she thought, smiling to herself. She stroked his dark red hair.

Wulf sat up abruptly. Between his eyes was the old familiar frown.

'I'm sorry,' he said. 'What have I done?'

'Don't be sorry,' said Fryth. 'I'm glad.' She took his hand. 'Anyway it's what *we* have done. It was as much my choice as yours.'

'I'm an outcast,' he said simply.

'And I am a free woman,' she replied. 'I am a free woman and I have chosen you.'

Fryth had already changed and was sitting by the fire when Eangyth returned from the shrine. She was glad to have escaped the questions her mother would inevitably have asked if she had been home first and seen her come in, flushed and dishevelled, long after the cattle. It was not that Fryth regretted what she'd done. On the contrary, she regretted only that the feelings Wulf had roused in her had been left unsatisfied. Next time, she promised herself, they would both know better. It was not what she had done that worried her, but rather whom she had chosen. She knew her mother could not approve of Wulf. He was excluded from the life of the tribe, and forbidden any kind of association with its women. He was an outcast and unlucky, and her mother, as the tribe's priestess, would be the first to insist that its laws should not be broken.

But, waiting for Eangyth, Fryth had made up her mind. It was too late, they had begun now, there could be no going back either for her or Wulf. They would have to be discreet that was all. Discretion would be justified if it spared her family knowledge of something that could not be undone, however wrong it was. She greeted her mother with a determined smile.

The next morning she went with Eangyth to watch the tree being painted. She caught Wulf's eye but his face was dark and anxious and she could not make him smile. He bent his head over the carving as she approached. Unobserved, she touched him lightly on the neck and saw with satisfaction his eyes close gently for a moment, and the colour rise in his cheeks.

Fryth had begun to learn her mother's arts. Eangyth introduced her to the rituals in the shrine. She taught Fryth that the daily offerings returned to Freya a small part of her gifts, both in thanksgiving for her care, and to ensure her goodwill so that that care would always continue.

Every day at dawn and dusk a fire was lit and fed with the aromatic herbs that grew in the shrine's precinct. As the scent of herbs rose in thick grey spirals, filling the air, flowers and bowls of food grown in their fields were laid beside the fire, and water from the holy spring was sprinkled over everything to purify the offerings. After the rites, the sanctified offerings were filled with special power and were used by Eangyth to make medicines, or, more directly, to feed the sick. On each quarter day, as it waxed and waned, a blood sacrifice was offered to the moon, the wanderer. The life of all wandering things was blood. Eangyth taught Fryth that only through these offerings in kind could the cycle of life continue, constantly feeding on itself – where else would it get food?

Fryth learned the ways in which a sorceress harnessed the energies in the natural world and how to use these energies in her magic. Animals brought men strength in sickness or in battle; wind and thunder carried madness and disease; plants and herbs could kill or cure, or produce healing dreams and visions; fire and water purified and healed.

In silence, breathing, fasting, songs and visions, Fryth learned about the spirit world and about the depths that existed in her own soul. She never regained the clarity and simplicity of her vision by the river, but she held on to the conviction it had brought her, and in all the work she was doing with her mother she felt that she was groping her way back to an understanding of its truth.

Fryth often travelled into the spirit world at the beating of her mother's drum, a large hoop of wood with a painted skin drawn tightly over it. She learned to submit completely to the powerful, and sometimes terrifying, forces that the spirit world unleashed on her. Eangyth warned that they might take her to the brink of madness, even death. Carefully, by slow degrees she drew Fryth deeper into the mysteries that she commanded.

On all her journeys the fox would come to Fryth, stepping lightly out from between the aspen trees, just as he had done at their first meeting. He led her down the windings of his secret world. She found she needed him to guide her through the labyrinth of experiences in this dangerous, demon-haunted place. She met her own demons first; fear and inexperience, and faceless future ills. She wrestled with these enemies in the course of many trances until if not defeated, they had at least been weakened in the battle. Only when she reached this stage would she be ready to fight the demons that afflicted other members of her tribe. But shortly after she began her training Eangyth, as she had promised, allowed her to take part in the consecration of the newly finished tree.

The original pillar had been taken down and given a warrior's funeral. Now, before the men left to join the Mercians, it was time to raise the new one in its place.

Fryth had not been inside the sacred grove since her initiation as a baby. Freya was always worshipped in sacred groves in the days before the English crossed the sea. Every day the priests would undertake the dangerous journey through the evil-infested forests. But the old country, Eangyth explained to Fryth, had been different. Life was harsh for everyone then. In this gentler land, Freya was satisfied with less and needed less appeasing.

'She makes things easier for us here,' Eangyth said. 'On the whole she is content with offerings from our village shrine. But, even so, there are times when we have to step outside our comfortable world and journey through danger. Danger overcome is like a purification. It leaves us stronger and refined.'

The forest represented danger to all the tribe, and to sanctify the pillar it needed to be carried through the forest to the sacred grove.

Twelve men, elders of the tribe, led by Cerdic, were chosen to carry the pillar. Edward was among them, and Eric the head woodworker. They were all tough, resilient men, but they shifted uneasily under the burden of the tree, and looked warily about as they made the winding journey to the centre of the wood. A few wore single blue beads on leather thongs about their necks; talismans to ward off evil spirits.

Eangyth and Fryth headed the procession, with Fryth gingerly leading a huge white bull by the bronze ring in his nose. The bull had been garlanded with leaves by the villagers before the procession had set off, and it walked heavily, heaving its flanks sorrowfully from time to time as if it knew its fate.

It was noon, and the sun, high above the clearing, flashed like lightning on the sacrificial knife as it came swiftly down. The bull sank to its knees and keeled over slowly. Cerdic and Fryth held out large jars in which they caught the flow of blood. The blood they could not catch ran over their hands and sank into the dry earth.

The pillar was held upright while Eangyth circled round it, sprinkling it with fresh blood. They joined hands round it.

'Pillar of the world,   rejoicing in blood.
Embrace our fate,   the pride of warriors,
Make it your own.   Strengthen our people
Give them joy in the hall!'

Fryth lit a fire and fed it with oil and herbs. The smoke rose to the sky in a thick black column, dwarfing the pillar. As it burned the men went one by one to the urn at the far end of the grove, the urn in which Fryth had once been immersed. They dipped their hands and faces into the urn's black water, snorting and blowing with the shock of its cold. Their purification over, they lashed the carcass of the bull to the pillar and set off back through the forest, like huntsmen returning with a kill.

A deep pit had been prepared to receive the pillar outside the hall where the old column had once stood. The bull's head, with its sharp curved horns was dropped into the bottom of the pit, facing the hall, then the pillar itself was carefully lowered in and packed tight with large stones. Finally, the earth was shovelled back and trodden firmly down. When the pillar was secure, a great cheer went up from the whole tribe. They crowded round, marvelling at its workmanship and the brilliant colours. Nobody touched it. They could feel its power.

Another feast was held that night, a quieter and more sober affair than Fryth's celebration, for the men were leaving the next day. Few boasts were made in the beer-hall after the roasted bull had been eaten. No one, it seemed, over-estimated his strength. As the drinking progressed, Edward left the hall and walked to his wife's house. He found Eangyth and Fryth resting from their day's exertions, scarcely talking. They made room for him beside the fire.

'I've made some new leggings for you,' said Eangyth. 'Fetch them from the box will you Fryth?' She took his hand. 'The winter will be cold.'

Edward seemed distracted. 'I never wanted this,' he said quietly, 'no good will come of it.'

'I know that, Edward, as well as you, but it's woven in our fate, there's nothing to be done.'

'Nothing has changed that you can see?' he asked without hope.

'You'll be safe, that at least I know,' said Eangyth. 'But I've told you that before.' Edward sighed. He took the leggings, kissing his wife gently on the forehead.

'He's not in the least like Wulf,' Fryth thought, watching Edward taking leave of his dearly loved wife. 'What gave him the courage to approach a sorceress? But . . . what gives Wulf the courage either?' Edward turned to her.

'I've come for you, Fryth,' he said. 'They want you in the

hall.' He squared his shoulders and grinned proudly, his fears
for tomorrow suddenly put by. 'Come with me.'

Fryth looked at Eangyth who nodded and smiled. She
followed Edward out of doors.

The hall was stiflingly hot and brightly lit. Fryth had never been
inside during a meeting of the men. She shrank a little at what
she saw. Flushed, beery faces, sweaty grease-smeared chests glist-
ening in the firelight. Edward sensed her hesitation.

'This is nothing,' he said cheerfully, 'the men haven't begun
to drink yet, and they're not likely to tonight.' He led her up
the centre of the hall between benches on either side filled with
shouting, laughing, back-slapping men. Occasionally there came
a rumbling belch, or a rasping hawk and spit.

The fire-pit smoked in front of the high table, and it was not
until they had passed through its miasma that she made out the
faces of Cerdic, and Hild, his toothy wife, sitting at the centre
of the table. Cerdic's huge limewood shield hung on the wall
above his chair. Fryth noticed then, above the smoke and
flaming torches, that several of the men had new, brightly
coloured shields over their places. The shield's jutting bosses
were shaped like women's breasts.

Cerdic's place was piled high with meat and bread but he was
not eating, and he had not touched the beer that filled his green
glass drinking horn. He turned the horn in his hands, tracing
with his eye the trails of white glass that circled its brim. He
looked up as Edward and Fryth approached.

'You've brought her at last!' He called out. He looked at his
glass and laughed, handing it to his page. 'If I was drinking
tonight I would ask you to serve me,' he said to Fryth, 'but
since I'm not,' he stretched, as if to squeeze out some little
irritation, 'perhaps you'd like to sing for us?' Fryth winced, she
looked imploringly at her father but he did not seen to notice
her discomfort. He was looking pleased and proud. Fryth had
no option; she took the harp. Cerdic thumped the table with
his fist and the hall fell silent. In the sudden hush, Fryth felt the

music rising in her again. Her song was long and intricate; its rhythm had the men pounding on the tables with the handles of their knives and they burst into delighted applause when it was over.

Breathless, Fryth kissed her father and excused herself to Cerdic, who pulled a silver ring from his finger and pressed it into her hand. His eyes were shining with pleasure.

Fryth made her way towards the door. The harp was moving down the hall and someone else began to sing;

'Beowulf spoke, son of Ecgtheow.
Sorrow not wise warrior, better it is
That a man avenge his friend than mourn. . . .'

A groan rose from the benches. Bones began to fly about. Fryth ducked out of the door.

She went straight to Wulf's workshop. Wulf often worked late and they had taken to meeting there after the other men had gone home. Fryth felt that she would always associate the smell of new wood-shaving with making love. She smelt them now and the thought made her laugh as she walked in.

'What is it?' asked Wulf, looking up. He put down his chisel.

'I was just thinking.'

'Of me, I hope,' he said, grabbing her round the waist and burying his face in her neck. She held him to her, and they lay down together on the sacks of shavings on the floor and made love slowly. Wulf groaned loudly and bit her breast, not gently. His teeth were very white, even and sharp, Fryth prized him loose. After a while she said,

'Cerdic gave me this.' She held up her hand, turning it in the light. The spiral ring hung loosely on her finger. 'It was for singing to him in the hall, I've just come from there.'

'A new song?' asked Wulf, twisting his head round to see the ring.

'No.' She had sung it to him the night before.

'I'm glad,' said Wulf. 'I shouldn't like to think of you singing a song that I don't know. I might never get to hear it.' Fryth knew where this was leading. In case he should grow melancholy she said quickly,

'You miss nothing in the beer-hall, I can tell you that, truly, nothing at all. A crowd of sweaty, drunken men.' She shuddered.

'I don't know what I miss.' He *was* growing melancholy. Fryth bit his ear. Wulf yelped. Then he smiled and pressed her down again among the sacks.

In the morning the men marched away. The old men and the boys and women were left to see the winter out together; the warriors would not return till seed-time. Wulf did not watch them go. He stayed in the workshop. It would be his all winter.

CHAPTER 5

After such a good harvest those who were left behind awaited the onset of winter cheerfully. The granaries were full and the lofts and storehouses well stocked. October was blood month, the month of slaughtering, when the fattened beasts were butchered and salted down for winter. The stockyards usually rang with the shouts and curses of the men. This year the women finished off the grisly work. Unlike the men, they tended to work silently, acknowledging the suffering of the animals waiting patiently for their bloody ends.

With so much food in store winter promised to be easy. The women had more free time, lacking men to care for, and took to meeting in each others' houses in the evenings, squatting round the fire singing songs, telling stories, gossiping and joking among themselves. There was a carefree feeling in the air despite the reason for the absence of the men, and the women were happy and optimistic.

Fryth's education continued. Eangyth taught her the meaning of the runes. They visited the forest grove together and cut a straight branch from an ash. Eangyth sliced it up into thin discs on each of which she cut a single glyph.

'These are our strongest magic,' she explained. 'Woden, the all-father, suffered for nine nights, hanging from a tree, before he grasped their wisdom for us.' She began to sing very softly.

' "On a windy tree I hung
Wounded with a spear.
Woden's gift to Woden,

Myself to myself
On that tree to man unknown,
Whose secret roots run into the dark.

Alone and friendless,
With none to succour me.
I stared into the depths
And saw the runes,
I seized them screaming
And fell back into the world.

Health I won that day,
And wisdom too." '

As she finished, a shivering in the trees above their heads filled the silence.

'The runes contain all the wisdom and truth of the old ways.' Eangyth said quietly. 'Since coming here those ways have changed in our tribe. Here, because the land, our Mother, welcomed us so lovingly we have gradually stopped worshipping the other gods.'

'I know their stories.'

'Some of them. Even *I* don't know them all. What I do know is that here in the runes we have the living power of all our ancient gods. We may no longer worship them, but their wisdom is still contained in these.' She let the thin light coloured discs run through her fingers. 'If we use them with understanding they can direct our lives.' She laid the discs out in an arc, face up. Fryth helped, turning them over slowly.

'Now,' said Eangyth, 'your own runes you already know, let's look at these.' She picked out three runes from the spread in front of her. 'Before the men went, Cerdic asked me to cast the runes to discover what their fate would be. These three fell.' She laid them out in front of Fryth. ᛉ ᚱ ᛉ

'Their message is quite clear.' Her finger was on the right hand rune. 'The first means pain, or perhaps necessity, the middle rune, a journey. And this rune,' she touched the last one in the row, 'means protection.'

'That's how you knew Edward will come home again.'

Eangyth smiled. 'Of course I did more than this to discover the fate of my own husband, but even from these I know he will be safe.'

Through the ensuing months Fryth learned the significance of the runes; the different ways of casting them and how to read what she had cast. She also discovered that intuition and long hours of contemplation brought their meaning home.

Eangyth told Fryth that the power of the runes would be enhanced if they were connected with her spirit messenger, the fox. They set a trap deep in the forest and took their living booty, snarling and writhing at the bottom of a sack, into the forest grove. The captive snapped its sharp pointed teeth in fury as they lifted it carefully from its prison. Eangyth gentled it in her hands, speaking to it softly, and it went quiet. Then she hung it by the neck from an ash branch until it died. When it was dead she slit its throat and smeared the red blood over the runes, staining them until they stood out against the pale wood.

'The fox died quietly,' she said, wiping her hands on her skirt. 'That's a good sign, he means to help you.'

Fryth made a cloak of the brown fox fur. Its grinning mask protected her neck and, from then on, a second pair of eyes looked out from behind her head.

Fryth continued to meet Wulf whenever she could. It was sometimes very late when she finished at the shrine, but he always waited for her. They had the workshop to themselves and made love on a small bed Wulf had set up in the corner. He sometimes spent the night there if he had been working late.

It was impossible that Fryth's friendship with Wulf should escape her mother's attention for long. Even if the evidence had not been there in her behaviour, Fryth knew enough of her mother's powers to be aware that she could find out in other ways. One night she came in very late. She had long since run out of reasonable excuses and made no effort to explain. She decided that perhaps Eangyth did not want to know. But she was wrong. That night Eangyth was waiting for her. She was holding a spindle with a whorl of pure cut crystal in her hand. She spun it rapidly as Fryth walked in, flashing rainbows of fire around the darkened room. Her face was serious.

'Wulf is an outcast, Fryth.' she said, with no preamble. Fryth was taken aback. Despite the fact that she knew this must come one day, she was unprepared for such a direct attack. She hesitated, fumbling with her cloak. It had been raining and the cloak was damp. She stood there, squeezing its thick folds in her fingers, saying nothing.

'He is excluded from the tribe because he is unlucky. His fate is bad and we must protect ourselves from it.'

Fryth found her voice. 'He's done nothing wrong.'

'It's not what he's done, Fryth, it's what he is. The gods would think we have no judgment if we allow someone with evil fate to live as one with us, they would lose their trust in us. That must never happen, surely you of all people can see that?'

'I can see Wulf working as a craftsman for us, *that* much I can see!' She was alarmed at the strength of her outraged feelings, they had been pent up for so long. She remembered talking to her father about Wulf's position. His answer then had failed to satisfy her. She did not hope for sympathy from her mother. She bit her lip, and to her shame she felt tears well into her eyes. She swallowed hard. Eangyth sighed and reached out for Fryth's hands but Fryth snatched them away, clasping them behind her back. She faced her mother defiantly.

'Wulf's done nothing wrong.' she repeated. 'It's us that do *him* wrong. Why do we use him as it suits us? And if the tribe does, why shouldn't I!'

'Fryth, I know Wulf himself has done nothing wrong.' She was trying to be reasonable. She looked intently at her daughter, searching her face. 'You really feel for him, don't you?'

'Oh, mother!' Fryth cried out. She flung herself down on the floor at Eangyth's feet, clasping her knees and looking up into her eyes. 'You must know what I am talking about. I can't help it if he's an outcast. You feel the same for Edward. I know you do. Besides,' she went on more calmly, 'not many men have their courage. Who else is there for me?'

'I'm not sure that it's courage, Fryth.' Eangyth said slowly. She was thinking over what Fryth had said, the main purpose of her argument temporarily forgotten. 'I think that men like Wulf and Edward have a magic of their own. Your father was the best musician in the tribe, and we all know what Wulf can do. I think that somehow it sets them apart, and it brings us closer to them. I'm sure that's why Edward felt able to choose me and I dare say the same is true of Wulf.' She paused, not happy with the drift of her thoughts. 'But even so,' she went on firmly,'Wulf *is* unlucky and he's not suitable for you. I admit his skill suggests he is not entirely forgotten by the gods, it's right that we should allow him that, but his fate's against him, and there's nothing to be done about it.'

'I can't stop now, mother, I can't, I need him.' Fryth said simply.

'I think often we don't know what we need,' said Eangyth wearily. 'You need the time to learn all I can teach you, and you need to please Freya. Nothing else has any importance.'

'You always have first claim,' said Fryth. 'And so does she.'

'I know that Fryth, I know that.' She sighed, 'but be careful all the same.'

It was her last word on the subject. Fryth was not sure if she had won a victory. She continued to meet Wulf, but no more openly than before.

Fryth already knew a great deal about medicines. She had often helped Eangyth to gather and prepare the plants and herbs that were stored about the house in jars and sacks. She knew which ones had to be picked by moonlight and which at noon. She knew which ones treated humans and which animals or even bees. Now Eangyth started to take Fryth when she visited sick villagers. Winter was her busiest time. The cold winds blew, bringing with them the spirits of disease and death. The old men's coughs, bearable in summer, turned mortal; children suffered fevers and infections of the throat and ears.

One evening Eangyth was called to the house of Rienmellt, a British bondswoman. Her little son Macha was very ill. He lay tossing and turning, burning with fever, unable to swallow the drinks that might cool him, since his throat was raw and swollen. Fryth accompanied her mother. It was the first time that she had visited this household as her mother's apprentice. She wore the fox-skin over her cloak. The exertions of her apprenticeship had burned dark rings, round Fryth's bright blue eyes. Her purposeful movements and slight frame contrasted sharply with her mother's tall, slow, stately presence. Her mother was the more imposing, yet the family drew back instinctively from the daughter as much as from the priestess.

Eangyth felt the boy's throat and forehead, she opened his mouth and breathed into it. Then she took his head gently in her hands and called him.

'Macha!' Then, a little louder. 'Macha!' Her voice was insistent, 'Macha, look at me!' The boy opened his eyes. He stared, without seeing, at Eangyth.

'Macha, I'm going to go on a journey for you. I'll find the spirit that's tormenting you and make him set you free. Watch and listen.' The boy fell back onto his pillow and closed his eyes again with a sigh. Eangyth seemed unconcerned. She bent over the bed and undid the mouth of the bag that hung at her waist, pulling out her eagle's feather and wolf's paw. Her eyes narrowed and a hissing noise escaped from between her lips as she flicked at the boy's body with the feather and shook the wolf's paw in the air above his head. Then she drew a circle on the floor beside the bed, squatted in it and taking a handful of leaves from the bag, she scattered them around her on the floor. The firelight cast a flickering glow over the sick-bed and the priestess in the circle. The white stripes on Eangyth's badger skin glistened, the small sharp ears were pricked.

The family watched intently from the shadows as Eangyth

beckoned to her daughter. Fryth squatted down beside her mother, but outside the circle. She carried a small drum. Fox and badger skins rippled in the firelight. Eangyth signalled to Fryth, who began to drum.

Softly at first, then growing louder and faster, the throbbing filled the room, Eangyth rocked backwards and forwards with each beat. Her head began to roll and shake and sweat broke out on her brow. Soon her head was thrashing and the drum-beat deafeningly loud, the confined space was caught and held fast in the rhythm of its tight-drawn skin. The walls pulsated and drew in round the little bed. The fox and badger skins seemed to swell and fill the room. The child writhed and moaned, clutching his burning throat.

Sweat was pouring from mother and daughter alike as the throbbing died away. Eangyth crawled out of the circle and collapsed, panting into Fryth's arms. The child lay still. Fryth held her mother's hands, they were as cold as ice, but her body was on fire. Macha's mother crept out of the shadows and moved to his bedside. She felt his body and smoothed his pale forehead.

'He's cooler now,' she whispered. Eangyth's strength was returning but her voice was drained and low.

'He will recover,' she said simply. She asked for water and tipped the dried leaves from the circle into the pot Rienmellt brought her, and then turned to Fryth.

'Give me the rune stave.' Fryth handed her a strip of wood. She had prepared it before they set out. Eangyth asked her to choose a healing rune. She had carved ⟨, the rune of fire and clarity.

'It signifies pain,' Fryth had explained, 'but also a light in the darkness, an opening and hope.'

'Good,' Eangyth had nodded, pleased with her choice. She dropped it now into the cup, breathed on it three times, then spat into it and held it to the boys lips, cradling his head in her arms. Fryth, looking on, saw in her gestures, not Eangyth the high priestess, but simply her mother whom she knew and loved, so many times she had seen her hold the boys like that, coaxing them to eat when they were sick.

'Macha, drink now, it will make you feel better. Drink.' The small boy opened his dark eyes. His face was drained and wan, but the flush of fever had abated. He looked with recognition into Eangyth's eyes and swallowed the water sip by sip as she tipped the cup. His mother let out her breath in a long sigh.

'Tomorrow give him half-cooked eggs. He must have nourishing food. Try milk with honey, and mix chicken fat with chervil for the pain.' Eangyth smiled, 'He'll soon recover.'

They received no thanks that night from the exhausted family, but on the following day a basket was left outside her gate filled with large white eggs. Eangyth added honey to the basket and sent it back with Godwin, asking for news of the child.

CHAPTER 6

These were the happiest months Wulf could remember since his father had left home. He was the only able-bodied man in the village now, if you did not count Harold the dwarf, or the idiot Thurston, and no one did. He ran the workshop single-handed, there was plenty to do. It was not the season for wood carving; general woodwork, making furniture and mending gates, cutting fence posts and hurdles occupied his time. Fryth visited him whenever she was free. They walked by the river in the frosty mornings and, returning to the workshop, which they had to themselves all winter long, made love on the little bed, or on the floor among the woodshavings.

The double lines between Wulf's eyes eased out and his face lost its habitual haunted look. The women needed him for many winter tasks. They had always been freer with him than the men were, being less concerned about the rules that made him an outcast. For the first time in his life he felt wanted and necessary.

Fryth needed him. The rigours of her apprenticeship, the hours of contemplation, the effort required to master a particular rite, or tune her body to the rhythms flowing from the natural world exhausted her. Besides these excercises, Eangyth kept her at work absorbing simple facts; which herbs for this specific illness or for that, the importance of the phases of the moon in working magic, the significance of semi-precious stones . . . and on and on. There were times when it was too much for Fryth and then she turned to Wulf, finding the answer to simpler questions in his arms.

She gave him Cerdic's ring. It did not fit on any of her small fingers. He hung it on a thong round his neck.

'They would ask me where I got it from,' he said, 'and anyway, what right has an outcast to wear silver.'

She had laughed at him, but she was disturbed by the gnawing bitterness which, she had quickly learned, coloured his whole life. She noticed that he was the most punctilious of all in conforming to the codes that ruled his life, as if, by accepting them, he could in some way weaken their power to hurt. It was either that or pride, she thought, which he wore like a second skin. Often, as in this case, his acquiescence maddened her.

'If you weren't punished by our laws, I'm certain you'd invent some torment for yourself, you thrive on them so much.'

'It isn't me who keeps the law alive,' he had answered shortly. He was stoking the fire, it had died right down and he was having trouble coaxing it back to life.

He shivered, hugging himself and hopping about. His body was thin and muscular, his skin very white. He looked at Fryth, who lay watching him with thoughtful eyes from the warmth of the woollen blankets. He went back to the bed and knelt beside her, taking her hands, folding them in his.

'I'd marry you, if they would let me.'

Fryth sighed. This was a subject she preferred to keep from entering her thoughts. She tried to change the mood.

'No one else would!' she said, only half-joking. 'I'm a powerful, dangerous woman.' She sat up suddenly and raised her arms above her head in a menacing gesture, rolling her eyes. The firelight shone on her sharp breasts. Wulf caught hold of her and buried his face between them.

'I'm safe down here!' His voice was muffled. 'Here I'm not afraid of you.'

'Prove to me you're not afraid,' she said. She took his head in her hands, forcing him to face her. He looked her deeply in the eyes. Then he smiled and with his mouth on hers he climbed onto the bed.

The question was set aside that night; as they lay together, panting and laughing in the firelight.

The Yule festival was a quiet affair that winter with no men to fuel the fires or drink the season through. The women and children brought branches of holly into their homes and Eangyth, with Fryth at her side now as a matter of course, lit the bonfire with newly kindled flame, bringing the fire down from heaven to light the depths of winter. Fryth sang a song to welcome the Yule fire as the women joined hands to dance round it. But there was no feast and there could be no rejoicing with the men away, facing danger in a foreign country.

New songs often came to Fryth now, as if carried on some current like shoals of fish in the river, shoals that fattened and increased. Encouraged by Wulf, she found that she could will a song to come, no longer waiting for the touch of inspiration, but summoning it, composing words and music for herself, rather as Wulf with his knife called the spirit from the wood. She made her songs for Wulf, but she sang them to the villagers too, and the women quickly picked them up, so that they became no longer Fryth's, but everyone's, and could be heard on every side, in the fields and in the village streets.

The villagers could hardly fail to notice how much time she spent with Wulf, but they were learning to respect her as a priestess, and no one now would dare to gossip about or displease her. Also, Fryth decided, they must have realized Eangyth was saying nothing too.

One evening shortly after the Yule bonfire Fryth went as usual to Wulf's workshop. It was late. The sun had long since set but she had been delayed by countless visitors. She had taken over the treatment of minor ailments from her mother, and the villagers trooped in to see her all day long. She spent the day treating coughs, worms, sores and itches, injuries and countless other troubles. It was wearisome and thankless and she longed for the hour or two that she could spare with Wulf.

He was sitting by the fire, and did not look up when she came in. At first she thought he had not heard her, but he slowly moved his head and she saw immediately that he was in pain.

'Wulf! What is it? Are you ill too?' She knelt beside him. Wulf groaned.

'I'm glad you've come . . .' His voice was weak, he was cradling his left arm.

'Wulf, what's the matter?'

'I've been waiting for you.' He held up the arm, it was gashed from elbow to wrist in a gaping wound. Fryth drew in her breath sharply.

'The axe slipped. It takes two men to split a plank.'

'Why didn't you call me? Why didn't you come.' She was already tearing up a sheet and starting to bind up the arm as tightly as she could.

'The bleeding got less, and anyway, I'm not allowed . . .' An outcast was not entitled to the sorceress' help.

'Wulf, Wulf, you're mad, I really think you'd rather die than give in!' She was angry now. 'You fool, you *might* have died. I've no patience with you. Anyone would think *you* made these laws, you enjoy them as much as if you had!' She finished tying the last knot. 'This is bad. I'll have to go home and fetch some proper bandages. Lie down, you've lost a lot of blood.' There was a dark stain on the floor, and bloodied cloths with which he had been trying to stop the bleeding, on the bench. Wulf sat quite still, allowing her to pull him this way and that as she bound up the wound, and now he lay down obediently at her command.

Presently Fryth returned. She dressed the wound properly and gave Wulf a strong narcotic drink to make him sleep. She was hardly gentle with him and as she left she heard him sigh. She saw this as more self-pity, and it made her angrier still.

Her annoyance lasted through the night. She was still angry as she performed the morning ritual with Eangyth.

'If he wants to suffer, let him suffer.' She thought as she went through the rite, lingering over every detail. She did collect some soil from the precinct, and water from the spring which she would use later to dress his wound, but by the time she got home the day's business was demanding her attention. It was not until late in the afternoon that she had time to go to Wulf. Her anger had cooled and she put together a basket of food for him. A day's fast would have done him no harm but he would be hungry now.

Eangyth's training was taking hold of Fryth, and long before she reached the workshop she began to sense something was wrong. She was running by the time she reached the lane in which the workshop stood, and was not at all surprised to see a little knot of people crowded round the door. She pushed her way through. No one had called her of course, but standing helplessly beside the bed were Wulf's mother, a thin grey woman, prematurely aged, and his half-grown sister. His mother spun round as she heard Fryth walk in. She grabbed her arm.

'Save him! Look!' She pointed wildly at the bed. 'He's dying, help him, please!' Her voice was shrill with panic. Fryth looked down at where Wulf lay. His face was the colour of ivory and beaded with sweat, his breathing was fast and shallow. She took his arm. She undid the binding as gently as she could, but Wulf was far beyond feeling any pain. An angry, thin red line ran from the now festering wound and disappeared under his arm. The gland there was swollen and hard, like an unripe plum. Wulf was usually such a careful worker, he never injured himself. To the demons of infection he was fresh meat.

Fryth was afraid. She knew Wulf's state was mortal. She hoped there was still time. She dressed the wound again, this time less tightly. She made the soil and water she had brought with her from the shrine into a paste and smeared it over the bandage, sealing it. As she worked she muttered the words of a charm. It was the most powerful she knew.

'I bind this wound with the best war-bandage.
May it neither burn nor burst,
May it neither grow nor deepen.
With this health-giving water I will heal you.
Feel no more pain than does this earth.
Earth and water bear away this hurt!'

Wulf lay very still. His body burned. Fryth could feel the heat he generated as she bent over him. She longed to call her mother, but she feared, with reason, that she would not come. There was no alternative; unpractised, unprepared and ill-equipped she would have to try to save him on her own.

She found a mallet and a block of wood. Removing her cloak she drew a cirle on the dusty floor, as she had been taught, and stepped inside. She beat the mallet on the wood, a slow, insistent drumming. She was drumming herself into the spirit world. She felt the room rocking and the walls close in. She took one last look at Wulf's face before a rushing darkness closed above her head. The journey was familiar to her now. Her fox appeared between the shimmering trees. He sniffed the air intently as if scenting her purpose, then, barking sharply, he turned and ran back into the trees.

A dark wood rose up behind them and the fox disappeared into it at a fast trot. Fryth had to run to keep up. The wood grew thicker and blotted out the light; brambles snared her feet and whipped her face. From the high black branches of the trees came the shrieks and rustles of night creatures, the hunting and the hunted. The trees began to ooze; thick, stinking matter rolled down their rough bark, their trunks closed in on her, pus and blood dripped from their branches. Her feet slithered on the slippery path. She stumbled and then stopped, despairing. The fox had gone.

A throbbing filled her head, and behind it she could hear a steady moan. She looked up and saw Wulf's body lodged in the suppurating branches of a tree. He was naked, sleeping peacefully, her silver ring was dangling from its thong round his neck. She forced her way towards him through the foul thicket, but its knotted, stinking branches reached out and enveloped her. She sank to her knees and closed her eyes. The wood had overpowered her. She could not go on.

Her head drooped down, but then, from a great distance, she heard one loud, high-pitched bark. The call was urgent. She struggled to her feet again and made a last despairing lunge, reaching desperately for Wulf. Her fingers closed on Cerdic's ring. She pulled, and slowly, easily, like a wire through clay she drew him through the mass of tangled branches until he lay, still sleeping peacefully, in her outstretched arms.

She could hear voices. How long she had been sitting there with Wulf she could not tell, but help had come at last. She tried to call out but no sound would come. Hands grasped her shoulders, she swayed in their comforting grip and opened her eyes. Large faces, white with fear, loomed down at her. She blinked, then opened her eyes wider. She saw the familiar workshop walls and smelled the smell of sawdust. She remembered then and smiled. She was lying in Wulf's mother's arms. Fryth could smell the hot sharp stink of fear in the woman's sweat, but Wulf was sleeping quietly now, his face had colour and he was breathing deeply and slowly. She had saved him all alone.

Fryth was ill for many days after this event. She lay half-conscious in her mother's bed. Eangyth tended her, while Wulf was nursed back to health by his mother and sister. Eangyth was not pleased. Her nursing stopped just short of harshness, and when Fryth was well enough to sit up and look about her, she spared her none of her pent-up fury.

Fryth had been irresponsible, criminally foolish. She was not being taught her mother's arts to waste them in an act of recklessness; an act the might very easily have led to her death. No one went into the underworld unprepared. Eangyth blamed herself, she said, she'd gone too fast with Fryth who was by nature far too self-assured. Look at the way she had refused to give Wulf up, when she knew that she was wrong both in the eyes of men, and far worse, of the gods. Well, where had that got her? She had been warned Wulf was unlucky, but would she heed the warning? No! Why? Because she, of course, knew best. What was to be done with such a foolish, stubborn girl!

Eangyth had been pacing round the room, now she came up to where Fryth lay cowering in bed, and clenching her fists, she let out an exasperated sigh. Fryth began to wish that she *had* died and Wulf as well. That would have been the end of her ill-fated career and love, at one kind blow. She wept, quietly at first, but then aloud as the tears ran down her cheeks. Let her mother think she was asking for pity, she needed it.

At last Eangyth relented. She had worked off all her anger, which was composed almost exclusively of fear. She became more gentle and later that evening, with harmony restored between them she got Fryth out of bed. She led her, wrapped warmly in a blanket, to the fire.

'I've been saving these,' she said, 'until you'd earned them.' Lying on the bench was a set of three girdle hangers, identical to hers. The keys of their mysteries.

'It seems you've earned them sooner than expected.' Her face was affectionate, even a little proud. 'I wouldn't have survived as you have done, despite your youth and inexperience. I think you will be greater than me.'

Fryth's saving of Wulf's life was the sensation of the winter. It occupied the villagers for weeks, and no one failed to notice the new hangers at her waist. They saw by them that she had come into her inheritance.

Wulf recovered more slowly. He regained his strength and fitness easily enough but there was a change in him. It was as if, Fryth thought, the purple scar that puckered his left arm had an echo somewhere deeper in his soul.

They continued to meet daily, as before, but there was a new reserve in him, one she could not broach. The frown was back between his eyes. His movements, even when he worked, were tense and restless. He was always glad to see her, but the happiness he had felt during the past few weeks was now somehow eluding him. He was struggling to regain it, but without success. He tried a rational explanation.

'I'm tired,' he said. 'My arm aches all the time and I have so much work to do. I'm slower since the accident.'

'Take on less work then,' Fryth suggested.

'And lose the payment. I must earn it while I can.' He left

unsaid the deeper concern, that he would lose the sense of being necessary and useful; that new and so much valued sense.

He worked late every evening now on the jobs that had accumulated while he had been ill. They seldom made love. Fryth would sit in a corner watching him. Sometimes she would try out a new song, which always pleased him, but often he worked, and she sat, in silence.

The evenings were getting longer. Spring was in the air, but it was very slow in coming. The first lambs were slipping into the shivering world in the chill hours before dawn. Fryth took her turn with the women in the sheepfold through the watches of the night. Sometimes she had no sleep at all. She would often have to go straight from lambing, as the sun rose, to perform the morning ritual, washing the blood and lanolin off her hands in the river before entering the shrine.

Exhaustion was sapping her patience with Wulf. One bruising night, after an evening in the workshop, in the course of which he'd barely said a word, she had gone directly to the sheepfold and wrestled through the small hours to deliver an old ewe of twins. These were the sheeps' last lambs. As they lay quivering in the light of Fryth's lamp the ewe's eyes fluttered then rolled up; her flanks shuddered and, with a weak sigh, she died.

Fryth was cast down as she wrapped the new-born lambs in her cloak to keep them warm. There were no spare ewes to take them on and few, in any case, would accept twins. It was difficult to hand-rear lambs and the chances of these two were slim. She sat wearily in the straw, clutching the little creatures to her breast, feeling the poignant frailty of their bony limbs. They were expendable she thought. She, Wulf, everything, was expendable so long as life, nature itself went on. Freya used the world of living things like a fungus growing on wood, sucking its very life away while she flourished and grew fat. She was indeed indifferent to suffering and pain, none of it mattered so long as *she* survived. Fryth looked down, and here the goddess was, living on in these small lambs, while their mother, bloody and rapidly stiffening, lay stretched out on the straw. Fryth staggered to her feet, hoisting the lambs up, one on each hip. They bleated mournfully. She must get them some milk. Godwin was good with lambs. She left him preparing a leather bottle of warm milk for them in the early light of dawn.

Eangyth was already at the shrine when Fryth arrived and they performed the ritual together. Fryth was angry with the goddess, she flung the holy water impatiently over the offerings. Eangyth took the jars from her with a look of surprise. She did not interrupt the ceremony, but when it was over she led Fryth out into the herb garden, withered now and brown, flattened by the frosts of winter.

It seemed that winter's death-throes were interminable and spring would never come. Fryth leaned against a crab-apple tree. She rubbed her cheek on its smooth bark. Its bare branches, pretty even in winter, made a canopy above her. She could feel the humming of its rising sap. The same force that killed the ewe would soon break out in leaf and fruit.

Eangyth said nothing but went back into the shrine leaving Fryth to her thoughts. Presently she returned, to find Fryth in the same attitude but with a gentler expression on her face. She gave her a handful of consecrated grain.

'You must make amends,' she said. 'Freya will not be treated in that way.'

Fryth asked for forgiveness. She prayed for the spirits of all dead things, and for the courage to accept the remorselessness of Fate. She lay down on the damp earth beneath the tree and, as she lay, the memory of her vision by the river bank came back to her. The huge, still, timeless world was once more beating in her heart. She saw it turning slowly, far beyond the reach of suffering and death; beyond, even, the reach of Fate itself.

She left the grain as an offering beneath the tree.

Fryth spent the rest of the day inside the precinct of the shrine. She had been learning the charm of the nine herbs. The charm that worked the magic of the most powerful herbs used in sorcery. It was long and difficult, and Fryth decided to stay in the herb garden working with the plants themselves, trying to absorb their potency, which was at its strongest in the early days of spring. It was gathering in the roots, waiting to burst out at the touch of the sun.

All nine herbs were among those growing in the precinct. The herbs were not tended like a domestic crop but allowed to grow unchecked in specially prepared beds set wide apart. Last year's growth now made a tangle of brown stalks over the bare earth. Fryth walked from bed to bed reciting the charm.

'Mugwort, oldest of herbs
Has power against three, against thirty
Against poison, infection,
And intruding enemies, ravaging the land.

Plantain, mother of herbs
Eastward turning, strong within.
Over it chariots creak, queens ride,
Brides tremble, bulls bellow.
Strength and power, fear and pride, all break against it.

Cress grows on a stone
It attacks poison and fights with the snake,
Reptiles slink by it, destroyer of their strength.

Deadnettle, milder than mightiest,
Drives out mild poisons,
Completes the cure.

Camomile is powerful food,
Infection cannot kill the man that eats it.

Wormwood, by seal sent
From foreign lands, over the waves of the sea,

Turns aside the power of strangers
And the harm of evil seekers.

Crab-apple purifies the house,
Banishes all evil spirits.

Chervil and fennel created by the Wise One
Hanging on the tree. He sent them into the seven worlds
To help the wretched and the fortunate alike.'

Fryth had been moving slowly from plant to plant as she went
through the charm, bending over each one in turn, drawing in
their strength, meditating on each verse. When finally this was
done she went back into the shrine. Hanging from the rafters
were bunches of herbs that had been gathered and dried the
previous summer. She collected a large bundle and fed it in
handfuls to the brazier. The small building filled with pungent
smoke. Fryth breathed the fumes in deeply until her head swam,
her arms hung down loosely at her sides and she began to sway
gently from side to side, rolling her head in a circular motion.
She closed her eyes as the fumes spiralled through her body,
passing into her blood and tingling in her veins. She could feel
herself being charged with their strength and energy. She had
acknowledged the power of the herbs. Now, in return, they
were investing her with that same power. Raising her arms above
her head she recited in a loud voice the words that Eangyth had
taught her would set the seal on this exchange.

'A snake came slithering in with poisonous thoughts
But Woden vanquished it. He took nine glorious herbs,
He struck the snake. It shivered into nine,
And scattered into the world. The herbs give me their power,
Their strength streams in me, like the waters of the sea.
I alone can use them, nine against nine.
Nine snakes from North, South, East or West, beware of
   me,

I have the power to scatter you again, and blow away your
poison.'

Gradually Fryth's head cleared. She felt light and strong and
full of energy. She sat quietly, feeling the energy humming in
her veins, until Eangyth arrived to perform the evening rite. All
the anguish and the anger of the morning was forgotten as Fryth
and Eangyth went through the ritual together. Fryth had reached
a new horizon in her spiritual journey, but she knew another
always stretched beyond, luring her onwards to some new and
greater understanding. The prospect filled her with exited awe.

Fryth found she had a new reserve of will when she visited
Wulf much later that night. He greeted her with his customary
frown and, scarcely looking at her, continued with his work.
He protested when she went up close to him and took the chisel
and mallet from his hands. The chisel had been slipping in its
groove from the weakness in his arm. Fryth held him at arms'
length, gripping his upper arms and pinning them to his side.
He squirmed a little, turning his head from her gaze, but by
degrees she drew his eyes to hers and held them. She looked
steadily at him, piercing through his taut defences, forcing him
to show the misery that lay beneath. He hung his head and
groaned. She led him to the narrow bed and lay down with him,
holding him closely in her arms. It was here that she had saved
his life and now it seemed she was going to have to save him
from himself, a new and far worse enemy.

She felt him rising, a small victory in itself after so long a
time. She started to make love to him. He lay impassively as
she sank down, watching her and holding still. She could almost
see his isolation as she moved against him.

'Wulf, Wulf,' she screamed, 'Where are you?' She collapsed
on him. Her face was wet with tears. He was crying too.

Slowly, like a block of wood coming to life beneath his knife,
he started to respond. He brushed away her tears with his
fingers. They felt cold and dry on her hot face. Then, pressing
close, he rolled over and looked down at her. He was gentle at

first, as if testing himself, and then ferocious. When he had finished they lay quite still, drained and exhausted in each other's arms.

After a while Wulf roused himself and threw some wood onto the fire. It was a fence-post he had prepared, but he let it go. They lay in front of the fire, Fryth holding Wulf in her arms watching the firelight gleaming on his dark red hair.

'I'd never known that life could be so good until this winter.' he said. 'It's strange that until they went away all I wanted was to be accepted by the men; to join the war-band and to sit with them in the hall.' There was still a yearning somewhere in his voice. 'And yet what I most dreaded . . .'

'Being left behind?'

Wulf nodded. '. . . Turned out to be the best thing that could have happened. Having you, and all this work, and the work-shop to myself.'

'Ourselves.'

'There's that,' he laughed. 'And being valued as a man in other ways as well; to be useful as a workman. You can't imagine what it meant to me to have a purpose. I don't need the war-band. I need respect.' Fryth stroked his arm.

'And then this accident.' He let out a long sigh. 'It brought home to me what my position really is. I lay long hours on this bed. The time you spend thinking is the worst.' He paused and pushed a lock of hair back from his forehead. Following the movement of his hand Fryth saw the two fine lines, deeply etched by the firelight, between his eyes.

'I thought and thought. What have I got? Nothing. All this is just foolish dreams. I'm still an outcast, the men will soon return. . . .'

'Am I a dream?' asked Fryth quietly.

'That's the worst!' cried Wulf vehemently. 'You're further from me than any of them.' He felt her arms tighten round him in response. 'It's true, you know its true. You can't deny it!' He felt her stir again. 'And if you do it only means you've chosen not to think about it. You've got so much else besides me. You have your work to do. It will always have first claim, even when you marry.' His voice sank. 'And if one thing's certain, it's that you'll never marry me.' He looked at her closely. She tried to find words of denial, but they would not come.

'You see,' he went on flatly, 'it's true. And shortly the men will come home and I'll go back into my corner, out of mind, a useful pair of hands. Only they're not so useful now, and I'm even less a man.' He buried his head in the crook of his wounded arm. The pain in his voice was almost too hard to bear.

'Oh Fryth, I dread the future now!'

She laid her cheek on the top of his head, breathing in the warm scent of his hair, compounded, as always with the spicy scent of wood shavings. There should be some medicine or charm for this, but Fryth knew that there was none. What troubled Wulf was intractable; the only cure she knew for his complaint she could not give.

'Wulf,' she said carefully, weighing her words. 'I think I would marry you outcast or not. Your being an outcast has never deterred me and it never will. But I *can't* marry yet, you know that well enough, maybe not for years.' She thought of the mysteries she had broached that day. She had as yet hardly touched on all there was to know. It might take a lifetime. She was prepared to give a lifetime to it. 'Maybe I shall never marry.'

Wulf pulled apart. He faced her squarely.

'Then where does that leave me? Your work already takes you away from me.' Fryth looked at him protestingly. 'Well, maybe it doesn't yet, but I know it will and so do you.' He slapped the floor with his open palm. It was a gesture of despair.

Fryth had no answer and no more was said that night, but they had reached a kind of understanding. Wulf was gentler now when they met, and more responsive. He talked openly to her of his unhappiness and his cloudy future. Sometimes he could forget himself and be happy for a while, but these times were all too brief. Fryth felt helpless when confronted with his pain; there was nothing she could do to change his fate.

CHAPTER 7

As the first buds of spring began to show the men started to return. They had marched away in a body, but they came back singly or in small groups. Once released from service by the Mercians each man's only aim was to get home as fast as possible. Those who travelled alone came fastest; the young men eager for their girls' arms, the farmers anxious to start ploughing and to get the seeds into the earth.

There was a great rejoicing in the village as they came. The women were glad to see their husbands and to be relieved of the heavy labour they had been forced to do all winter. The children were pleased to have their fathers back, the girls their lovers and the old men their brave sons. All clamoured for tales of adventure, deeds of blood, and adversity overcome. The war-band did its best to satisfy the thirst for entertainment in those they had left behind, but it emerged that there was little to tell. All but two came home safely and unharmed. The two who died had died of fever, not of wounds.

There had been a great victory against the Northumbrians but the men of Fryth's tribe had done little of the fighting. They had been a small and insignificant component of the Mercian army. Cerdic's warriors, together with other bands from Middle Anglia, had been left in the rear while Penda and his ally Cadwallon, a king from the western British lands, marched to meet the Northumbrians. Penda and Cadwallon fought a glorious battle against King Edwin. Edwin had been killed and his army utterly defeated. Cerdic's men were in the rear to cover Penda, should he need to make a hasty retreat.

They spent the winter on the borders, squaring up to small

bands of Northumbrians sent to harry them. There were occasional clashes, but these were merely echoes of the real fighting further north, and the men of Fryth's village saw the long months out in boredom and discomfort, kept together only by their friendship for each other and the firm bond of loyalty that tied them to Cerdic. He had done what he could to keep up their morale with exercises and, when food was easily foraged, with feasting, but they were very glad indeed to see the end of the winter campaigning.

The men did their best to satisfy the stay-at-homes with stories of the lands through which they had passed; the dense and murky woods, wide echoing marshes thick with waterfowl, and strange tribes of dark and wiry British who lived in boats and wore garments made entirely out of feathers. The people of Northumbria were not unlike themselves, they said, but some worshipped a strange god, born in the rising sun. They practised weird and disgusting rites, feeding on human flesh! They had rejected the old gods; it was no wonder that the Mercians had so easily defeated them.

Edward was one of the first to arrive. He came home in the middle of a bright spring morning. Eangyth had been kneading the week's bread in a large wooden trough which she had carried out into the yard to make the most of the warm sunshine. It was hard work pounding the spongy, resistant dough and Eangyth had paused to catch her breath, unbending her back and wiping a floury hand across her brow. As she straightened up, the yard gate opened and a tall figure blocked the threshold. He stood there for a moment, stooping to lean his shield against the door-post.

The light was behind him and for one split second Eangyth wondered who it was. In the next her arms were round Edward's neck, there was flour in his hair and traces of sticky dough across his shoulders. He dropped his pack and lifted her into the air, spinning her round. Then they stood, not speaking, locked together. Athelmar came running out of the house chasing a small puppy, one of this year's litter. Seeing Edward,

Athelmar pulled up short, then whooped and flinging his arms in the air, he hurled himself at both his parents. They staggered slightly as he crashed into them, locking his arms around his father's legs. Godwin, Guthlac and Fryth, hearing the commotion, came outside and the entire family were joyfully reunited.

Edward looked thin and pale. There were grey streaks in his beard and his face was engrained with sweat-smeared dirt. His clothes were torn and ragged, he was bare-legged and his shoes were worn right through. He hugged them all repeatedly, breathing in their warmth, saying over and over again how good it was to be home. Eangyth led him indoors. First he ate enormously, asking for more and more, managing between mouthfuls, since the children would not wait, to tell the story of the winter campaign. Then he washed himself and changed his clothes.

'I exchanged my leggings for a barrel of fish!' he said as he strapped his leather thongs round an old checked pair Eangyth found for him. His voice was deep and resonant, it seemed to fill the room. In his absence they had all forgotten quite how big and loud he was. He saw Eangyth frown and laughed, 'I decided that I was more likely to starve than freeze to death. Our worst enemy was hunger, except when we could find a friendly village. Here! I'd quite forgotten. Did someone bring my pack in from the yard? There's something in it you must see.' The pack was produced and Edward rummaged through it, pulling out various grimy belongings. At the very bottom was a little leather bag. He shook its contents onto his palm.

'Look.' He held out his hand.

'What are they?' asked Fryth. She peered at the three, thin, silver discs lying in the middle of her father's calloused hand.

'They're pictures, look closely, here.' He pointed at one with a thick finger.

'Oh, yes!' said Godwin wonderingly. 'I can see a boat, look there's its oars, and there are little men in it.'

'And this one has half a man's face!' Eangyth was fascinated.

'Turn it over,' said Edward, 'and there's the boat on the other side. They're all the same.'

'They're lovely, father,' said Fryth. 'How did you get them?'

'Are they booty?' Godwin's eyes sparkled.

'Not at all,' replied Edward. 'There was no opportunity for that. No, I was given these by a Northumbrian chief. He liked my songs. I sang to him a great deal. We camped a few days beside his village.'

'Why didn't he fight you then?' asked Godwin, 'I thought you went to kill Northumbrians, not to sing to them.' There was a hint of disappointment in his voice. Edward turned to Eangyth, directing his answer to her.

'It's as I said, the Northumbrians are our brothers too. This village wouldn't accept Edwin as their king because of his new religion. They weren't over eager to help us, but they wouldn't fight us either. I got the fish from them, and their chief liked music. His harper had taken the new religion and left him over a year ago.' Edward grinned. 'Poor man, he was quite starved of good singing, he couldn't hear enough.'

'But what about the fighting, father, did you kill anybody?'

'I never got the chance. We were attacked a couple of times, but they ran away when they heard the rattle of our spears. They were being beaten further north, you see, and were probably trying to conserve their strength.'

'They couldn't fight another battle though, not after Penda killed their leader, could they?' There was triumph in Godwin's voice.

'I think they lost their heart for battle. Edwin was a great king.'

Fryth was turning one of the silver discs over in the light. The half-face was fat. It looked well fed and jowly, too human to be a spirit or a demon. She handed it back to her father who slipped all three into their bag.

'What about this new god, father, did you learn anything about him?'

'No, I told you we met only followers of our gods. But you

hear some curious tales. These Northumbrians are supposed to eat and drink human flesh and blood.' A series of disgusted and disgusting noises came from the boys. 'It doesn't sound very pleasant, does it?' said Edward. 'Talking of which, I'm hungry again.'

'I'm not sure there's anything left!' Eangyth looked amused.

'Well, then,' answered Edward, 'I think I'll take to worshipping this Northumbrian god. Now, where shall I begin!' He rolled his eyes and, pouncing on Guthlac with a loud growl, and started chewing at his neck.

By the time the last man had returned, the home-coming heroes were already beginning to repeat and embellish the tales of their adventures, and the the village quickly returned to its normal ways.

To ensure the co-operation of Freya in the coming growing season the cutting of the first furrow of spring was attended by an elaborate ceremony. This always took place in the same field, one that contained three of her favoured haunts; a small standing stone, worn smooth by the attentions of generations of villagers; a low, twisted oak tree which grew in the middle of the field surrounded by a narrow circle of rough grass untouched by the plough; and a little spring, whose water trickled down a well-cleared field drain to feed the village pond.

In the days that led up to the ceremony Eangyth and Fryth gathered a strip of bark from each evergreen tree growing on the land, and a leaf from every plant whose leaves were showing in the early spring. They took their harvest to the shrine and steeped it for several days in water from the sacred spring. Meanwhile they collected milk from every yielding cow, and flour made with every type of grain: barley, wheat and rye. They mixed the milk together in one jar, and baked a single loaf from the three flours. Finally, they prepared jars of the best oil and honey in the village stores.

On the morning of the field-ceremony the two women were out before daybreak. They cut four turves, one from each corner of the field, and in the light of the rising sun they anointed the undersides of each turf with the infusion of bark and leaves and with the milk, oil and honey. As they did so they chanted softly together, repeating again and again,

'Grow and multiply and fill the Earth.
Grow and multiply and fill the Earth. . . .'

They carried the turves to the shrine and laid them, green side up, in the white circle of sand behind the tree. The turves lay all morning in the shrine. Eangyth and Fryth returned at noon, accompanied by the whole village, dressed in holiday clothes. A great procession followed the turf back to the field. Cerdic brought up the rear leading two, lumbering, brown oxen, yolked together, ready for the plough.

The procession halted at the sacred oak in the centre of the field and made a wide circle round it. Fryth cut four strips from its bark and marked them with the rune of harvest, ϕ , signifying a fertile season. The procession reformed. Fryth carried the rune staves and Eangyth the turf. Starting in the north they walked slowly, following the sun, round the edge of the field replacing the divots one by one. Before each turf was pressed back into place Fryth threw a rune stave into the hole as if it were a seed that she was sowing. Then the village moved to the standing stone, forming another circle round it. The two priestesses stood on either side of the stone and, turning to the east, began to chant the *Acerbot*, the incantation of fertility:

'Erce, Erce, Erce!
Eastwards we stand, favours we pray for.
To the guardian of the heavens,
To the Earth we pray, and Sky.
To the Holy Mother of the Earth,
And the might of heaven's high hall.
That we may with the gods' good grace
Pronounce this charm,

And with our steadfast thoughts
Waken these seeds for our people's use,
Fill this earth by our firm belief,
And make the meadows beautiful.'

With arms outspread and heads flung back, the two women turned round three times and lay face down. All the people did the same.

As the villagers lay still, a light rain began to fall. It came on steadily. Heavy clouds had been building up throughout the morning. Complaints were heard as the village scrambled to its feet. Why did it always rain during their most important festivals?

The rites continued. They made a horse-shoe round the spring, There was a movement in the crowd and a Briton, one of the poorest in the village, who owned a meagre plot of land, was pushed into the open space where Fryth and Eangyth were standing by the spring. He had come prepared and handed Eangyth a small bag of fresh seed corn, receiving another from her in return, twice its size. Eangyth scattered his seed round the spring.

The plough-shares had been stacked at the edge of the field and now the village moved to where they stood, polished and gleaming in the streaming rain. Eric, the carpenter, stepped forward. He bored a small hole in the handle of a new plough and Eangyth pressed leaves of the nine chief herbs and fat and salt into the hole. Then Cerdic hitched the large brown oxen to the plough, spat on his hands, and grasped its handles. Straining and blowing under his cracking whip, the oxen started plodding slowly down the field. The harness creaked, the plough-share bit and the soil curled over it in a fresh wet wave. The first furrow of spring lay open to the sky.

One last thing remained. Fryth broke the loaf baked with flour of every kind of grain and laid it in the first furrow. The whole tribe said a final prayer:

'Field filled with food for us
In our Mother's name be blessed.
Be secure from every harm.
Grow and flourish, fill with fertile gifts,
Bright corn. May each grain prosper us.'

The ceremony ended, the growing season had begun. The sodden crowd went quietly home to warm themselves and dry off by the fire.

The Mercians kept the bargain they had struck with Cerdic. In return for their services his men were given a weight of raw silver, mined in the country of Cadwallon, Penda's British ally. The heavy silver bars were laid out like spoils of war beneath the new wooden pillar and the whole village came to marvel at such riches, proud that their brave men had warranted this payment. The question of what was best to do with it arose. The silver was their prize and not to be idly spent on ordinary needs. A meeting was called in the hall. The women packed in with the men, squeezing in behind the benches.

Several suggestions were made; it should be cast into rings, one for each adult, stored against some future disaster, given to the shrine. Finally one young warrior spoke up.

'We saw many new things in Northumbria. They're far richer than we'll ever be. For myself, I have never forgotten the beer-hall in one village we passed through.' He looked round at his companions. 'Do you remember? It was the one with gold-bound doors.' The men remembered and a murmur of assent was heard. 'Great plates of gold,' the young man went on, 'beautifully decorated. Perhaps we could do the same, with our silver.'

'I'm sure it wasn't gold,' said Cerdic. 'Much more likely bronze, but I do remember seeing them. They were certainly a splendid sight. What do you think?' He turned to the assembled company. 'If it can be done it would certainly make a worthy memorial to our campaign.'

Everyone agreed that it was an excellent idea, and Leofric, who had thought of it, was slapped heartily of the back for making such a good suggestion. Cerdic was so pleased that he handed him a ring. It was a small one but it made the seasoned warrior blush with pleasure.

Eric was asked to work out how it could be done. Nothing like it had been attempted in the village before. Eric called his men together in the shop. Wulf was there, occupying his old place in the shadows, furthest from the fire. He listened to the men a while, hearing various impractical suggestions, then, quietly, he interrupted. The men gave him his say.

'We should ask Gadd how to handle silver, that's a jeweller's job. But I know he makes moulds for his brooches and I think we could work on something like his lines. Perhaps if we were to carve some panels to fix to the door, like his moulds only bigger, and then ask him to make the silver into sheets, we could beat the silver over the carved panels till it fitted like a skin.'

The men were willing to try out Wulf's idea, and Eric suggested that Wulf should pay a visit to Gadd's workshop to ask him to help. Wulf readily agreed to go.

Wulf and Fryth could no longer meet in the workshop. Wulf had removed the bed on the day the first man had come home. But in the longer evenings they often had time to walk a little way out of the village to be alone together. Fryth had been afraid for Wulf when the men started to come home. She dreaded the return of his black mood, but on the whole he had taken it very well, slipping back without too much complaint into his insignificant position in the tribe. He was never truly content, but it seemed that he had worked out the worst of his anger and frustration in those dark winter days.

One evening they walked, as they often did, to a small clearing in a coppice not being worked. A woodman had built a little hut in the clearing. It was half collapsed but Wulf had propped up its sagging ridge-pole with a forked branch and it afforded them a little shelter from the rain that seemed to fall incessantly that spring.

'We didn't get much work done today,' Wulf was full of excitement when he met Fryth outside the shrine, 'one of the shepherds came down from the fold this morning with a story of a wolf. Apparently it took two lambs from underneath his nose. His dogs didn't even bark!' A wolf was almost unheard of in their lands and Fryth was sceptical.

'How could he be sure?' she asked. 'It was much more likely to be a fox, I should think.' The wet leaves on the woodland floor clung uncomfortably round her ankles and she bent down to sweep them off. Wulf pushed her from behind impatiently.

'Well, he swears he saw its pug-marks in the mud, there's plenty of that up there at the moment. It was a wolf, he says, no doubt about it. Anyway there was no stopping Eric, he spent all day sharpening his spear, so did most of the others. They're out now, hunting it.'

'It'll have cubs to feed,' said Fryth thoughtfully. She was silent for a moment, picking her way between the trees. 'A wolf is not a good sign. It means the coming of hard times.' Wulf was unconcerned. They had reached the clearing. He caught her hand, smiling. They drew together and went into the hut.

'Even so,' she said as they walked home, 'I hope the men don't catch it.'

But they did. In the morning the body of a large she-wolf lay stiffening on the ground outside the hall. Her rough pelt had been draggled into points by the soaking rain and her teats were full. Somewhere her cubs were crying out for milk, and shortly they would die. Eric and the other men, several holding musty sacks over their heads and shoulders to keep off the downpour, capered round the body laughing with excitement. They were elated by their success.

'Look at those sharp teeth!' shouted Sigurd, one of the huntsmen, prodding the grimacing jaws with his spear. Cerdic came out of the hall to investigate the cause of the commotion.

He thanked them gravely. Wolves did not make good neighbours.

Only Eangyth and Fryth were displeased. A wolf was a beast of ill-omen, bringing famine, war and death. Something would have to be done quickly to avert this fate. The spirit of the dead she-wolf must be appeased or they would soon have a family of hostile wolf-spirits to contend with. It might already be too late.

Later in the day Eangyth went to Cerdic. She explained her fears to him and he saw at once the danger they were in.

'What do you suggest we do?' he asked, alarmed.

'The best thing we can do would be to commemorate this visit on our new silver doors. The wolf spirits will be flattered and appeased.'

'How can we do that?' asked Cerdic anxiously, 'what will please them?'

'It is a wolf spirit that swallows up the sun at the end of every day.'

'And spits it out every morning.' Cerdic's face filled with understanding. 'Of course! What would please her more than that we should picture her on our doors like that? There was an old man, older than my grandfather, who had the image on the lid of his pouch. It's long since buried with him but I still remember it. The sky-father's head was surrounded by fire. . . .'

'And gripped on either side by two wolves, one swallowing him as the other spits him out?'

Cerdic nodded eagerly. 'We must tell the craftsmen to get to work. It should satisfy the wolf-spirits to see their story on our doors. I hope it will be enough to avert their anger.'

Eric was summoned to be given his instructions. He seemed unmoved by the prospect of the bad fate that his hunting might have brought on all the tribe. Rather, he was proud that his night's hunting was going to get such a prominent memorial.

Wulf directed the carving of the panels, keeping for himself the most intricate parts of the design. The sky-god's head, ringed with flame, was framed by the fearsome wide-open jaws of two wolves, one on either side of his face, and he was held at the feet and shoulders by their sharp claws.

When the carving was under way Wulf paid Gadd a visit. Gadd lived alone a few miles downriver from the village and Wulf spent several days with him learning how to manage silver. He was fascinated by Gadd's art. It required as steady a hand and keen an eye as his own, but it was far more delicate.

'And opulent,' Gadd said. 'There's nothing like working with precious metal.' He had a rich, deep voice, it went with his luxurious trade. He showed Wulf how to prepare a mould, how to mix the alloys and to handle molten metal. Wulf was a quick pupil and Gadd was impressed.

'You'd make a good goldsmith, my boy,' he said. He was not given to friendly gestures or soft words except in the rituals of buying and selling. 'Such talent deserves a finer medium than wood.' He fingered a small trial piece, newly unmoulded, that Wulf had made under his direction. 'Of course you have a lot to learn, but you have the makings, and with me to teach you . . .' He paused, lost in thought. Wulf said nothing, he had been listening quietly, his eyes fixed on the two halves of the mould lying on the bench in front of him.

'Skilled apprentices are gold themselves,' Gadd was thinking aloud now. 'I've never found one even approaching good enough until . . .' He cleared his throat and sniffed, then went on more loudly, 'I'd be willing to take on a lad like you. You have real promise.' Wulf continued to stare at the bench, scarcely daring to breathe. This was an opportunity he had never dreamed of.

'I'm an outcast.' It came out as a whisper.

'What's that to me?' Gadd simply brushed aside this huge objection. 'Half the year I'm travelling, who's going to know what your status is? As foreigners we'll both be outcasts of a kind. But we'll be welcomed everywhere, I promise you. An artist has no need of a lord or war-band.' He gripped Wulf's shoulder, the shoulder of his left arm, the one that was weaker now.

'I need an answer straight away, summer's coming and I'll be leaving soon. You'll have to start your training on the road. No harm in that,' Gadd added, more to himself than Wulf. The idea of an assistant was growing more attractive all the time.

For Wulf the idea of apprenticing himself to Gadd was as attractive as the feel of the river bed to the foot of a drowning man. He returned to the village with the Mercian silver beaten into thin sheets, and his mind made up.

He was ecstatic as he broke the news to Fryth. 'It's the only chance I'll ever have of getting away from here. A real chance to make something of myself at last. Gadd's a good craftsman, the right sort of master to have, but I can be better than him, I know that. Not to be an outcast! Not pitied and ignored, but welcomed – he said we would be – rewarded even!' He broke off, overwhelmed.

Wulf was pacing round the little hut, his face bright with joy. Fryth listened in silence.

'We'll be travelling north, possibly as far as Northumbria. Gadd says there's real wealth there and a liking for rich things. He's even sold his jewellery in the court. One trip will set my mother up for winter, longer probably, and make up for the time I'm away. . . .' His voice broke off again, his last words were hanging in the air between them as he turned and looked at Fryth.

She pushed at a twig with the toe of her shoe, looking at the little pattern it made on the dusty floor. Then she dragged her foot across the pattern and obliterated it. Her sense of loss and pain surprised her. She had been the one with other plans, now suddenly it was Wulf who was putting distance between them. Had he said when he was leaving?

'When?' she said aloud and there was desolation in her voice. Wulf stopped pacing and came towards her. He put his arms tightly round her.

'I told you,' he said softly. 'It must be soon. But I'll be back, and, after all you know, you have *your* work to do.' He said this not unkindly, and Fryth could not disagree.

The silver panels were completed and fixed to the beer-hall's stout doors. Their beauty and exquisite workmanship were a testament to Wulf's great skill and the whole tribe felt enriched, basking in their bright reflection.

The last thing Wulf did before he left the village was to go to the hall. He stood in front of the silver-panelled doors and stretched out his arms. He ran his fingertips lingeringly over their shiny surfaces, then dropped his arms to his sides, turned abruptly and walked away without looking back.

He had parted from Fryth earlier. They met in the early morning outside the shrine. Fryth hung a small bronze box round his neck. It contained a rune stave to ward off evil spirits, and another to recommend him to benign ones. Wulf slipped the box under his shirt.

'Don't follow me,' he said, 'I'd rather leave you here.' She was clinging to his hands and he gently disentangled them. He kissed her and she stood quite still, watching him walk down the path towards the river. She could hear his feet echoing on the plank bridge that crossed it as she turned and went back into the shrine.

She prayed that Wulf would be fulfilled in what he was setting out to do. She cast the runes for him and it was well past noon before she left the shrine, so long and thoughtfully had she pondered on their obscure message.

CHAPTER 8

Fryth's work now had her undivided attention. With Wulf gone she devoted herself entirely to developing her arts. She became so absorbed in studying, either with her mother or in seclusion on her own, that, although she scarcely dared admit it and offend his travelling spirit, there were days when she did not think of Wulf at all. She missed his quiet, attentive company and his strong eager body, but, without the distraction of his presence, her spiritual life was growing richer day by day. With this growth came the certainty that it was what was most important to her.

Since her outburst when Fryth had saved his life, Eangyth had never mentioned Wulf's name, and when he went she had not offered one word of comfort to her daughter. Fryth had asked for none. She knew that Wulf's going had come as a relief to Eangyth, so she was taken by surprise when one morning her mother held out her crystal ball to Fryth and said,

'It's time you learned the use of this, let us see if you can discover how Wulf is faring.'

Fryth looked up with a jerk at the mention of Wulf's name.

'It should not be too difficult for you,' Eangyth continued evenly, 'your thread is woven in with his.' She paused. 'Or has been.'

Eangyth sounded practical and not unkind, but Fryth, still startled, could not find the words to talk of Wulf with her mother. Instead she assumed the air of a diligent pupil.

'What am I to do?' she asked in what she hoped was a matter-of-fact manner, taking the crystal ball. Eangyth, sensing a danger passed, adopted the same brisk tone.

'Since you will be looking, not through time, but distance, the crystal is not used on its own; that takes much practice, the magic is far more powerful. You must fill a bowl with water and put the crystal into it, praying all the while for an answer to your query.'

'As if I were casting runes?'

'Exactly! You see, you're already half-way there. The crystal will give its answer to the water.' Eangyth picked up a small slotted spoon which she kept with the crystal in its bag. 'When you think it has done its work lift it from the water with this spoon; be very careful to spill none. Then watch. If you have questioned from your heart, you will see the answer in the water.'

'Let me try!' cried Fryth. She almost snatched the spoon from her mother, then realized that, by her eagerness, her feelings were betrayed. But Eangyth only smiled.

'Not here,' she said gently, 'Edward and the boys are bound to interrupt you. Go to the shrine this evening and see what comes.'

Fryth followed Eangyth's instructions carefully. She prepared herself by summoning the dragon energy that lay coiled around the centre of the world. The windings of the serpent's fiery tail would link her with the place where Wulf was standing. She prayed for success.

The last drop from the slotted spoon splashed back into the bowl and gradually the ripples cleared. Fryth stared at the dark surface of the water. All she saw at first was the reflection of her own face and glittering eyes. Then, by degrees, the glitter turned to fire and there, behind the fire, was Wulf. He was working a pair of leather bellows. She recognized at once his look of quiet concentration. His face was calm, fuller than when he had left, and his frown was gone. A shadow fell across him and he looked up and smiled. The shadow would be Gadd. It swelled and filled the bowl with darkness and the vision was gone.

That night Fryth told her mother that she had seen Wulf and that he was well and happy. Eangyth put an arm round Fryth's shoulder and squeezed it comfortingly.

'I'm glad,' she said, 'I'm glad.' She bent, and laid her fair head on Fryth's dark hair. Fryth felt that a narrow gulf between them had been bridged.

Summer was well advanced by now but the rains continued and the wind was always chill. The sky-father on the beer-hall doors and his attendant wolves shone more with rain-drops than with the summer sun.

There was more activity than usual in the village all summer long. A steady stream of messengers passed between the Mercians and Cerdic. Despite the famous victory of the previous winter, Penda could not afford to ease the pressure on Northumbria. Cadwallon had remained in the north with his army, and he needed reinforcements. Cerdic was bound by the unbreakable chains of loyalty that tied a man to his war-lord and could not refuse to fight again. But neither he nor his own men wanted to return to the battle grounds before the end of the growing season. Penda's heralds received the courtesy and hospitality due to their exalted office, and there were long discussions and many oaths and protestations of loyalty and support. But Cerdic was cunning and he was playing for time. He made demands, suggestions, questioned this tactic or that. Each new matter was taken back to Penda's court for answer and all the time Cerdic spun out the messengers' frequent visits with feasting.

Fryth was much in demand at these feasts. Her fame as a singer was spreading. It was even suggested that the arrival of Peada, one of Penda's own sons, was less for the encouragement of Cerdic than to satisfy his own desire to hear Fryth sing. Peada was a large, gaunt, raw-boned man. He looked tired and strained, and his colourless eyes with their sandy lashes were red-rimmed. The effort of keeping the alliance together was plainly taking its toll. Fryth had a stool at the end of the high table. On his first night Peada leant across to her, mead splashing from his horn, his mouth full.

'I hear you have a famous voice,' he said. His own was harsh and he had the flat-vowelled Mercian accent. 'I'd welcome a new song.'

'My songs aren't songs of war or heroes,' Fryth warned as she took the harp. 'This one,' she said, 'is a song of love.' The song was short. She had composed it for Wulf after he had left. The intensity of her feelings as she composed it, full of loss and longing, renewed themselves as she sang.

'My thoughts journeyed far to join my Wulf
When rain slapped the earth and I sat apart weeping.
Wulf, my Wulf, my yearnings for you
. . . have made me ill.
I am sick of love, not of starvation . . .
How easily they can sever that which was never
Truly at one, the song of us two together.'

The dark mood of the song hung in the air like a pall. There was a long silence, and then, Peada began to clap. His two large, bony hands slowly knocked together, the only sound in the packed hall. Then, gradually, everyone joined in. Peada's ugly face had softened and a gentle look had come into his eyes. He was drinking from an enormous silver-mounted drinking horn, his own. He thrust it at Fryth.

'Take this,' he said. Fryth hesitated, she drew back a little. 'Take it, please.' He shook the last few drops onto the table. 'It's a small thing to repay a great gift like yours.' Eager hands reached out and passed the horn to Fryth. She saw faces, still moved, fill with pride. She took the horn for Wulf's sake. He, who would never drink with these companions, would drink from it to her.

'Thank you, my lord,' she said. 'Truly, my song is not worthy of such attention.' She bowed. Cerdic, beaming, bowed too.

'We all thank you, gracious lord,' he said. 'The lady Fryth's songs are one of the glories of our tribe.' He bowed again. 'No doubt she'll sing again tomorrow, if you wish.' He caught Fryth's eye and gave her a conspiratorial look.

'Of course, my lord,' said Fryth, who understood what Cerdic was about, 'and the following night if I am required.' Peada looked pleased.

'How good of you,' he said. 'It is a privilege to hear such music, I'll gladly stay to hear some more.'

'Meanwhile, my lord,' said Cerdic hurriedly, wanting to ration the songs as an incentive to Peada to prolong his stay, 'meanwhile, the question of our troop acting under Cadwallon's orders. I'm not sure that a Briton . . .' Peada's attention was distracted and Fryth slipped out of the hall.

Cerdic strung out Peada's visit for a week and Fryth sang to him every night. The Mercian embassy responded to her songs with genuine delight, and Fryth enjoyed performing to them. They took many of her songs home with them, fixed in their memories.

Fryth noticed a change in her mother that summer. Eangyth said nothing to her, but Fryth sensed an urgency about her. Eangyth drove her on, at times even burdened her, with practices, visions, dreams and secret knowledge. Her mother appeared to be relieved at each new understanding reached by Fryth, as if one more aspect of her craft had at last been made safe. But if she was more involved than ever in Fryth's education, Eangyth was becoming less concerned to carry out her priestly functions. Fryth now took over more and more of her mother's work.

As she grew into her rôle as a chief priestess, Fryth saw Eangyth gradually withdrawing from the rigours of that rôle. Her mother's face filled out, her eyes softened, and her gestures became less measured and controlled. Now she seldom visited the spirit world, preferring to leave the arduous journeys to Fryth. The change in Eangyth was imperceptable to all but

Fryth, but she saw it, and accepted it, knowing that the time was coming when she would have to carry on alone.

There was a change too in the villagers. The constant comings and goings of the Mercians unsettled them. There was a feeling of unease, a general pessimism in the air. The omens were not good. Cattle were falling sick, ponies lame, milk was turning sour straight from the cow, cooking pots over-turned on the fire. There were countless instances of the work of elves and demons. The people felt threatened as never before by evil spirits.

Much of Fryth's time was devoted to helping the tribe to ward off the evil spirits. The women especially, fearing for their husbands and sons, would come to her for help, bringing little offerings to the shrine, asking for Freya's favour. Fryth took the gifts and hung them on the tree in the centre of the shrine. In exchange she would give the women rune staves carved with the rune of protection. Sometimes she suggested they should visit one of the spirit places in the ceremonial field and make their prayers there. Narrow paths were beaten through the growing corn, and little groups of women were often to be seen pressing themselves against the tree and stone or drinking from the spring.

Cerdic's delaying tactics succeeded. The corn was slowly ripening in the fields, the beasts fattening in the meadows, and the men were still at home. The weather had not improved and the harvest would be meagre in comparison with the previous year. It was not so bad as to be seriously worrying, but it would need careful husbanding through the winter. The men would carry shorter rations to the fighting and rely on what they could forage to see them through. Fryth pitied the people through whose lands they would be travelling. Their harvests were going to be no better.

When the harvest was over, and the celebrations finished, the war-band once more prepared for winter campaigning. The village rang with the sound of whetstones as each man sharpened his long spear. Some carried heavy battle daggers with single, lethal cutting edges. Others made do with smaller everyday knives. Cerdic carried his chieftain's sword. It was the pride of the warriors, an ancient weapon passed down in Cerdic's family for generations. Its name was Wyrmfah, chosen for the sinuous, serpentine coils that could clearly be seen in its bluish sheen. They were created when the sword was forged. Three strands of white-hot steel had been plaited together, then beaten flat to make an almost unbreakable blade. It had been far too long, according to the warriors, since Wyrmfah had tasted blood.

Cerdic knew that this winter his men would be in the front line. The protracted wranglings in the beer-hall all summer long had resulted in Penda promising Cerdic a more prominent part in the fighting. It would have been hard to persuade his men to return to the idleness and discomfort of the previous winter's campaign. He was pleased of course to have achieved this promotion for his men, and joined with them in boasting of the deeds they would all perform, but he knew that they were going to face great dangers, and he was only too aware that they lacked experience when it came to real fighting. He needed some gesture to reinforce the men's moral, one that would carry them in good spirits through the winter.

He went on his own at dawn to meet the two priestesses as they emerged from the shrine. Fryth was the first to come out. Cerdic was standing with his back to the gate, staring at the river running past. He turned quickly when he heard it creak open. His face was anxious, but he composed himself as Fryth greeted him. He offered her the same respect these days as he gave her mother, and he dropped his eyes from her clear gaze. The fox's mask stood up behind her head. Its sharp angles reinforced the air of alert tension that always attended Fryth when she was about her work.

Eangyth came out, walking slowly, and joined them. She was almost languid now, and the contrast between mother and daughter was even more marked. The two women listened gravely to Cerdic as he asked them for advice. He wanted some powerful magic to strengthen his men. Fryth and Eangyth promised to consider the matter and to pray for guidance. They went back into the shrine to consult the spirits and Cerdic returned to the village. He would have his answer later in the day.

He met the priestesses outside the beer-hall as the sun was setting. The silver-plated doors cast a pearly light over their serious faces. None of then underestimated the difficulties that lay ahead. Eangyth recalled the bloody vision she had had the night the compact with the Mercians had first been made.

'Freya has given us her answer,' she said. 'There's little we can do to ward off the danger that's coming. But if we know we have done everything we can to help ourselves, at least we can confront our fate with firm minds.'

'The horse-spirit came to me in the shrine,' said Fryth. 'It is the spirit of warriors, and the strength of our tribe.'

'You must take all that strength for yourself,' Eangyth said. 'You must make the horse sacrifice. None of our generation have seen it done, but, if there ever was a time for it, the time is now. It will give you, and the men, courage and protection.'

Cerdic was excited by the prospect of performing such an ancient and sacred ritual. The horse sacrifice would certainly enhance his position in the eyes of both gods and men. It had once been part of a great ritual of conquest. At special times a stallion had been released to wander at will over the face of the earth. The tribe would follow it for one whole year, doing battle with all the peoples through whose lands it passed. At the end of the year the stallion would be sacrificed by the tribal chief in a great ceremony. In this way, with the help of the horse spirit, his lands and influence were extended and his status increased. The old men and women had heard of the horse sacrifice from their grandparents, who in turn had heard it from theirs. The year-long ritual had long since ceased. Now, on the very rare occasions when the ceremony was performed, the stallion was sacrificed with no preliminaries, and its head set up on a pole to watch over the people and their lands.

The stallion chosen was a large, grey, thick-set animal, which had already sired many foals, ensuring the continuance of his line. Cerdic himself performed the sacrifice so that the stallion's strength would pass directly into him. After he had dispatched the horse, the warriors filed past, dipping their spears in his steaming blood. His head was raised high on a pole above the gable of the beer-hall, to be picked clean by kites and ravens. The stallion's body was given a warrior's funeral. It was cremated on a massive pyre and buried by Fryth with great honour in the village cemetery. Unlike all other sacrificial animals, it was not part of the ceremonial feast. The horse was too sacred to be eaten.

Godwin joined the men on the day of the sacrifice. He had been pressing his father to let him take his place in the men's hall all summer long. He could not bear the thought of being left behind when the men went north again, and eventually wore down the opposition of both his parents. To his delight his voice began to break at harvest-time and Edward had no option but, with great reluctance, to give way. Godwin was small, like Fryth, but strong and active. His new shield practically hid him from view, but he carried it proudly and wielded it with ease.

Eangyth took Godwin to the shrine alone and hedged him round with charms. He came back smiling, full of confidence, but from that day Fryth saw the change in Eangyth accelerate. She still went with Fryth to the shrine for the daily rituals but now she would take no part in them. She looked on as Fryth performed them on her own. She would no longer consult the spirits or cast the runes. Fryth knew without asking that her mother had already discovered more than she wished to know about the future. As for herself, Fryth felt she did not need to look ahead. The most important thing was to prepare herself to confront her fate, however it chose to come.

As the day of the war-band's departure approached Eangyth grew increasingly withdrawn. She spent long hours by herself in the shrine, praying by the little spring. One morning she put a restraining hand on Fryth's arm as she was about to leave the shrine. She drew back into its dark recesses, and Fryth saw that she had been making preparations to cast a spell. She had laid out a bowl filled with butter, a bunch of herbs and three small knives. Signalling to Fryth to watch, Eangyth took the bowl to the brazier and put it on the coals. When the butter in the bowl began to bubble, she added the herbs. There were three: deadnettle, wormwood and mugwort. The herbs shrivelled at once, curling and twisting in the boiling fat. When a few thin black strands were all that were left of them Eangyth plunged the three knives into the pot, murmering softly as she did so,

'A smith sat and forged a little knife,
Out little blade, wound me not!
Six smiths sat; they made war spears,
Out spear, out! Pierce me not!
Fly spears, fly and strike the mountain tops,
Strike me not!'

When she had finished, Eangyth took Fryth into the precinct. She gave her the knives, still hot and slippery with butter, and Fryth held them cautiously.

'I've never used that charm before,' said Eangyth, 'and I never will again.' Her face was weary, and her expression sorrowful. 'I want you to learn the rest of it. Before the men leave you must say it over them. I can't do it, I no longer have the strength.' Fryth put down the knives and took her mother's hand,

'Whatever you want of me I'll do,' she said. 'Whatever comes I will be with you. Teach me the charm now.' Eangyth looked at Fryth, squeezed her hand and smiled.

Fryth committed the charm to memory and charged herself with its magic. Eangyth gave two of the knives to Edward and Godwin; the third, Fryth kept until the time came for the men to go.

Fryth feared for the warriors, and dreaded the departure of her father and Godwin. At the same time she knew that as the autumn drew on Wulf would soon be home. She found that she was longing to see him, to lie with him in the woodman's hut, and to hear the tales of his adventures. She could not resolve the conflict; all she could do was to spend as much time as possible with Edward and Godwin. Edward was as doubtful as ever about the sense of the alliance, but Godwin was bursting with excitement and longing to go. His delight at his new status as a warrior was infectious. His optimism encouraged Fryth and she allowed herself to be pleased for him. This in a way brought her some comfort.

She made one more attempt to see Wulf on his travels. The crystal ball was hers now, Eangyth would not use it any more. She saw him clearly enough, but not this time with Gadd. He was standing with another man, a stranger with an oddly shaven head. Wulf was gazing at this stranger, his face was rapt and full of joy. Once more Fryth was relieved to see him safe and well.

At last the call from Mercia came. The men in the war-band took leave of their families and mustered outside the hall where Fryth was waiting for them, standing in front of the silver doors. She raised her arms, throwing back her fox-skin cloak to reveal her round bronze brooches. The warriors gazed at the broken wheels of the sun glinting on her breast as Fryth pronounced the battle charm Eangyth had taught her in the shrine. She sent her spirit out with the warriors,

'Under the lime-wood, the light shield
On the field of slaughter, where the hags of battle rally,
Screaming as they guide the spears,
I will return their venom,
A speeding arrow against them;
Shatter the spear that would wound our warrior.
If he is struck in skin, or flesh,
Or in the bone, I will succour him.
If iron strikes him, it shall melt away.
Against the shot of elves and demons I will defend him.'

Fryth gave Cerdic the third knife wrapped in a linen cloth and he put it in his tunic. As he thrust it in, its point pierced through the cloth and scratched the skin of his throat. A thin, red line of blood welled into the scratch. Cerdic touched the spot. He pulled his hand away and stared at the smear of blood on his finger tips. He turned white. Hastily, Fryth stepped forward and clasped him by the shoulders. She kissed him on each cheek, pulling his tunic closed over the scratch. Cerdic came to his senses before any of his men noticed the mishap. He took a deep breath, shouted an order, and the warriors marched away with the words of the battle charm still ringing in their ears. Eangyth did not watch them go. She remained inside her house, staring at the fire.

CHAPTER 9

Winter came on fast, the autumn was wet and blustery, just as summer had been, but colder. The women, once more left in charge, prepared for the annual slaughtering. Blood month had come round again. The beasts were no fatter than the harvest had been and fewer barrels were needed for the salt meat.

Fryth was helping to make the cure that was always mixed before the first days of butchering. Her arms were steeped in brine, she could feel it prickling the small cuts and scratches on her hands. The salt tubs had been set out in a paddock just outside the village smallholdings, near the killing grounds. The northern road ran past the paddock, across the river valley and up the wooded ridge on the far side. The women were hard at work when suddenly one called out,

'Strangers coming! Look up the road!' Another immediately reached for the axe that lay at her feet. Danger was always lurking now, with war in the air and no men at home.

Fryth knew at once it was Wulf. She sensed him long before she made his features out. Hastily she dried her salty hands on her skirt and rolled her sleeves down over her reddened arms. She was half-way to meet him when she saw that his companion was not Gadd. He was walking with a stranger, a tall man with a stoop. As they approached, she saw the stranger had a shaven head. All that had been left by the razor was a narrow ring of hair encircling his crown, and he was beardless too. His face was red and weatherbeaten. Fryth halted, puzzled. She felt a faint prick of alarm. Wulf must have seen that it was her by now but he did not quicken his stride. He came towards her steadily, keeping pace with his companion. At last, all three stood together in the middle of the road. Fryth was the first to speak.

'Hello, Wulf.' She clasped her hands behind her back. She could hear the strained formality in her voice. 'Welcome home!' She unclasped her hands and reclasped them in front. Wulf met her eye then glanced uneasily at his companion. Fryth looked down at her old stained skirt. She laughed, embarrassed. 'You must excuse me.' she turned to the red-faced stranger. 'We're making brine.'

At last Wulf found his tongue. 'It's good to be home, it's been so long . . . Osgar,' he touched the stranger's shoulder,'. . . he's travelled with me . . .' His voice trailed off. The man inclined his head and raised his right hand, palm outwards, to shoulder height.

'God bless you, my daughter,' he said. His voice was deep and resonant. He had an unfamiliar accent, but his eyes were warm and friendly. Wulf was silent, staring at the ground.

'Yes, well,' Fryth cleared her throat. This was not the home-coming she had envisaged when she had dreamed of Wulf's return. Evidently Osgar was Wulf's guest.

'You must take Osgar to greet your mother,' she said. 'I'll wait for you later, Wulf, by the gate of the shrine.' She was sure she saw Wulf flinch, but she went on. 'I'll be there at dusk.'

'Very well, we'll meet then.' He was still staring at the ground. Then he looked up. 'Come, Osgar, I'll take you to my home.' He said this with a smile, the first of their meeting. His smile included Fryth but he looked away when she smiled back.

The travellers walked on into the village and Fryth returnd to the salting tubs disturbed in mind and spirit. The women were full of questions.

'Has he made his fortune?'

'Will he buy his father's freedom?'

'Who was that bald man?'

'Why has he brought a stranger home? He looks unfit for labouring. We don't want another mouth to feed.'

Their voices buzzed in Fryth's ears as she bent over the tub, stirring the slimy mixture with a shaggy wooden paddle. The puzzle of Wulf's odd behaviour and the enigmatic stranger was too much for her, but let it wait till evening; she'd find out soon enough.

She went alone to the shrine that evening. It seemed full of anxious spirits. A pot of spring water lay overturned on the floor, its contents splashed across the sand. She knew that she had left it upright in the morning. She prayed for guidance and felt compelled to draw a rune of protection in the soft puddle in the sand. She scarcely knew what it was she wished to be protected from.

At last the ritual was over. Fryth glanced once round the shrine making sure that everything was in its proper place, then she drew a deep breath and walked out to meet Wulf.

It was already nearly dark and he was carrying a small lamp. It cast a ruddy glow on the ground beneath him and softened the sharp drawn angles on his face. Fryth went up to him and wrapped her arms round him, but with a sinking heart she felt him stiffen and she stood back quickly, dropping her arms to her sides. She looked at him. His face was full of something not unlike regret.

'I'm sorry,' he said.

She took his arm. 'This much at least he'll let me do,' she thought.

'Let's walk a little way,' she said aloud. They walked in silence, Fryth leading Wulf like a blind man by the arm. She had not planned the walk but presently they found themselves outside the little woodman's hut. The roof had sagged again but the evening was dry and Fryth made a small fire in the open air, lighting it with Wulf's lamp. The smoke curled up, grey against the blacker night, and tiny sparks flickered.

They sat a little apart watching the fire, saying nothing. Eventually Wulf drew breath.

'Something has happened,' he said.

'I can see that,' Fryth could hear the harshness in her voice.

'You're going to have to try to understand.' He fell silent again.

'Yes?' She was impatient. 'Yes? What do I have to understand?' Wulf opened his mouth, then closed it. 'How can I begin to understand unless you tell me?' Fryth went on. '*What* has happened? Who is that man?' She paused, her exasperation was unsettling him even more. She said, more gently. 'Please try to tell me Wulf.'

'You'll have to try to understand.' He hesitated, seeing her eyes flash, then he tried a different tack. 'I met Osgar in the north, I'd been alone for weeks.'

'Alone? What happened to Gadd? Why isn't he with you? Is he dead?'

'No he's not dead as far as I know, I expect he'll be home soon. I haven't seen him since I left him.' Fryth was astonished.

'Since you left him? Why did you leave him, Wulf? What has happened?' Her voice was rising.

'I told you. You're going to have to listen to a long story.' Fryth sighed. She propped her chin on her fist.

'I'm ready,' she said. 'Go on.' Wulf drew in a deep breath, he looked up at the sky.

'Things went very well for a while after we set off. I started work straight away. Gadd is a good teacher, a difficult man to live with and not a very pleasant character, but a good master. I was learning fast, enjoying myself, starting to feel free for the first time in my life.'

'I saw you,' Fryth interrupted. 'I saw you looking well and happy, I had a vision of you. . . .' A shadow crossed Wulf's face and he went on quickly, cutting her short.

'Gadd paid me well. He gave me the wastings from my silver work and I traded it for things, my saddlebags were filling up. And then we reached Northumbria. . . .' Fryth looked at him expectantly, waiting for him to continue. 'Gadd had said the real money was there.' Wulf laughed harshly. 'Well, that might have been true once, but things are very different now.'

'We killed their king; no wonder things are different.'

'That was just the beginning for them. Cadwallon's still there.' Fryth nodded.

'I know.'

'Yes, but what you don't know is what he's doing up there. He's a foul monster, Fryth, his men are destroying Northumbria, burning, torturing, stealing, murdering. They're killing everyone: little children, old men, old women, everyone. Except the young women, they don't kill them, at least not as soon as they find them.' Fryth screwed up her face. 'Those that survive,' Wulf continued, 'they enslave. It's better to be killed at once than captured by the British.'

'My father never told me this,' said Fryth quietly.

'He never saw it, but he'll be seeing it now.' Wulf closed his eyes as if to shut out the memory, then he opened them wide. 'I saw it,' he went on, 'Gadd and I travelled right into the thick of it. Gadd did make some profit, but not through selling jewellery.' Wulf laughed bitterly. 'No, he was buying the stuff. Silver, even gold, from starving Northumbrians and all of course for practically nothing. You should have seen how he battened on them!' He laughed again. 'I had no more opportunity to learn his trade.' He stood up and stretched a little, flexing the fingers of his left hand. 'I went a woodworker and have come home a woodworker.'

Wulf started pacing up and down. Fryth reached up a hand to check him, but he evaded her grasp and went on pacing restlessly.

'I wanted to come home. I was sickened by everything I saw, by everything Gadd and I were doing.'

'But *you* were doing nothing surely?'

'I was with him, that was bad enough. I told him I couldn't go on. He was very hard on me. He said he should have known I wouldn't be able to take it; that villagers and churls should stay at home and not venture into a world too big and lively for their small minds and narrow experience.'

'I've seen nothing of the world.' Fryth interrupted; she thought a moment; 'but our warriors survived it, churls that they are!'

'Yes, but they go together, stay together, like a village on the move, it's not the same. Anyway Gadd let me go, I think he was glad to in the end.' He stopped pacing and turned to face Fryth across the fire. The flames leaped and crackled between them.

'It was on my way home that I met Osgar.' Fryth looked up. 'He was travelling like me, but with a different purpose.' Wulf skirted the fire and sat down at Fryth's side, closer now.

'You must understand that I was all alone.' His voice was earnest, his face close to hers. 'I'd never been alone before, cut off from everything and everyone I knew.' He took Fryth's hand in both of his and turned it over, examining it closely as if reminding himself of its familiar contours.

'I'd seen such things. The careless cruelty I've suffered all my life seemed kindness in comparison.'

'Oh, Wulf!' Fryth squeezed his hand. She realized that this was the first time since his return that he'd touched her of his own accord. He turned and looked at her. His face was in the shadows as he spoke.

'I knew that fate was hard, God knows I'd done my best to accept my own, at least I knew its cause, but up there there was no cause. These people had done nothing wrong and still they were ensnared.'

'Everyone's Fate is different, Wulf,' Fryth said quietly. 'The thing is to be ready to endure whatever comes.' Her eyes became distant; she was thinking of her own.

'Of course you'd say that.' Wulf cut off her thoughts. 'It's what we've been taught to believe.'

'What do you mean, Wulf? That's not a lesson, that's a fact.'

'I thought it was then. I looked at my own life. Everything I knew told me that the life we lead here, even at its best, is futile, meaningless and full of pain. We're born, we suffer and we die. And nothing we can do will ever improve our lives.'

'Improve? How would things improve?' Fryth was taken aback. Her eyebrows drew together in a puzzled frown. 'Does the earth improve? Does water? Do the trees? They *are*, that's all. And so are we. What do you want, Wulf, what are you saying?'

'I warned you this would be difficult.' He sighed and fell silent. Fryth stroked his hand.

'You've been through an ordeal.' she said gently, humouring him, 'I can see how it's upset you. Perhaps we should stop for now.' She slid her hand up his leg and pressed against him but, to her surprise, Wulf leapt to his feet, pushing her away.

'No, I must finish.' He spoke convulsively. Fryth felt a little shiver of fear. Wulf's behaviour was unnerving, there was something dangerous about him, something she could not reach. He had started pacing again.

'I was walking home; the route was long, I hardly knew the way. Anyway the landmarks were changing all the time as Cadwallon burnt them down. I had plenty of time to dwell on my thoughts.'

'Just like the time when you were ill.'

'Yes, but worse, you weren't there to help me.' She smiled then; she had not lost him altogether, at least he had kept the memory of her in his mind. 'By the time I'd been on the road by myself for a couple of days I was having thoughts of killing myself, there and then. I could see no other way of cheating Fate.'

'Or doing its will.'

'I thought of that as well, don't worry. It's probably what kept me going. Anyway, one morning I passed through a badly devastated village. There was nothing new in that; I simply held my nose and hurried on. Then I noticed there was life in the ruins. Sheets and skins had been stretched over the shells of burnt-out houses to make shelters. I heard voices coming from one of them. It was a long time since I'd asked directions so I put my head inside the door, well, it wasn't a door, just a flap, made by a cloak. There were people sitting in a ring inside. In the middle of the ring was a little wooden box, beautifully carved and covered with a sheet of beaten silver, just like my doors.'

'The idea came from Northumbria, didn't it?'

'Yes, you can imagine it caught my eye, I wanted a better look. I thought perhaps they'd sell it to me.'

'So you had learned something from Gadd, after all.'

'I would have given them a fair price. But it never came to that. No one seemed to notice me so I slipped in to wait until whatever was going on had finished. A man was speaking, and truly Fryth, I'd never seen attention like I saw on those poor faces, all thin and worn and bruised. He seemed to have them under some kind of spell.'

Fryth narrowed her eyes, 'Go on.'

'Well I listened too. He was talking about Fate. I could hardly believe it. It was as if he knew what I'd been thinking all those days, as if he'd deliberately crossed my path to answer me. He said that what we call Fate is what happens to us because we're ignorant of the truth about the gods. He said that once we knew the truth, Fate would lose its power over us.' Fryth shifted uneasily. Where was all this leading?

'This man, the one who spoke, was Osgar I suppose?'

'No, not Osgar, one of his companions, a foreigner, a real one, not English. His name was James. The Deacon they called him.'

'A real foreigner.' Light was beginning to dawn in Fryth's mind. 'Had he got anything to do with this new religion, the one the followers of King Edwin took up?'

'I wish you could have seen him Fryth.' Wulf went on excitedly, ignoring her question, 'his eyes were black, but they burned like fire!'

'But was he a follower of this new religion, Wulf?' Fryth was insistent.

'I'm trying to tell you about it, listen to me, Fryth!' Now it was Fryth's turn to rise to her feet. She faced Wulf.

'He was, wasn't he? That's what all this is about. This foreign magician has bewitched you. What did you say? "It was as if he had them under a spell." Well no doubt he had, and you as well. Wulf, this is very dangerous. This new religion has destroyed Northumbria, if it can do that it will certainly destroy you!'

'Please listen, Fryth.' There was desperation in his voice. 'It's not what you think.'

'My father told me they eat human flesh.' She shuddered.

'It's not like that, please let me go on.' Fryth sighed. She sat down again, her face was dark and anxious.

'I'll tell you what happened to me, but I can't tell you about the new religion, I shouldn't do it justice; I don't know enough yet. That's why Osgar has come with me. I want him to tell the whole village. I want everyone to know the things I've learned.'

'Osgar's one of them, of course, he must be a sorcerer too.' Fryth was thoughtful. 'What kind of sorcerer tells anyone and everyone all he knows? No wonder their magic is so dangerous if its secrets are open to anyone to use.'

'They aren't secrets!'

'What was in that box?' said Fryth, suddenly remembering the silver-covered box that had caught Wulf's eye.

'I don't know, I never got a chance to see.'

'No secrets? None at all?' she cried sarcastically.

'No. You hear the whole story and then you can choose to be initiated. After that you can take part in the rites. I haven't got that far.'

'Oh, Wulf, don't go any further! Leave it now. There's danger coming, I've seen what Fate has in store for all our people. What will happen if we offend the gods? Now more than ever before we need to please them.'

'Our people?' said Wulf coldly. '*Your* people, you mean. Remember I'm an outcast.' Fryth shivered; she saw a great divide opening between herself and Wulf. She piled more wood onto the fire. She decided to let him have his say. At least then she should know exactly what it was that she would have to face in him.

'All right,' she said cautiously, 'tell me everything; what happened when you met these men; why you've brought Osgar home with you. I'm listening.'

She took his hand and pulled him down beside her. She composed herself and Wulf continued with his story. He was calmer now, they were trying to make allowances for each other.

'I listened to James in that ruined hut telling the people about this new god. His followers call themselves Christians, after his name.' A log collapsed into the fire, sending up a shower of sparks. Fryth watched them leap into the sky then flicker out into the darkness. 'James told us that his god had overthrown the old gods in a bloody battle long ago; that he had died in the fight but then come back to life. It all happened far away, which is why the story has taken so long to reach us.'

Wulf saw the look of incredulity on Fryth's face and shook his head. 'I told you I couldn't do this justice. Osgar will explain. But of all the things James said, one I knew would change my life. He said his god asked us to forgive each other for the wrongs we do to each other. He said it was an evil thing to take revenge; that if somebody harms you a thousand times you should forgive him a thousand times. This was wonderful to me, Fryth. I saw at once that if James is right and this new god has overthrown the old, then the old laws must be overthrown as well. That my father's wrong must be forgiven, and I can live a man's life in the world!'

'What do you mean, overthrown the old?' Fryth could keep silent no longer. 'The gods are here, they're all around us, listen to the trees, watch the fire.'

'James said that we are ignorant about the gods. God made the trees and stones but he is not in them. He is altogether bigger than anything on this earth.'

Fryth shook her head as if to shake off some persistent fly. She struggled not to argue. How could she argue against this madness.

'He said we are gripped by fear and ignorance, and that if we accepted the truth of what he was saying about our gods and his new god, nothing on earth would have the power to hurt us. I looked round at those poor people. They were suffering terrible hardship, and yet his words gave them hope and happiness.' Wulf's eyes shone. 'As for me,' he continued. 'I was utterly compelled. When James finished he picked up his box — I'd forgotten all about it — I tried to get to him but the people were crowding round, so I waited outside the shelter until he came out. He saw me standing there and he came up to me and said he hadn't seen my face before. I told him I was a stranger and he invited me to go back with him to his camp. That was where I met Osgar and the others.'

'Who were the others?'

'They were all Northumbrians, Christians. King Edwin brought a foreign priest from a southern country to convert his people to Christianity. James came with him. They had a great deal of success.'

'And brought about Edwin's and his country's ruin. The gods will not protect those who deny them.'

'Fryth, listen to me, these Christians are good men. Believe me, the Northumbrians would be much worse off than they are now if it wasn't for men like James and Osgar. Edwin's foreign priest, Paulinus, fled the country before Cadwallon could find and kill him, but James stayed on. He is always in danger, but that doesn't deter him. He travels up and down the country, not only preaching, but helping to rebuild houses, clear out wells, tend the sick and dying. His concern and loving kindness for the people win as many people for the new religion as his words.'

'Both have won you, it seems. I have hardly understood a word, Wulf. I don't see how these men who feast on human flesh and blood, who deny the spirits, who deny our Mother, can do anything but harm. By bringing Osgar here you have put us all in great danger. There are evil spirits everywhere since the wars began. They're hovering over us like kites, waiting to attack.'

They had talked the night out. Dawn was beginning to break in the eastern sky. The fire had sunk to glowing embers. Fryth stood up stiffly, she stretched herself and shivered. A barn owl drifted over the clearing. Seeing Wulf and Fryth, it banked steeply, then flew swiftly away over the trees.

'They don't eat human flesh, Fryth.' Wulf said wearily. 'They cherish life, they want people to be happy.'

Fryth started to walk home. She set off without waiting for Wulf. She felt quite dazed. Only one thing seemed clear; she knew Wulf well, she knew his propensity for suffering and self-torture. It was easy to imagine how in Northumbria, lonely and scared, confronted with bloody horrors of all kinds, his mind might have become unhinged. What else could account for all this? She knew how much he valued kindness and respect and his capacity for returning love for love. These foreigners had shown him kindness and reassurance when he most needed them. They had healed his wounded spirit, but at the same time it seemed, had filled his poor oppressed brain with dangerous nonsense.

He walked behind her, saying nothing. The sun was coming up, she looked back at Wulf and saw his downcast face. What had he expected of her? What *could* he have expected of her? She wanted to comfort him and slowed down, letting him catch up with her.

'Wulf?'

'Yes?'

'You didn't really think I could accept all this, did you. You know what I am.'

'I don't know, Fryth, I don't know what to say. Many like you have accepted it.' Fryth snorted in disbelief. 'It's true.' Wulf went on. 'Paulinus converted the high priest of Northumbria himself. Do you know what this priest Coifi did? He rode up to his temple on a stallion and threw a spear into it! He's still alive. He's become a very holy man.'

Fryth sighed a great sigh that turned into a yawn. It was too much for her. She couldn't bear to hear another word. They were reaching the village. She parted from Wulf with a brief word of goodbye at the river and turned towards the shrine.

She needed to collect her troubled thoughts and to ask Freya for her help in facing the danger that was threatening the tribe.

She sat by the spring in the shrine surrounded by the objects of the morning ritual. The sun was striking a shaft of gold through the door, picking out the bowl of grain, the splash-marks made by sprinkled water and the small handful of autumn flowers. The air was still pungent with the scent of smouldering herbs. The sound of the bubbling spring water grew louder and louder and Fryth prayed to the spirit in the water. She felt her head swell and fill with light, and she sat motionless, waiting.

After a while, in the stillness, a large spider came crawling across the floor and onto Fryth's outstretched hand. It was caught up in the shreds of its own web which trailed behind it in a dusty bundle. Fryth watched as it made its painful way over her knuckles. As it crawled, she began to whisper the words of a charm.

'Spider spirit, come inside
Bring your web, trap sorrow in your hand.
Tie your bridle round her neck.
Ride her roughshod over our borders
Out of our land. Free us from danger.'

The spider was crawling up her arm, feeling the air with its legs like a blind man. It found one of her round bronze brooches and hoisted itself onto its outer ring. As the spider picked its way across the image of the sun in the centre of the brooch, the tattered remains of its web became entangled in the fret-work, in an angle of the sun's rays, and was torn off. Released abruptly from its burden, the spider jerked forwards and then fell, hitting the floor with a soft thud. It scuttled away into the shadows.

Fryth left the shrine, deeply disturbed. The charm was a powerful one, but the spider spirit had been disarmed. She had asked for help, and received this evil omen in reply. She did not wish to carry the burden of this message back into the village so she walked a little way away from it, following the river, to collect her thoughts. The river banks were lined with reeds, they bent and rustled in the swiftly flowing current. Fryth paused to listen. The river spirit soothed her as it often had. She took off the brooch on which the spider's web had come to grief and washed it in the water at the rivers edge. The last shreds of the web floated out over the surface of the water and were swept away downstream. Fryth gazed down at the swirling water and slowly shook her head. The river spirit had taken away the omen, but in her heart Fryth knew that the evil it portended still remained. She spat into the river, casting a little of her defensive magic powers after the spider's web.

Fryth went home and found Eangyth waiting anxiously for her return. She did not ask for news of Wulf, but launched immediately into a story of her own.

'I had a visitor last night Fryth, after you'd gone with Wulf. The stranger Wulf brought with him came to see me. He walked straight into the house, unannounced.' Fryth raised her eyebrows. He must be very sure of his own powers, she thought, to dare to meet a sorceress indoors. Eangyth read her thoughts.

'He's either very confident or very ignorant. He'd been told I was the priestess here. He said he'd called to warn me that he'd come to lead what he called "my lost sheep" into the fold.'

Fryth sighed wearily. Suddenly she felt extremely tired.

'Wulf told me a little about him last night. He's utterly beguiled by Osgar and his foreign god.'

'You've heard about this new religion then?'

'Wulf tried to tell me but none of what he said made sense.'

'It seems that Osgar thinks he can persuade our people to adopt his god,' Eangyth said. Fryth grunted.

'What does he mean? Is that how a stranger should behave? How can foreigners have such affrontery!'

'He was very pleasant to me, very courteous, but his manner was strange. You know how you would treat a child playing with a sharp knife? He behaved like that. He moved and spoke very warily, in case the knife should slip and cut either him or me.' Fryth shuddered, remembering what had happened to Cerdic.

'The knife he's afraid of is our magic, of course!' Eangyth went on.

'And well he might be afraid. From what Wulf told me his magic is of a different kind. Apparently the priests of this foreign god tell everyone his mysteries. Wulf tried to tell me something about it himself. It seemed to me to be nothing but a jumble of foolishness.'

'It may be foolish but it has possessed Wulf, and most of Northumbria by all accounts. Besides we can't ignore the omens. We know that we're facing troubled times. What could be worse than to offend the gods and lose their favour.'

Fryth told her mother about the evil omen she had just encountered in the shrine. Eangyth shivered. She pulled the eagle's feather from her box and flicked it at the air around her head.

'I think this new god is a sun god.' she said uneasily, 'which means what happened to the spider is the more alarming. I am beginning to see things more clearly now. If Osgar's god is a sun god, then the third rune of your vision, the sun rune, must have been pointing to this meeting.' Fryth fingered her brooches,

'You made me wear this sign,' she said. She looked across at where Eangyth was sitting. The long eagle quill quivered in her mother's hand. and the eagle-spirits glittered on her brooches.

'Now I know why I did. Your Fate is tied up with this god, that's certain now.'

'Wulf's fate is tied up with him as well, it seems. He says it's brought him happiness.'

'Osgar kept using that word to me. I told him that pleasing the gods is not done for our happiness, but theirs. He knows very little about the work of a priest!'

'I am afraid for Wulf,' Fryth continued. 'He met these people when he was despairing, utterly alone. They showed kindness to him, befriended him, no wonder he was impressed. We know they're capturing a great many despairing minds in Northumbria.'

'Well what are we to do? Osgar's a brave man and he has every intention of carrying out what he calls his "mission" here.'

'I don't think we should allow Osgar to stay, at least not if he's going to upset the tribe and disturb the spirits. Our people aren't despairing, but they are uneasy, and a prey to evil.'

'I'm not sure that it's safe to cross the man, Fryth, not until we've found out a little more about his god and how dangerous he is. We don't want to add his anger to our other troubles.'

'I can't believe we're not strong enough to withstand the anger of a foreign god!'

'I'm not sure. All that we know about this warns us to be on our guard. But –' Eangyth pursed her lips, 'if you are right then there can be no harm in letting Osgar have his say, and if you aren't, well, we'll have learned something about what we have to face.'

Fryth put a hand to her brooches. 'So you want to let him stay?'

'I think it's best to let him play the shepherd if he wishes. Perhaps we'll discover that his magic's only soft words and loving-kindness in the end.'

'I hope you're right.' said Fryth quietly.

Eangyth's face took on the withdrawn expression that Fryth had grown used to recently. She walked slowly over to her loom and picked up the shuttle.

'He wanted an answer this morning, Fryth.' she said. 'Will you go and tell him?'

Fryth found Wulf and Osgar outside the beer-hall. Wulf was showing his new friend the silver-panelled doors. High above on the gable flagstaff the sacrificial horse's head, by now almost stripped bare, gazed down at them from empty eye sockets. The last flies of autumn were buzzing in fitful bursts about the shreds of flesh that still clung to its bones. Wulf had been telling Osgar the story of the hunting of the wolf. Osgar was shaking his head and Fryth caught the tail end of what he was saying.

'. . . only men have spirits, created in God's image. It is sinful nonsense to imagine that God's image is to be found in wolves, or any other animals.' Wulf was looking abashed and his expression turned to sheer embarrassment as Fryth approached. She smiled politely and bowed to Osgar. She was wearing her fox-skin cloak. Her mother's eagle's feather and wolf's paw dangled from her waist. She turned to Wulf.

'Your friend is welcome in our village.' She spoke with the voice of authority and Osgar's eyes widened a little. Fryth realized that Wulf had not explained her position to him. With Cerdic away, she and her mother spoke for the village in all things. She smiled again and said, with just a hint of patronage.

'I hope he will feel free to do exactly as he wishes.'

'Thank you, lady, 'Osgar returned her smile. 'I always have but one wish and that is to serve my God.'

'Just as I serve my gods.'

She left them standing there, Wulf white-faced and Osgar making a gesture over his chest with his right hand. She glanced back before she left the square and saw the stranger, hands clasped, sinking to his knees in front of the silver doors.

Osgar stayed in the village for a fortnight. He set out his little wooden shrine by the river beside the women's washing pool. It was a simple wooden box, obviously humbler than Deacon James's. When he was speaking he placed two straight pieces of wood fixed together in the shape of a cross on top of this travelling shrine. He kept them inside the box. No one discovered what else was in it.

The women gathered round eagerly to listen to Osgar. They were pleased by any diversion from their daily exertions. He spoke to them in a soft, gentle voice about his new religion. Of sin and death and of his God dying bloodily on the cross. Of love and redemption and of duties to each other and to God. He spoke about his God's family, his mother and his father and about his birth watched over by the stars and animals. He said that they were misguided in their beliefs and mistaken in the things they worshipped. He told them that if they believed that what he said was true they should ask to be purified by him in holy water. Only after they had been washed in this way would his God accept them and forgive their sins.

Osgar's words were such a jumble of contradictions that the women were soon thoroughly confused. They found it difficult to accept that their belief in blood sacrifice, in the spirits of trees and water and animals should be wrong and sinful when the same spirits obviously took part in his god's story. They were puzzled by Osgar's talk of love, since he threatened them with endless torture if they would not accept his words. They were shocked to be asked to forgive injuries and insults and thereby bring dishonour and the taint of cowardice on themselves and their families.

The women may not have understood or appreciated Osgar's message but to begin with they enjoyed the entertainment it afforded. They loved to hear new stories and all agreed that Osgar told them well. Besides he was a well-set man and not bad looking, despite his ugly shaven head. They made him welcome and he was gratified at first by the numbers who came to listen to his preaching. It was not long, however, before he began to realize what little effect he was having on their souls. They would appear to take in what he was saying but, rather than ask him to explain the more obscure aspects of his message, they would nod and click their teeth and then interrupt to say that he had put them in mind of another good story, had he heard of . . . ? As if he had been telling fireside tales.

An additional humiliation came when one of the younger women waylaid him one evening in a narrow passageway between two houses as he was walking home. She hung one arm round his neck and groped him with the other, pushing him against the wall. Osgar wrenched himself free, calling out loudly against the devil and all his works.

'You should have seen him jump!' the girl reported to a fascinated audience that night. She sniffed derisively. 'And after all he says about love.'

As the second week of Osgar's stay progressed it was evident that he was having no success. It was true that Harold, the dwarf, and the idiot, Thurston, seemed to accept his message. They took to sitting at his side when he preached, nodding their heads vigorously at everything he said. He welcomed them and treated them with a kindness and respect that they had never experienced from their own people, but Osgar was losing hope of converting even one of the more important members of the tribe. His frustration began to show.

He started to get angry with his patient audience, telling them more forcefully that unless they believed in the love of his God they would certainly be damned eternally and burn in hell. This only served as more evidence, to those who thought about it, of the peculiar mixture of bliss and torment in his religion. What was worse, he warned them that when they visited and worshipped the spirits in their sacred rocks and springs and trees, they were, in their ignorance, consorting with demons. He said their priestesses, who led them in these heathen, sinful practices were agents of the devil.

The women were affronted. They began to murmur among themselves and attendance at his meetings rapidly dropped off. They all agreed he told a good story, but to entertain them with tales of his foreign god was one thing; to offend their gods was quite another matter, and a dangerous one. They would hear no more.

Eangyth and Fryth were relieved at this turn of events. They had watched Osgar at his work from a discreet distance, and had questioned members of his audience privately. They both failed to come any closer to the import of his message but it was quite clear that Osgar would have to go before the spirits of the place became offended by his presence. Fryth decided to tackle Wulf.

She found him deep in conversation with the Christian. Osgar leaped up and crossed himself at the sight of Fryth. Thurston, who was sitting at his feet, made a clumsy effort to imitate the gesture; Osgar smiled indulgently and patted his head. Ignoring them both, Fryth addressed Wulf.

'I'd like to speak to you Wulf. Alone.' She added the last

firmly. Wulf looked at Osgar, who nodded, then made the sign of the cross over him with outstretched hand. Wulf followed Fryth who led him to the gateway of the shrine, where she stopped. She had said nothing as they walked, but now she turned to face him.

'We have let Osgar have his say, Wulf. We have tried to make him welcome. But it's not right for guests to offend their hosts or for strangers to insult the spirits of a place. We can't allow this to go on. It's time for him to leave.' Wulf sighed and shook his head.

'I did hope . . .'

'What did you hope, Wulf? That we would give up all that we know to be right, everything that makes us safe in this world, at the word of one strange Northumbrian! How could you hope for that?'

'What he says is true, Fryth, I know it, I feel it in my heart and mind.' Fryth walked slowly back down the path towards the river. She reached the bridge and leaned against its rails, staring at the water rushing underneath. A shoal of small grey fishes, heads upstream, were browsing among the weeds, flicking their tails from time to time in order to keep in the same place. Fryth did not look up when Wulf joined her.

'What evidence is there for what he says?' she said to the river as Wulf placed his elbows beside hers on the rail. 'You must have more than feelings.' She turned her head and looked at him. 'I *know* what I know, Wulf, I know the goddess's power. I have felt it, certainly, but I know it in my blood and heart and brain. I've seen it with my eyes.' Fryth's eyes were flashing and Wulf looked away.

'How can your Osgar claim his god has overthrown the gods I live with every day?' Wulf opened his mouth to speak, but Fryth cut him off with an impatient gesture, striking the bridge with her fist. 'No, I must speak. If people begin to believe that our gods are dead, what will become of the Earth, our Mother? Osgar's god is a sky god, born in the east like the sun, but I've heard no mention of the goddess from him.' Wulf looked back at the shrine. The high plank walls of its stockade completely hid the building within from view.

'James and Osgar say that their God is the only god. He made the earth and rules it, alone.' Wulf shifted awkwardly, his eyes still would not meet Fryth's.

'Yes, and only fools could possibly accept such ignorance. I don't know how they live in those foreign countries, perhaps there are no women there. You can't make life here in our land without a female, Wulf.' she said this slowly, as if explaining to a child. 'The earth is our mother. No sun god could create life on his own.' Fryth turned round and leant back against the rail. 'What worries me.' she went on more gently. 'Is what will happen if Freya is denied. She is powerful and dangerous. She requires our sacrifices and our obedience. I think there will be no end to her vengeance if we neglect her. That's why Osgar must go before he does any harm.'

'Why don't you tell him to his face, Fryth?' Wulf was regaining his composure.

'I don't know what to say to him. I'm sure he wouldn't listen to me. There'd be no point in meeting him. I just want him to go. I'm afraid of his words, I was not prepared for the shock of what he says.'

'We have never considered our beliefs.' said Wulf quietly. 'It's sometimes difficult to find the words. I think that's where the strength of the Christians lies, they think so deeply. Oh, I know the women chose not to take Osgar seriously, but I had questions that needed answering. The Christians had the answers to all my questions.' Fryth grunted and looked down at the river again. Her shadow fell across the shoal of little fish. They flicked their tails as one and darted out of sight under the bridge.

'It's a good thing that not everyone's like you, Wulf,' she said.

'I wish you could have met the Deacon, Fryth.' Wulf gripped the rail, holding it at arms' length. 'Osgar's a good man, but he's one of us, a churl as Gadd would say. He attracts the lost and the downhearted like Harold and Thurston. . . .'

'Or like you in Northumbria.'

'If you like, but my needs were different. You asked me why I thought things should improve. If you had led a life like mine you'd know why I needed to believe that things might be better. James showed me a way.'

'I think he's misleading you. He's wrong about so many things.' There was tension in Fryth's face. She pressed her fists against her temples. 'I've never had to think as hard as this before.'

'You've never had to think at all,' said Wulf. Fryth frowned, and Wulf went on hastily. 'I mean you've never been called into question. This new religion isn't going to go away Fryth, you're going to have to find your answers.'

'My powers as a sorceress will not go away either, Wulf. I can prepare myself. You of all people can't deny my knowledge.' She looked him in the eye. 'Have you told Osgar how this agent of what he calls the "devil" saved your life?'

'No,' replied Wulf, 'I haven't, but I know what he would say.'

'What.'

'James would say,' said Wulf carefully, 'that it was his God working in you in spite of yourself.'

'Oh, well!' Fryth breathed out a long sigh of capitulation. 'It seems this god keeps *all* the good to himself.' She laughed. 'At least these foreign magicians are subtle. They make worth adversaries.' Wulf picked up the last remark.

'*We* are at odds now, Fryth,' he said sadly. 'I know I could persuade you if I had the understanding, but I am just beginning.'

'You do intend to go on, then.'

'I must. I'll leave with Osgar, I've told him I want to be initiated. He says there's a Christian community not very far from here, no more than two days journey.' Fryth's eyes widened in disbelief. 'Yes, even among us Middle Angles. You see, it really isn't going to go away.' His face became earnest. 'Oh, Fryth, we know so little of the world in our small tribe. How can we possible claim to know the truth of anything when everything we know is so limited!'

Fryth thought of her meditations, her magic and her secret knowledge. She knew they reached the heights and depths of everything, far beyond what the world of men with all its various truths could offer. But how would Wulf know this? All she said was, 'It's true I know very little about the world.' Wulf nodded, but Fryth went on firmly. 'Even so, what I do know is that wherever we go and whatever we do, we are simply wanderers on the face of our Mother Earth; always at the mercy of Freya.'

'I used to think the same, but now I know different. I'm going to go with Osgar to the Christians and ask to join them.'

Fryth shrugged her shoulders and sighed. 'I can't stop you, Wulf, I know. I shan't try again.' She had a sudden thought. 'But what about your mother and sister? How will they manage among the Christians, or has Osgar turned them into Christians too?'

'No,' he bit his lips, 'no they won't be persuaded. I shall have to leave them here.'

'But Wulf, what will they do, how will they survive? You *can't* leave them here without you!' Wulf hesitated, he spoke faintly and without conviction.

'Osgar says a sign of true devotion is to forsake your family to follow Christ.' Fryth gasped.

'I don't believe it, you can't have heard him right!' Wulf nodded awkwardly. 'But this religion breaks down everything that's sacred!' She grasped him by the arms and shook him. 'Wulf, they've driven you mad.'

'Osgar says I must have faith, if I do what's right and pray for them no harm will come to them. Besides,' here he was on firmer ground. 'I've asked them to come with me, truly, I've begged them, Fryth, but they won't.'

'How can you expect them to give up what very little they have, what little they know, to risk everything with you? How could they do that, Wulf, if they can't share your "faith"? How could you ask them to?'

'I have to do it, Fryth.' Wulf said quietly. 'I have to go; I know I'm right. God will protect them.'

'No one else will,' said Fryth with conviction. She walked back to the shrine and started to pull open the gate of the stockade. Wulf followed her, He put a hand on the gate, pushed it shut again and leaned against it. He looked steadily at Fryth.

'We'll leave tomorrow,' he said. 'I don't think I'll be coming back. Will you wish me luck?' Fryth said nothing. She took him in her arms and held him for a moment, pressing her forehead against his chest. Then she let him go.

'Luck is a gift of the goddess, Wulf,' she said. 'I wish you luck, and her protection.' She opened the gate again and went inside, shutting it behind her.

Wulf and Osgar left the next day. Thurston and Harold left with them, trotting and stumbling, one on either side of the tall priest. Osgar raised his hand in blessing to everyone they passed.

CHAPTER 10

Fryth did not see them go. She woke early after a fitful sleep. Wulf's parting words had echoed in her head all night. She remembered, as she woke, the runes that she had cast for him on the day he left with Gadd. She slipped quietly out of bed and crossed over to the hearth. The embers of last night's fire were glowing dully among the ashes. She smoothed some ashes down and thoughtfully traced the same runes in them with her forefinger. ᛉ ᚠ ᚷ ᚱ A journey, a gift, wealth and pain. She had been baffled by their odd conjunctions when she had first cast them all those weeks ago. Now their meaning was less obscure.

She sighed, blurred the symbols with her hand, and stood up. She wiped her hands together, rubbing off the ash, then threw some kindling on the fire. The dry twigs caught quickly and soon the morning fire was crackling on the hearth. Woken by its noise, Guthlac and Athelmar scrambled from their beds. The day had begun.

Winter set in hard soon after Wulf left. The village pond froze a good month earlier than usual and the fields were crisped and blackened by the early frosts. The women ventured out of doors as little as possible, and Fryth was working even harder than usual, combating the demons of disease in a population weakened by the cold. There were many deaths among the old and young even before the Yule festival, which for the second year in succession was a very quiet affair. Food supplies were holding out, but only just, and in the long dark nights that followed

Yule the firelight cast deep shadows in many hollow cheeks when the women gathered together in the evenings.

Some families fared worse than others, and Eangyth and Fryth made a special point of asking the better off to help the poor, the bondspeople and the landless British. This was usually willingly done but, calling one morning on Ethelreda, a woman with more property than most, who was always open-handed, Fryth was surprised to meet with a hostile refusal.

'Why should I hand out from what little I have every day if they come and steal from me at night? At this rate they'll have everything and I shall be left with nothing.'

Ethelreda's store of corn had been raided in the night. The thief's footprints were clearly visible in the dusty floor around the sacks. Stealing was quite uncommon in the community, where differences in wealth, though they existed, were slight. This hard winter had stretched the difference considerably, despite Fryth and Eangyth's efforts. Thefts would weaken their case when it came to persuading the villagers to help each other, and something had to be done quickly to prevent a repetition.

That same afternoon Fryth announced to the village that she was going to cast a spell to catch the thief. At her request Ethelreda flung open her barn doors and the villagers crowded round to see what she would do. No one dared to enter the building, but they packed tightly in the doorway, craning their necks and blocking out the light.

In the dimness of the barn they saw Fryth, dressed in her fox-skin cloak, circling the footprints on the floor. She had scattered dried leaves of mugwort in the dusty marks and now she was shaking the eagle's feather and wolf's paw over them. Hissing and gnashing her teeth, she crouched down, balancing on the balls of her feet. She laid the feather and wolf's paw down carefully beside her and undid the pouch at her waist. In it was a beeswax taper and a fire-steel. Still hissing, she lit the taper and carefully allowed three drops of wax to drip into the footprint in front of her. Then she stood up and walked slowly round the barn, leaving three more drops of wax in each corner. Finally, coming back to the centre, she crouched down again, allowing three last drops to fall.

The onlookers heard a humming sound. It seemed not to be emanating from Fryth, but rather from the air around her. The sound swelled and the transfixed villagers felt the barn begin to rock. Dust filled the air and swirled round the still form of Fryth, squatting in the centre of the floor. The light from her taper cast a deep red glow over her face, as if she were sweating blood. She shifted, still crouching, and spread her feet wide apart, raising her arms to shoulder height; her elbows were bent and her fingers stretched out like claws, the fox's bushy tail hanging down her back brushed the floor between her legs. They could hear her hissing through the humming noise and trembled at the sound.

Fryth began to whisper,

'Cowardly creeping thief of harvest. . .
Shrivel like coal on the hearth,
Shrink like dung on the wall,
Spill like water in the pail.'

Her voice grew louder:

'Dwindle to a linseed grain,
Smaller than a worm's hip-bone,
More delicate than thistledown.
Die like wood in the fire. . . .'

She was shrieking now, her voice echoed in the rafters,

'Be utterly consumed, be nothing at all!'

The crowd let out a sigh and a shiver rippled though it. Fryth leaped to her feet. Her eyes were glaring and sweat was dripping from her forehead. She closed her eyes and swayed gently to and fro, muttering under her breath, but so quietly that only those standing on the threshold itself could hear her.

> 'Mugwort oldest of herbs,
> Has power against three, against thirty,
> Against poison, and infection.'

Her voice dropped lower still:

> 'Against intruding enemies, ravaging the land.'

Fryth opened her eyes and looked about her. After a long pause Eangyth emerged from the shadows of the barn where she had been watching Fryth, taking no part herself in the proceedings. She wrapped a woollen cloak around her daughter, who was shivering and dizzy from her exertions. The crowd outside the door melted away, and Fryth and Eangyth walked out into the cold evening air to go home and wait upon events.

No further robberies took place, but there was no immediate evidence among the village population that the spell was working either. Then, a few nights later, as they were preparing for bed, there came a soft, timid, knocking at Eangyth's door. Fryth went to answer it. She was often called out in the night these unhealthy days. A slight figure, shrouded in a threadbare cloak, was standing on the threshold.

'Please come,' said a muffled voice, one that Fryth recognized with a start as belonging to Wulf's mother. 'My daughter is sick, I think she's going to die.' Her voice was desolate, utterly forlorn. Fryth marvelled at the courage that had brought her to the door and was glad that she, and not her mother, had opened it.

'I'm going out.' she called to Eangyth over her shoulder, 'you go to bed.' She slipped out through the half-open door, shutting it quickly behind her before Eangyth could see who had called her. She followed Wulf's mother through the dark streets, shivering in the biting cold. She'd had no time to find her cloak. The woman kept up a brisk pace, saying nothing, but wringing her hands all the while. Soon they reached her house. It was ragged with neglect, and as they stepped inside Fryth felt the draughts leaking in through the tattered thatch and crumbling wattle walls. Wulf's sister was lying on a pile of sacks on the floor beside the hearth. No fire was lit, and all the light there was came from a small rush wick in a bowl of mutton fat.

Fryth looked down and caught her breath. The girl was wasted, practically shrivelled up. Her eyes were tightly shut, her face was the colour of yellow wax and a hoarse rattling came from her chest with each painful, slow drawn breath. Fryth recognized the signs. She turned to her mother and said as gently as she could, 'There's nothing I can do. She's past my help. It can't be long now.' She knelt beside the shabby bed and took the dying hand in her own. It was feather-light and curled stiffly, like the claw of a bird. The mother moaned hopelessly, she clenched her fists and began to beat her breast. Fryth stayed where she was, holding the wasted hand. As she knelt there, understanding came to her, and she knew that Wulf's sister was the thief. She looked up suddenly at Wulf's mother, who saw at once the knowledge in Fryth's face. Instantly, her moaning stopped, and she hung her head.

'I didn't dare to call on you,' she said, her voice barely above a whisper. 'I kept hoping that she might survive, but now,' her voice cracked and she began to wail again, 'it's over. My lady, she . . . I . . .' Fryth stood up, shook her head and reached out to the woman.

'Please don't call me that,' she said, still shaking her head.

'My lady,' Wulf's mother cried out more loudly still, 'we are so poor, no one is allowed to help us. She couldn't bear to see me going hungry. She said we'd suffered enough, I couldn't stop her.'

Fryth knew that stubborness all too well. She swallowed hard, 'Better this way,' she said quietly, 'than a hanging.' The law would have no mercy on an outcast; both women knew that.

'Better this way altogether!' Wulf's mother cried out fiercely. 'What hope was there for either of us? Better that she *should* die, and I with her.' She turned on Fryth, her voice shrill, 'Why don't you curse me, too?' She beat on her temples with clenched fists.

'Hush, hush,' said Fryth, looking down at the dying girl. Wulf's mother dropped to her knees beside her daughter, cradling the unconscious girl in her thin arms. The girl shuddered slightly, her breathing fluttered, and she was dead. The mother's head sank down over the fair head clutched to her breast. She rocked back and forth in silent agony.

Fryth's body filled with painful weariness. What could she do? What was there to be done? Rage mounted in her, against Fate, against the savage laws of men and, most of all, against Wulf whose mad selfishness had led to this. At this last thought her mind cleared. She drew a deep breath. Wulf might be the cause; he was also the only solution now.

'Listen, Eadburgh,' It was the first time she'd called Wulf's mother by her name. 'Listen!' She gripped the woman's shoulder, forcing her to cease the rocking motion. 'There's nothing left for you here. You must get away as soon as possible. You must go to Wulf.' She felt Wulf's mother stiffen. 'There's no alternative,' she went on urgently. 'He told me that he'd asked you to go with him and that you'd refused, and who would blame you, but now you've got to go.' Eadburgh gently laid her daughter's head back onto the rough sacking. She sat back on her heels and looked up at Fryth, who sensed at once that there would be no argument.

'You'll find him. Follow the road he took and ask. I'll make arrangements for you, you won't go hungry on the road. And one thing we do know, however crazed these people are, they're kind, they won't turn you away. Get ready now, you must leave at once. Tomorrow, when the news gets out,' she nodded at the shrunken corpse, 'your life won't be worth a candle flame. I'll deal with the burial.' In being practical, she was in some way staving off the horror of the night.

'An outcast's grave,' said Eadburgh bitterly.

'Leave now and spare yourself that,' said Fryth. Eadburgh shrugged her shoulders, she was numb with grief. Slowly, like a sleepwalker, strenuously avoiding looking at where her daughter's body lay, she started to put her meagre belongings together. Fryth left her making preparations, and returned a short while later carrying a bundle of food and a heavy knife. Eadburgh shivered at the sight of it but hung it from her belt. She took the food gratefully.

Fryth walked a little of the route that Wulf had taken with Eadburgh. It was a pitch black night, and the frosty air was thick with malevolent spirits. Fryth whispered many protective charms over Wulf's mother as they walked. No one who had any choice travelled at night. Where there was no choice it was impossible to be too well protected.

Wulf's family house stood empty in the misty dawn. Fryth pushed the door closed behind her against prying eyes. While it was still dark she had taken the body, lighter than a little child's, and buried it in a shallow grave at the edge of the village cemetery. She had no time to give it the proper rites, but she did leave a bowl of milk beside the head in the grave. She had helped the living woman on her journey, and now she gave Wulf's dead sister some succour for the road that she would travel, wherever she was bound. The village needed her to take that road. It would not do for her spirit to return, looking for the help she had been denied in life. To make quite sure that it would have to make its journey, Fryth returned to the house as the sun was rising and sprinkled it with water from the holy spring. No ghost would find a welcome in a hallowed place.

The house would crumble now, and sink back into the earth from which it had been made, but the family which had lived in it would be forgotten long before all traces of its walls had disappeared. Standing at its door in the morning light, Fryth put her head in her hands and wept.

News was beginning to filter back to the village from the north. Wulf's friend, Osgar, was not the only stranger to pass through the village that winter. Small bands of men were on the road, vagabonds made homeless by the devastations of war, soldiers on the run from this side or from that, eager to put themselves as far away from capture as possible. The village pieced the news together bit by bit. The Mercian army had met with a reverse in Northumbria. The Northumbrians had mustered under a new king, Oswald, another Christian and a mighty warrior. He had given the Northumbrians new heart and they were fighting back.

Then, as before when the first buds began to show, the men themselves returned. They came home in a body this time, and a very small one. Cerdic was not among them, nor was Edward, nor were most of the older of the chief's companions.

The news was simply told, and quickly too. The sooner it was conveyed to the stunned audience of waiting women the better for all concerned. Cadwallon was defeated. There had been a terrible battle in which the village war-band had borne the brunt of Oswald's fierce attack. They had been in the vanguard of Cadwallon's troops, according to the promise Cerdic had extracted from the Mercians. The men had fought bravely, hand to hand, but they had been overwhelmed. Cerdic had been killed almost at once, cut down by a dozen Northumbrian blades. His companions had chosen to die with him rather than to run and save themselves. Edward was one of those stout friends, true to the traditions of his kind, so frequently exalted in the beer-hall and so suddenly made real in flesh and flowing blood. Those men who had returned had tried to die with their companions, but, seeing the day was his, Oswald had called off his troops. He called it mercy. They only felt disgrace.

The disaster was absolute. The very heart of the tribe had been torn out. There was not a woman in the village who had not lost a husband or son. Godwin had died with his father. Edward went down first and Godwin had been killed trying to protect his father's body with his outsize shield.

Fryth had nowhere to look for comfort in her grief. There was no consolation, no source of pride. All the dead warriors, farmers, shepherds, woodworkers, had died defeated in a cause that was not theirs. They themselves, acccording to the laws and traditions by which they had lived, could have wished for no better and more honourable death; but the women, left alone with a handful of young and broken-spirited men, could hardly share that wish, or the beer-hall pride that led to its fulfilment.

Eangyth aged overnight at the news of her double loss. She seemed to shrink before Fryth's eyes. She shed no tears but her soul appeared to wilt within her. She sat long hours by the fire, absently fingering her beads or the keys at her waist.

'I saw this. I saw it coming clearly,' she would repeat over and over again, 'and still it is too hard to bear.' She had not lost her wits, but she had lost her heart and Fryth could not console her.

Fryth was the only priestess in the village now. Freya, even in their dreadful plight, could not be neglected, or still worse might come. Fryth rallied the village as best she could. She never left the house without dressing in the full regalia. During the winter months she had embroidered her dark blue cloak with yellow suns and moons, and over this she wore her fox skin. The eagle's feather and wolf's paw dangled from her waist beside her shining girdle hangers, and to them now she added her mother's crystal ball and slotted spoon. Her slight figure and purposeful gait, and her intense expression with its quick blue eyes became the focus of the village. She encouraged and exhorted its depressed inhabitants incessantly; insisting that life must go on, if not as normal, then at least in some new pattern they would have to devise for themselves.

There was no one obviously suited to replace Cerdic as leader of the tribe. All the older and experienced men were dead. The shattered remnants of the war-band avoided the beer-hall, which had stood empty since the men had left. It was as if they felt unworthy of it and ill-equipped to confront the spirits of the dead warriors they thought must be thronging its vacant benches, and damp, black hearth. Fryth called a meeting outside the hall. The village gathered underneath the sacred pillar. Its paint, after almost two years, still glowed brightly in the clear spring sun. Fryth was carrying Cerdic's chieftain's sword. It had been rescued from his body by the survivors of the battle. Oswald had ordered his army not to plunder, but rather to allow their vanquished enemies decent burial, and so Wyrmfah had been saved. Fryth held the sword in front of her for all the tribe to see. A sigh rippled through the crowd.

'A tribe is not a tribe without a chief,' she said to them. She had no need to raise her voice for the villagers were standing in heavy silence. 'Cerdic has left no successor,' she said, 'and it is difficult to choose between those who are left.' She looked round for opposition but there was a general murmur of assent. 'But we must have a new chieftain.' The little crowd murmured in agreement again. 'Therefore I suggest we cast the runes. Whoever is chosen in that way will have Freya's blessing and command the respect of us all.'

'How will that be done?' someone called out from the crowd.

'If we agree to this I'll show you. First, let's see if it's what people want.'

Leofric stepped forward. He was the young man at whose suggestion the silver panels for the doors had been made,

'If we want a leader I think we've no alternative. There isn't one of us who's worthy to replace Cerdic, but if his spirit sees that whoever sits in his place has been chosen by Freya, it will be satisfied and not think we've dishonoured him.'

'No one wants to replace him,' put in another survivor, 'but we must have a new leader. Whoever is chosen in this way, even if he doesn't want it, will know the task was meant for him.' Fryth was pleased with the response.

'Are we agreed, then?' Fryth asked.

'We are!' They spoke as one voice.

'Then I'll make arrangements. It shall be done at the most auspicious time. Soon it will be the thirteenth day of the moon, and Freya's day. It will be best to cast them then.'

Fryth thought she felt a lightening of spirits as the crowd dispersed. Simply to be meeting together, discussing things together as they were used to doing in the hall, coming to a joint decision, acted on the tribe to good effect. It was like watching a sick man returning from the brink of death, still scarcely living, still with long days of suffering before him, but on the mend.

On the thirteenth day the tribe assembled once more beside the pillar. All the men of fighting age, and there were very few, stood in a group in front of the rest. Fryth was with them. She held a bundle of rune staves in her hand, all were blank except one, which she had marked with ↑ , the rune of Tiw, the god of war and warrior chieftains. On the ground in front of her was a large black cock. Its scaly yellow legs were lashed together by a leather thong. It had stopped thrashing its powerful wings, and lay a tattered heap of iridescence in the dust.

Fryth held the rune staves in the air above her head, calling on Freya to show herself and make her choice. Then she threw the thin strips of wood onto the ground. The marked rune fell face down.

A hush fell over the company. In the sudden silence, far above their heads, a skein of geese, returning north from winter pastures, winged across the open sky. In formation the geese exactly echoed the shape of the Tiw rune. As they came on, their mournful honking could be heard, growing louder and louder. When they were immediately overhead a fresh leader pressed to the front. He wheeled, then swooped down over the village rooftops towards the water meadows by the river. The whole flock coasted after him, out of sight.

'Freya has answered me!' Fryth turned to the young warriors, 'She is here. Make your choices.'

One by one the young men came forward to pick up the staves. Some moved quickly, snatching up the nearest stick with no deliberation. Others lingered, moving their outstretched hands hesitantly over the wooden slips, touching one here and one there in an agony of indecision. Most curled their fingers round the rune staves secretively, holding them to their chests, hiding them from view. Six, seven, eight had their turn and then it came to Leofric. He strode out of the crowd and stooped resolutely over the nearest stave. He did not try to conceal its message but held it out in front of him. Etched on its white undersurface was the rune of Tiw. He turned to Fryth, who took him by the hand and led him to the pillar. He stood with his back against it facing the crowd. A great cheer broke out. Freya had chosen well.

Fryth sacrificed the cock, catching its blood in a wooden cup. She smeared the chieftain's rune stave with blood, and sprinkled some on Leofric.

'This blood heralds a new dawn,' she told the people. 'Leofric is our leader now. He is Freya's choice, he will serve us well.' She beckoned to Guthlac, her brother, who was standing in the crowd. He came forward, carrying Wyrmfah. Fryth dipped the chieftain's blade in the bright cock's blood then handed Leofric the sword. A louder cheer rose from the tribe; a small piece of their honour was preserved.

'And now,' said Fryth, 'Leofric must lead his warriors back into the hall.' She gestured to Leofric to open wide the silver-covered doors. He shot back their double wooden bolts, flung them open and, with Fryth at his side, he led the men inside. A new fire was lying ready on the hearth, Fryth's secret work. Diffidently, the little band of warriors filed into the building. They stood in silence, shuffling their feet and looking round as if they were seeing it for the first time. The air seemed to throng with the spirits of dead men, they could almost hear their voices and their echoing laughter. Nearly all the young men shuddered. The hair on the backs of their necks stood up.

Sensing their disquiet, Fryth stepped quickly to the hearth-pit in the centre of the hall.

'The spirits of the dead are feasting even now in the high hall of the gods,' she said, 'the hall which welcomes only those who die in battle. There is no greater joy for warriors, they are happy, they have no reason to return. Now I shall sanctify the benches ready to receive new heroes.' She knew the language of the beer-hall well. The young men visibly relaxed. Their shoulders straightened and their heads came up.

Fryth took the wooden cup and dipped a thick horse-hair brush into the cock's red blood. She flicked the blood at the benches, the high table and the hearth. Then she turned and sprinkled the men with the last drops.

Without being asked, Leofric knew what was fitting now. As Fryth put down her brush, he picked up the fire-steel that she had placed beside the fire. The wood was soaked in pitch, it kindled in seconds and soon it was blazing up. Its bright orange flames chased the dark shadows from the corners of the roof, and with them, the last traces of the men's unease. One began to sing, softly at first, but then with growing confidence. Gradually all the other men joined in, settling themselves at the benches, beating gently on the tables with their knives. Leofric made his way to the high table and sat down gingerly, testing himself, seeing how it felt. He looked round the hall. There were more empty spaces than there were full ones, the men were bunched together on the benches near the top, but they had reclaimed the hall. He drew in a deep breath and called for beer. A shout went up and two men went out to fetch the casks. Fryth, smiling to herself, followed them into the sunshine.

Having a new leader, however young and inexperienced, restored a little vigour to the tribe, but there were no illusions about the difficulties they faced. The workforce was seriously diminished. Now children, including Fryth's young brothers, were drawn into the struggle for survival. They grew up very quickly that spring, taking their turn at the plough, wrestling with the oxen and the thick black soil both at once; helping with the lambing though the cold spring nights; even battling with the blacksmith's tools and potters' clay. They learned these unaccustomed crafts fast.

Fryth led the field ceremony that year. She gathered all the elements of the ritual, baked the loaf and cut the turves herself. Eangyth remained at home beside the fire. Leofric guided the plough down its first furrow. There was no holiday mood, but the villagers were both pleased by the way their young chieftain held himself, and encouraged by Fryth's firm will. She had lost as much as any of them and her courage gave them strength. By the time the grain was ripening in the fields they had regained some of their lost heart. The beer-hall was alive again, the harp went round and battle-hardened warriors sang songs of war, the truth of which they all could vouch for.

The war was never very far away. Cadwallon might have been killed and his army defeated, but Penda's strength had hardly been diminished by his ally's death. By persuading the Briton to fight for him, he had preserved his own life and the greater part of the Mercian army. So it was that scarcely a week passed without some small war-band marching through the village. Penda was mustering on the Northumbrian border again. The village men showed little inclination to join the travelling bands and no effort was made to persuade them. The Mercians could see that they were very young and had lost the heart for battle. Lacking an experienced leader they would be of very little use. The villagers were able to get on with what mattered most, growing food.

The visiting soldiers brought their share of troubles none the less. Barns had to be securely locked at night and guard dogs set. The soldiers cut down trees at the forest edge in great numbers to feed their camp fires, and trampled down the fields. A girl, fetching water from the river as the evening drew in, was raped.

Worst of all, the unprecedented movement of men about the countryside brought with it new demons of disease; sweating fevers, rotting boils, all kinds of horrible contagion. Fryth was constantly at work among the sick, and in many cases she was powerless against this battalion of foreign devils. She pursued them in the spirit world but they laughed at her magic, and escaped. The depleted village dwindled even more.

By the onset of winter Fryth was exhausted, but the pressure had begun to ease. Freya had been good to them and the winter stores were well stocked. The warrior bands diminished as the army gathered further north. Fryth found time to give way to her tiredness. She spent more time at home with Eangyth and her two young brothers. She pitied Athelmar and Guthlac, forced out of childhood prematurely. She valued the help they gave in the village fields and on her father's lands, which they had inherited, and on Eangyth's, which Edward used to work for her. She repaid them as best she could by trying to recreate their shattered family life. She was so busy that it was not always possible, but as the evenings grew shorter they would sometimes sit together by the fire, as they once had done with Edward and Godwin, and tell stories, and Fryth would sing to them. She no longer sang to the tribe, she found the music would not come.

Eangyth had always been a comfortable companion. She had once been forceful and decisive too, but now she was never anything but gentle. She was ageing visibly. Silver showed in her hair and her shoulders were stooped. Fryth often felt a pang as she looked at her mother sitting hunched up, staring into the fire. She was proud to have worked with her when she was at the height of her powers, and thankful to have learned her magic from such a source. But now Eangyth's own fires were dying low. Fryth no longer asked her mother for advice in her work, but she often turned to her for comfort and support when exhaustion overcame her in the struggle against the demons of illness and despair. She learnt new skills from Eangyth at this time: patience, sympathy, a ready ear and a soothing tongue. Fryth needed them in these troubled times and Eangyth taught them to her without knowing it, as they sat together by the fire.

Life was settling into its new pattern, but some things did not change. Fryth still performed the ceremonies morning and evening in the shrine. Propitiating Freya was more important than ever, now that existence had become so precarious. She lit the Yule fire, as had always been done, with a new-kindled flame. It blazed up merrily, signifying hope in the midst of winter's darkness; and for the first time in two years the people danced. Winter was seen out in reasonable comfort; the harvest had been good and anyway there were fewer mouths to feed. Even so it was with some relief that the village, more or less intact, heralded the return of spring.

It was not long, however, before their relief was tempered with resentment. It seemed that there was going to be no end to war. Soldiers were on the road again, hardened and more troublesome after the rigours of their indecisive winter campaigning. There were cattle thefts and crops were taken from the fields. The men organized themselves into a defence group, keeping watch over the stockyards and the fields and barns at night, but when one of them was killed in a brief and bloody skirmish with some Mercian men, they gave up. Let the soldiers take what they would, the world had changed and the tribe would have to accept the change with all the difficulties it brought. The marauders continued their depredations unchecked, but they were never very large in number and the village could support the continuous slight drain on its resources.

One morning in early autumn, Fryth left the darkness of the cave-like shrine and walked out into the crisp daylight. She had been praying for an easy winter. The branches of the central tree had shivered gently and a humming filled the air. Fryth felt that Freya had heard her. Her spirits were light as she shut the gate of the enclosure carefully behind her, turning a key in the newly-fitted lock. She sniffed the air, it carried dry weather. As she raised her head, something in the shadows cast by the corner of the enclosure wall caught her eye. It looked like a sack, or a bundle of rags. She sniffed again, this time in irritation, catching a sweet, rotten smell in her nostrils. Then the bundle of rags moaned.

Instantly she was kneeling beside it, feeling through the tattered clothing for the body underneath. She tried to prize its hunched form open, catching her breath when she saw dried blood on the rags. The man groaned again, then straightened out and rolled over on his back, arms out, palms upwards in a gesture of surrender. A great sigh shuddered through his body and he lay as still as death. His beard and hair were straggling and matted, dark with filth and blood, but as the shadow moved off his body and the strong morning sunlight fell across it, Fryth saw that beneath the filth the hair was auburn. The bloody, tattered and unconscious figure was Wulf.

Fryth cried aloud. She wrenched off her cloak, the fox skin falling unceremoniously to the ground, and wedged it under his head. She ran to the stream that ran out under the enclosure wall and cupped some water in her hands. Kneeling beside Wulf's head she held the water to his lips. They were swollen and clotted with blood. She tried to force them open but with no success. The water trickled through her fingers, adding to the dark stains on his clothes. Fryth called his name again and again, but there was no response. She leaped to her feet, looking about her wildly, but no one was in sight. She started running to the village to get help.

The centre of the village was astir. Men and women were gathered in a knot in the village square, shouting and gesticulating excitedly. The knot broke open as they heard her cries for help. In its centre was the cause of the commotion, the tall shambling figure of Thurston, the idiot. Fryth scarcely had time to register his presence before she was on her way back, hurrying to the shrine, accompanied by two strong youths whose help she had enlisted.

They carried Wulf into the village, and at Fryth's insistence they took him to the carpenter's workshop. They cleared a space on the cluttered floor while someone ran to fetch a mattress. Wulf's breath was rattling in his chest as they laid him down. They withdrew quietly leaving Fryth alone with him, closing the door behind them. Fryth peeled off Wulf's tattered clothes, biting her lips at the hideous wounds she revealed, retching at the stench of putrefaction. Wulf's skin, which had always been pale, was almost transparent now, bloodless, gleaming like ivory between the blackened wounds. Three objects, clotted with blood, hung on separate thongs around his neck. Fryth removed them carefully, wrapped them in a rag, and put them in her pouch. Wulf's heartbeat staggered feebly in his chest with each hoarse breath he took. As Fryth wiped away the mottled foam that fringed his lips, a shaft of sunlight struck across the dusty floor. The door opened softly and poor witless Thurston, with his habitual, lop-sided, dribbling grin, came tiptoeing in.

Stiffly, Fryth moved back allowing Thurston to approach. Still grinning foolishly, he crouched over Wulf, laying his head on the heaving chest, stroking Wulf's cheeks with large, fumbling, clumsy hands. As Thurston stroked, Wulf's mouth suddenly dropped open. Thurston gurgled soothingly, pushing at Wulf's jaw with his fingers, trying to close it again. But Wulf's mouth would not stay closed.

Gently, Fryth reached out for Thurston's hands. She pulled him to his feet and, stumbling a little, blinded by tears, she led him out into the sunshine.

Thurston was incapable of rational speech but, although they would never learn the story from him, everyone could guess what must have happened. The Christian community, they knew, was not very far away. Evidently one of the marauding Mercian war-bands, maybe even one of those that had been troubling them, had come across Wulf's Christian outpost. Naturally, the Mercians would regard all Christians as the enemy, and had slaughtered Wulf and his companions. How Thurston had been spared to bring Wulf home to die would remain a mystery for ever, but his courage and his devotion moved them all.

Fryth thought of Osgar's kindly smile and dangerous talk; of Eadburgh, Wulf's mother – now she would never know if she had reached her son – and of all the poor Christians with whom Wulf had lived. They had trusted in the foreign god and not one was living now to recant, or to refute their foolish claim that the gods were not indifferent to the fate of men.

It was not until several days after she had buried Wulf beside his sister that Fryth remembered the amulets she had taken from round his neck. She pulled the bloody rag in which she had wrapped them from the depths of her pouch, untied the bundle and turned them over in her hands. They were rusty with dried blood. One was a small wooden cross. She could see the golden gleam of yew beneath the stains. Yew had been Wulf's favourite wood for carving little things. Besides the cross there was the bronze box which still contained the charms that she had given him when he had first set out with Gadd; and, black with tarnish, Cerdic's ring, the first fruits of her singing.

Fryth knelt on the floor of her mother's house, clutching Wulf's pitiful legacy in both her hands, bending her head, pressing them to her forehead as the tears ran down her cheeks.

That night she took them to the shrine and washed them in the sacred spring. She rinsed the bloodstains from the cross and burnished the ring with sand. The spring ran murky and she sat and watched it as it cleared. It always did run clear. Despite cruelty, suffering and death, Freya would not be polluted. Fryth lit the brazier and piled it high with leaves of aromatic sage to purify the air.

She knew what was required of her. Freya had always acknowledged her devotion and reponded to her magic. She knew that she belonged here in the village shrine, doing the goddess's will. She held Wulf's cross in her left hand; *he* had had no certainties, nowhere he had truly belonged. The box containing the rune staves she had given him was in her other hand. She cupped cross and amulet in her open palms, weighing one against the other. Wulf must have done this too, she thought. Perhaps, for him, the cross had outweighed her magic; but, she opened the box and lifted out the little strips of wood, these were proof that he had not denied it altogether.

Wulf had continuously turned over in his mind the unhappiness of his situation, trying to make sense of it. She never had the need to think, he had said, and he had been right. If something was known, filling the heart and blood and breath, there was no need to think about it. Thinking only brought unhappiness and indecision. She rubbed the cross lightly on her skirt bringing up a soft shine in the golden, almost grainless wood.

Christianity was for thinkers, people who were sure of nothing, people whose spirits were hollow and open to invasion.

Fryth stared at the cross intently. Her eyes closed and her head began to sway. Darkness enveloped her and held her for a long time. When at last she opened her eyes she was gripping Wulf's cross so tightly that her knuckles were white and bloodless and she had to prise the fingers open to make them let it go. She turned the cross over in her hands, The yew was her tree, Wulf's talisman had a meaning for her as well.

'A rough tree outside, inside steadfast.
Firm fire-guardian, fed by deep roots,
A joy to our native land.'

In a quick, decisive, movement she hung the cross round her own neck, pushing it out of sight under her dress. 'Let the change come,' she said aloud. Freya was powerful. Surely her magic was strong enough to withstand the power of thought.

CHAPTER 11

Eangyth had been growing increasingly frail and, in the fourth winter of Leofric's chieftainship, she died. She had forseen her death and warned Fryth to prepare for it. She herself was even eager for it, always hopeful that her journey would reunite her with her husband. Eangyth spent most of her last weeks lying in the great family bed. Fryth nursed her tenderly, coaxing her to eat, talking quietly to her about the old days, the days before Edward and Godwin had marched away. Once they discussed Eangyth's property, which Fryth would inherit after her mother's death. Left unspoken was the fear both of them shared, that Fryth was unlikely to enjoy her wealth as her mother and grandmother had done before her, and the subject was not mentioned again. Sometimes Fryth sang to her mother. In particular Eangyth liked to hear Fryth's initiation song, the first song that had ever come to her. She said it brought back the happy life they once had known. Sometimes Fryth would sit in silence beside Eangyth's bed, holding her hand. When they had worked together it had always been in silence, and in silence Fryth felt the deepest communion with her mother, an understanding that needed no words.

On the night that Eangyth died, she asked Fryth to help her up. Fryth dressed her mother in her old regalia. She draped the grizzled badger skin about Eangyth's shrunken shoulders, and for the last time hung the crystal ball and shining girdle-hangers at her waist. Exhausted by the effort, Eangyth lay back again against the pillows, and Fryth and her two surviving sons gathered round her bed. Her eyes glittered with their old fire as she gestured to her daughter to take the drum.

Fryth lifted her mother's wide-mouthed drum onto her knee and softly, with a beat no louder than the gentlest pulse, she drummed her spirit into its last journey. Eangyth's breathing stopped and the fire in her eyes dimmed, and then went out.

In all that she had suffered, Fryth knew that she had not learned what loss was until now. Eangyth's death emptied her soul. She went through the rest of that winter in a daze. The daily round of household occupations hardly registered in her numbed brain; only when performing the rituals in the shrine did she feel even half alive, since they brought her closer to her mother's spirit. She raised a cairn of stones on Eangyth's grave and when at her lowest ebb she would revive herself by drawing on the energy they transmitted to her from the spirit world

Soon after Eangyth's death Fryth's brothers, still a pair of beardless boys, left home. The roving war-bands were not so much in evidence now, Penda's army was growing more organized as he continued the fight against King Oswald. Messengers, well-disciplined fighting men, had come to the village to make the call to arms. Leofric swore new oaths of loyalty to Penda and led the village's handful of warriors to join the Mercian army. Memories of recent disasters were put out of mind as the promise of a glorious battle with Oswald's troops enticed them from the thankless struggle in the short-handed fields. The prospect of adventure was a reward for the hard work that had been forced on her brothers since the death of Edward, and Fryth did not have the heart to deny them. The young men's going left the land less well-tended still, and worse defended.

The war, despite their hopes, went badly. Suddenly Mercian soldiers on the run were everywhere, plundering where they could, hiding in the forest from Northumbrians who pursued them furiously, for the first time penetrating deeply into Penda's territories as they hunted down their quarry. Frequently small bands of wounded men would struggle into the village, demanding help, commandeering provisions from the already meagre stores, talking of skirmishes with the enemy not more than one day's march away.

The crisis that had been building up for years had come at last. Fryth's tribe had no resources left to withstand the onslaught of warfare in their midst. All the security they had known, everything they valued, their independence, their peaceful lives, the life blood of the tribe itself, had gradually been drained away, leaving them defenceless and afraid. Fryth had no comfort for them, no large gesture that might rekindle their hearts. She knew that Fate was inexorable. Why should it be otherwise for them? She bent over the spring that welled up in the shrine day after day, listening for any hint from the spirit that might guide the tribe in their despair. At last, to her surprise, since it had been so long, a song came to her. As it formed itself on her lips she knew that it was the voice of Freya working in her.

'. . . He who has lived with it knows
What cruel company sorrow can be.
We, who long have lacked a loving word,
From war-lord and dear friends, live in this loneliness,
Sorrow and despair are the only companions
Of those who send their hearts over the frozen waters.
Wearily seeking departed friends.'

Fryth's own heart ached as the song filled it, and the shadows in the shrine darkened. The inspiration of the goddess offered little consolation:

'. . . This world dwindles and passes away.
Until he has suffered his share of world's winters
No one is wise. And the wise man must be patient.
Nothing in the Kingdom of earth is easy,
All life beneath the heavens is in the hands of Fate.
Possessions fail, friends fail, families fail,
No one lives forever in the wilderness of this world.'

Fryth left the shrine and called the tribe together under the sacred column. She sang the song to them and they understood it well; all that was left to them was acceptance and endurance, and they had a strong reserve of both. In some strange, sorrowful way, Fryth could see that it brought them peace.

The following evening, as she left the shrine and walked slowly towards the bridge, wondering what fresh disturbances awaited her return, Fryth was roused from her thoughtful state by a commotion in the reeds at the river's edge. The reeds were clashing together, and from somewhere in their depths came a snarling and a snapping sound. Suddenly the reeds parted and a blurred shape, brown and white and yelping, came hurtling out, colliding with Fryth and falling in a heap at her feet. It was a large dog fox. Its legs and muzzle were covered in blood, its ears torn and bleeding, its brush was bedraggled and covered with river mud. The fox picked itself up, shook each paw gingerly, then arched its neck and licked its white breast. It looked at Fryth with narrow, yellow eyes, and limped slowly away into the woods behind the shrine.

All Fryth's senses were alert, her muscles tense. She stood stock still for a long moment, watching and listening. But everything was still again. The light breeze brought only the murmur of voices from the village, and the river gurgled on its way. No sound came from the reeds. Cautiously, Fryth tiptoed to the water's edge and parted the reeds with her hands. In their centre was a hollow formed by flattened, bloodstained stalks, the site of a desperate struggle. Looking down, Fryth saw what kind of a struggle it had been. Lying stretched out, quite dead, was the square, grey body of a badger, the stark, black and white stripes on its head were in almost shocking contrast with the muddy browns and greens on which it lay. Its mouth stretched open over pointed, blood-smeared teeth.

Fryth pushed her way through the stiff, rustling reeds. The muddy water at the river's edge closed round her ankles as she dragged the badger's body from its last battle-field. Its weight surprised her. She was panting with the effort by the time it lay at her feet on the grass. She knelt beside it and turned it over on its back. It was a sow, an old one, one that had suckled many cubs. Its great age, Fryth saw at once, had given the fox the victory in what otherwise must have been an unequal fight. In any case a battle between these two animals was something she had never seen before. She sat back on her heels, pondering on the meaning of such an event.

The badger had been her mother's spirit guide, the fox was hers. Fryth gazed at the rough pelt of the beast in front of her. It seemed that this death was an echo from the spirit world. The old badger had been overthrown. Her own fox-spirit now reigned supreme. Fryth knew what she must do. She must offer the badger back to Freya who had sent her to her mother. Reverently, she gathered the dead animal into her arms and, staggering slightly under the heavy load, rose to her feet. Without pausing to look back, she crossed the bridge and, taking the road that skirted the village, set off towards the forest. Alone, with night falling, with no torch to light her way, she took the badger's body to the sacred grove.

The night was dark and the way home wearisomely long. The tiredness of misery dragged at Fryth's legs, slowing her down.

It was long before she smelt the smoke, or heard the cries, that she felt the old familiar pricking sensation in the hairs on the back of her neck and broke into a run. Several times she stumbled in the dark, and once she fell headlong. The fox skin was snatched from her shoulders by an overhanging branch. The long bronze girdle-hangers crashed against her knees. She was hindered by them and by her flapping cloak. Without stopping, she tore off both belt and cloak, catching her string of beads as she did so. The beads cascaded down over her flying feet.

Her breath was searing her lungs when finally she emerged from the forest and stood quite still in the fields at its edge.

The village was on fire. Dark shapes were moving among the

smoke and flames, silhouetted against the bright glare. The air was alive with screaming and loud shouts. A roof crashed down with an enormous explosion, hurling a sheet of flame and sparks into the night sky.Every now and then Fryth, still motionless, caught the glint of weapons in the firelight. Horses and cattle were bellowing, thrashing and churning in their stockades.

She never knew how long she stood there, watching the Northumbrians at their slaughter. By degrees the cries and moaning died away. The dark shapes clotted together in small groups and started moving on. The houses were still burning fiercely and the sky above the village had turned a lurid orange, streaked with red. Fryth stepped back into the shadows as a small group of soldiers passed close by her. She saw with a start that one had a huge silver-mounted drinking horn under his arm. She could feel her breath coming slowly, passing over her lips and tongue like milk. Thoughts floated through her mind and vanished like the sparks flickering out in the sky above her. She started walking slowly, as if waist deep in water. She felt no fear, only the vaguest unease that she would not find her way with the houses burning down. Something dropped onto her foot, she glanced down. It was her brooch, slowly she put her hand up to her shoulders, the other had gone. It must have fallen further back. She did not stop, but kept on walking at a steady pace.

Something flashed passed her, yowling piteously, an acrid smell followed in its wake. It was a half-burned dog. She was in the village now it seemed. Shadows were scurrying in the blazing ruins and from somewhere came a hideous, rhythmic screaming; the screaming filled her ears until she thought her head would burst, and then abruptly stopped.

A man bumped into her, a stranger, carrying a blazing faggot in his hand. A Northumbrian, looking for booty. He caught her arm and jerked her round. Fryth found herself looking into his eyes, she could see the flames' reflection flickering in them. His eyes began to travel over her, suddenly they opened wide.

'What in God's name . . . ?' he shouted above the roar of the fires.

'We thought this was a pagan place!' Fryth glanced down; Wulf's cross of yew hung down outside her dress. He had seen Wulf's cross. He took her for a Christian! He was calling to his friends. In an instant Fryth's brain cleared. She felt her spirit rising as if through fathoms of still water, surfacing in the smokey glare, gasping for life. She knew she must say nothing. She clutched Wulf's cross and held it up before her face. Two more men came running up.

'A Christian! There's a Christian here!' Her captor was shouting in amazement. He looked down at the front of Fryth's dress. It was smeared with badger's blood.

'Those heathen bastards! Don't you worry girl, you're safe with us, we'll get you away from here.' The others crowded round. Fryth stayed mute but her brain was working furiously. How was she to survive? One way alone had any possibility. She would soon give herself away if she talked. Their blood must have time to cool before she spoke to them. This meant a good day's journey, possibly even more. There was only one way to avoid talking altogether. She closed her eyes and began to sway, slowly at first, then faster, and faster still.

'Catch her! She's going to faint!' Strong arms held her, but she did not feel them tighten round her.

Her fox came stepping lightly out from between the shaking aspen trees. He greeted her with his welcoming bark, and led her away on the start of what was to be her longest journey in the spirit world.

PART II

THE PAGAN

CHAPTER 12

Fryth woke with a start. It was dark. Shutters had been closed across the windows of the little white room and a small oil lamp was flickering on the floor beside her bed. This time she knew at once where she was.

'In Heruteu,' she whispered into her pillow, 'in Northumbria, by the sea.' She sighed deeply and closed her eyes. There was no sound, everything was hushed and still.

For a long while she lay motionless, hovering between sleep and waking, until she was roused gently by the sound of music. It came drifting through the silence into her room. Somewhere close by men and women were singing, unaccompanied. She could hear deep bass voices rumbling beneath a sweeter, higher sound. Fryth had never heard such music. It rose and fell, swelled and diminished. Each voice seemed to sing a different tune, and yet, she thought, the tunes flowed so naturally together that after all it must be a single song that they were singing.

Fryth lay captivated by a magic that was entirely new to her. When the singing finally died away she cried out for it to start again. But silence had fallen. Presently she heard the sound of many shuffling feet outside her window, crunching on what must be a gravel path. Before the sound of the last footstep had ceased she heard a murmuring outside her door. It opened slowly, letting in a gust of cold night air. The strange, raw, salty smell she had noticed earlier in the day intensified. A bulky figure filled the doorway for a moment, then stepped into the room.

A large, imposing woman, dressed in a voluminous brown garment, stood looking down at Fryth. Her abundant frame cast a deep shadow on the floor behind her and half-way up the wall. Fryth heaved herself into a sitting position, and leaned back against the wall. This simple movement cost her a tremendous effort which must have shown in her face, for the fat woman's expression was instantly concerned.

'Please,' she said, her voice was deep and rich, 'you mustn't strain yourself. Lie back. Look, I'll sit beside you.' She squatted lightly down beside the bed. She had that disquieting agility and grace that sometimes attends a bulky body. The woman took Fryth's shoulders gently in her hands and helped her to lie flat again. Fryth sighed, a sigh that was half a yawn.

'You're very tired you must rest. My name is Heiu, I am Abbess here. You are in my care. I have brought you here from York where I took charge of you. Do you know that you have been unconscious for over two weeks?' Fryth nodded feebly. 'You were in some kind of trance. A troop of soldiers were carrying you. They said they had carried you with them from Middle Anglia. Is that right?' Fryth nodded again, '. . . and all the way you had not stirred. They had decided you must be enchanted and had grown afraid of you. They were going to abandon you, to leave you to die; but I saw the cross lying on your breast.' Fryth reached up a claw-like hand. Wulf's cross was still lying there!

'It was for the cross I saved you. . . .' Heiu paused. She looked thoughtfully at Fryth as if about to ask her something, but then appeared to change her mind. She rose slowly to her feet.

'I'll ask you nothing more tonight,' she sighed, 'except your name.' Fryth told her. 'Well, Fryth, I'll come again tomorrow. We'll go now, Hubert.' Fryth raised her head, puzzled, and saw for the first time, in the shadows, quiet and motionless, the small figure of a man. He must have been behind her, thought Fryth, no wonder she had not noticed him. She saw that he had the same tufted hair as Osgar. He was staring at her. She returned his gaze with the same intensity: neither looked away until Heiu moved to the door, blocking the stare with her body.

'God bless you, my daughter,' she said softly. The little man slid out of the room. Heiu was making a more stately progress when Fryth called out.

'Madam!' Heiu turned in the doorway. 'What is an Abbess?'

'Leader, you could say – a spiritual leader.' She smiled and was gone. Fryth turned her face into the pillow as a wave of loneliness and grief washed over her.

'I am an Abbess too,' she said aloud.

The beautiful music she had heard that evening haunted Fryth's dreams, and as she lay dozing in the thin, dawn light it came floating back again. She listened entranced to all the separate voices weaving one rich song. The pattern that they wove was rare and intricate, composed as much of light and colour as of sound. She wrapped it round her like a cloak and felt that she could never hear enough.

The two women who had been with her when she had first woken from her long trance, brought her a breakfast of fish and eggs and bread. She ate ravenously and drank huge quantities of milk. She could feel the nourishment stirring her thin blood. She was too weak to hold even the smallest bowl, but the women nursed her carefully, feeding her like a baby. They told her their names were Cwen and Bebba. They called themselves nuns. Both were dressed in the same shapeless brown dress as their Abbess. Cwen was short and fair, with bright blue eyes and chapped red cheeks; Bebba was thin and grey-haired, her skin was pale and her fingers long and white. Both had pleasant, calm, smiling faces. It was obvious to Fryth that they were pleased and excited to be associated with a miracle, but they were wary too; every time they entered the room they would make the sign of the cross in the air in front of them.

From that first morning Cwen and Bebba were always considerate and gentle with Fryth. They brought extra woollen blankets for her bed, for the cool night air struck through her wasted body to the bone. They propped her up on thick straw-stuffed pillows, and they fed her almost every hour with nourishing food which they had specially prepared themselves.

Fryth felt at ease with them at once and relaxed under their kindly attentions.

She had to be careful even so. As Bebba helped her to eat her first breakfast, holding a bowl of milk to Fryth's lips, her fingers brushed against Wulf's cross.

'And how do you come to be wearing this?' It was obviously a question she had been waiting to ask. 'Where have you met the Grace of our Lord and Saviour?'

Weak as she was, Fryth knew she must be circumspect. She told them of Osgar's visit to her tribe, how he had preached to them and told them of his god.

'The god Osgar spoke of is obviously a mighty power,' she said artlessly, 'so I took to wearing his sign, in the hope that I might obtain some strength from it.' Cwen and Bebba tutted and looked grave.

'Such ignorance!'

'Such boldness! It's a wonder you weren't struck down. But God is good, He forgives an ignorant heart. . . .'

'. . . or a half-taught one. It's a pity this Osgar didn't stay to finish his good work.'

Fryth knew that it would not be sensible to be too open about her past, so she did not mention her part in Osgar's departure from the village. She said merely that he had not been made to feel welcome and hinted that she regretted this. The women seemed to accept what she told them, and took it in good part. Fryth discovered that they had been born and bred as Christians, and that they tolerated what they saw as ignorance; treating it with pity, rather than anger or contempt. From that first day, Fryth saw that Eangyth had been right. The Christians chose to see her ways as childlike, something to be put right gently rather than bitterly confronted; to be led away from, to be grown out of.

Fryth had reason to be grateful for the tolerant attitude of those in whose care she found herself. They preached love and compassion and tried to live accordingly. Despite the fact that she was a pagan, and that the mysterious trance in which she had arrived was plainly evidence to them of diabolic influence, they treated their frail charge with tenderness. But they saw it as their duty to fight the devils which they considered to be in possession of her soul.

Heiu commenced the battle for her soul at once. In daylight she looked less massive than she had in the shadowy lamplight of the previous evening, but she was still a very imposing woman; tall and fair and stout. Her face was ruddy and weather-beaten, like Cwen's it had been coarsened by the wind and sun, and her eyes were a deep blue. Her expression was serene and kindly, but Fryth sensed an iron will beneath the composed features. She was obviously a woman of decision, certain of her powers. Knowingly to have taken an enchanted girl into her care was proof enough of that.

The white bird floated past the window as Heiu sat down beside Fryth's bed. She wasted no time in pleasantries, cutting short Fryth's speech of thanks for rescuing her.

'This is a monastery,' she said.

'A what?'

'A monastery, a community of men and women, monks and nuns, who have devoted their lives to the service of Christ. It is the first monastery in Northumbria to have women among its members.' She said this with some pride, and paused to allow its full effect to sink in.

'Are women usually unwilling to live in monasteries then?' asked Fryth, puzzled. Heiu failed to grasp the implication of the question.

'I was guided to establish this foundation less than a year ago,' she went on. 'We have started in a small way, but we shall grow.' Fryth looked about the room. So it was newly built. Her mind was wandering. She stroked the smooth, white, chalky wall.

'What is this?' she asked. 'I've never seen a wall so smooth and white.'

'Plaster, made with lime. We burnish it. My monastery will be beautiful in every detail; everything we make is for the greater glory of our Creator. Craftsmen came from Gaul to help us. They are master-builders.' Fryth though of her village shrine, dark and cave-like, like a living thing, composed of living things. She looked up, and out of the window. The sun had crept into its frame, its bright glare filled the room and rebounded from the glossy walls. Fryth sighed. Heiu put out a large dimpled hand and stroked her forehead. Her hand was firm and cool.

'Where is Gaul?' asked Fryth turning her face to the Abbess, seeing a bright, white village in her mind. Heiu laughed.

'I suspect there is a great deal you do not know, besides the love of Christ,' she said, not unkindly. 'We have a lot to talk about. But first you must regain your strength, there'll be plenty of time when you have recovered.' She rose to her feet, shaking out her full brown robe as she did so. A smell of lavender wafted over Fryth. Heiu looked down at her and smiled.

'I'll come again,' she said and left the room. Her sandals creaked softly as she walked.

Like a sick animal, Fryth knew instinctively what would most hasten her recovery. Of first importance was not to dwell on her wretched situation. Long years of training had perfected her ability to still her mind. Remorselessly she forced out racing thoughts, the gnawing anxieties and painful memories. As far as possible she emptied herself of all thought.

She ate ravenously; she slept; and when she was not sleeping she lay quite still, breathing slowly and evenly. Each day that passed was measured by the glorious music that floated into her room at regular intervals. It lifted her spirits and filled the emptiness she struggled to achieve with light and peace.

Sometimes she lay so motionless and quiet that her nurses were afraid she might have slipped back into her trance. But she would turn her head and greet them with a smile. She sensed a mounting awe in Cwen and Bebba, and decided that this was no cause for regret. It was just as well that they should have some respect for her powers, since they had no respect for her beliefs. They told her repeatedly that she was a heathen. It was through no fault of her own of course, how could she know otherwise, coming as she did from a benighted land? But she must learn that the gods she worshipped were in reality aspects of the Devil, the Anti-Christ, who roamed about the world battening on all the ignorant souls he could find.

Fryth lay still and listened in silence to Cwen and Bebba's lectures. She offered no resistance, and her aquiescence encouraged them to think their efforts were not being wasted. Fryth inwardly marvelled at their complacency, but she tried to give no indication of her feelings. They were good to her and their kindness warmed her sorrowing heart.

Gradually she put on weight. The knuckles of her fingers no longer stood out like knots. The skin on her arms began to tighten as the flesh filled it out. She could sit up with no effort, and on one memorable day, stood upright on tottering feet. Cwen and Bebba held her arms. It was their triumph as much as hers.

'You weigh at least as much as a feather now!' laughed Bebba.

'When once you were just thistle-down.' Cwen squeezed her arm affectionately. They were leading her to the window. Fryth faltered; her heart was pounding. These four walls had been her universe for so long. She felt safe within them, protected, she did not want to look beyond them. She had already seen enough of the world. She was content to stay in this white box until she died. Her knees sagged.

'Don't make me!' she cried out. 'Please! I can't bear it. I don't want to know!' The two women were startled by her outburst. They looked at each other and shook their heads. They tried to soothe her, coaxing her gently, pinioned between them, to the window.

'But its beautiful, our monastery.'

'People come from miles around just to see what we have done. Come look. . . .'

'You must see where you are!'

'You don't understand!' wailed Fryth. 'I don't want any more than this.' She was twisting her head about, trying to bury her chin in her neck, anything to avoid raising her eyes. In that instant a shriek split the air overhead, it was the white bird. Slowly Fryth looked up and out

The bird had gone. She breathed in deeply, grasped the window-sill and looked about her. She saw bright thatch, white walls, gravel path, and bees, drowsily working the last of autumn flowers. Gradually the jumble of impressions formed itself into a coherent whole.

From where she looked out she could see two long, low buildings. Each had six windows and six doors, like a row of little sheds joined together. Fryth saw that she was in one of an opposing pair of similar buildings. A vegetable patch, bordered with flowers, filled the space between. A man was walking among the cabbages and beans with two buckets dangling from a yoke across his shoulders. Gravel paths criss-crossed the vegetable garden. They connected with a central path that linked three larger buildings set at either end of the rows of houses, one at one end, two at the other. Fryth guessed at once that the single larger building must be the monastery's shrine. Like the others it was white, but it had no windows. Double doors, firmly closed and unadorned, were in its gable end. Above them, almost disappearing into the shaggy golden thatch, was fixed a high wooden cross.

There was a wide gap between the houses opposite and through it Fryth could see a field of rough, brown, cropped grass stretching behind the houses into the near distance. There, on the horizon, where the field should have met the pale blue sky, was a thin band of darker blue.

'The sea!' Fryth cried out. 'The sea!' She turned a face that was wet with tears to her two companions. 'I've never seen the sea.' Her knees gave way entirely and she sank to the floor.

Cwen and Bebba helped Fryth back to her bed and she lay down trembling. Cwen was frowning anxiously.

'Whatever's got into her? She seemed so much better.' Bebba knelt down and took her hand. She peered into Fryth's face. 'I am better, I am' cried Fryth, 'I'm *much* better, and I am so grateful to you, believe me I am! I don't know what it was that frightened me, I really don't. Your monastery is beautiful, quite beautiful.' She spoke from her heart and what she said was true in all but one respect. She knew very well what it was she feared – the future. How was she going to rebuild her shattered life in this alien place?

Cwen and Bebba left her. Worn out, she fell asleep almost immediately and the white bird sailed through her dreams all night.

Fryth saw little of Heiu during the weeks of her convalescence, but Cwen and Bebba often brought greetings from the Abbess, and enquiries as to the progress Fryth was making. The nights were growing colder and Heiu ordered a fire to be built on the new hearth in Fryth's room. Cwen built it up for her and lit it from a pot of charcoal brought from the kitchen.

'It's a long time since I've done this,' she said, snapping a stick across her knee. 'We're not allowed fires in our cells. The flesh is weak and must be subdued.'

'Why, Cwen?' It was the type of question that Fryth was constantly asking. 'Why make yourselves more uncomfortable than you need? The earth provides us with good wood and fire, why not make use of them?' Cwen shook her head, grunting as she broke another stick.

'It's for that reason. We're told not to rely on the things of earth but to look beyond to the things of heaven. Too much comfort here and we would forget our true destination.' She smiled cheerfully and it was Fryth's turn to shake her head.

When Cwen had gone she slipped out of bed and settled herself beside the newly kindled fire. The sticks were crackling merrily and the grey smoke was already smudging the new yellow thatch as it twisted towards the smoke-hole in the roof.

Fryth gazed into the red heart of the fire, feeling vaguely comforted. Here at last was something familiar to her. The hearth-fire held the spirit of home. Fryth thought of Cwen, and all the others in this place. They had cut themselves off from even this, the simplest of the spirits of the earth. Her daily encounters with the strange, unnatural beliefs of the Christians had not brought her any closer to understanding them. To call the mother that nourished and protected them the Devil, to deny themselves the benefits she offered in the hope that this would bring them reward after death, seemed to Fryth a terrible perversion. It led to a reversal of all certainties of life. What would kinship mean where religion put itself above the ties of blood? Had not Wulf been led to abandon his family, with dreadful consequences? For how long would Freya continue to support a land that denied her?

Fryth shivered. She threw a fresh log on the fire. As the flames spurted up a new thought came to her. Even in Northumbria the flowers grew and the seasons turned. Obviously there would still be those who had not abandoned the old ways, Freya must even now be getting her due from people who refused to accept the Christians' religion. Fryth felt, for the first time since she had woken in this place, the surging of the goddess's power on her blood. She had neglected her for too long. Thoughtfully she traced the rune of hail in the ashes on the brand-new hearth.

'Whitest of wheat,' she whispered,
'Whirls from the sky,
Whipped by wild winds, turns into water.'

She was a grain of hail, carried by cruel winds into this foreign country. Now she would become water, silent and invisible, nourishing the old ways.

That night she kept back a little of her food. She gathered some leaves of the creeper that grew round her window, tinged with autumn gold, and she made an offering to Freya. The act felt strange and clumsy, but a familiar humming filled the air and Fryth knew that the spirits of the place had welcomed a new devotee.

From that day she performed her rituals night and morning, keeping a bowl of water by the fire to purify the hearth. Her nurses suspected nothing. Fryth's offerings were everyday things, completely unremarkable before they became part of her ceremonies, and she was careful to offer everything to the fire-spirit when she had finished.

That she was once more performing, even in the most inadequate way, her magic, was the greatest restorative to Fryth's health. She could feel her strength of mind and body growing daily. She was able to contemplate her situation without panic or despair. Walking was no longer an effort, and she was eating normally again. Cwen and Bebba, seeing that she was nearly recovered, summoned Heiu to see the change their careful nursing had wrought in her.

Heiu came alone. Fryth was sitting by the fire when she came in, staring at its glowing heart. She stood up and offered Heiu her stool. Heiu nodded. She moved the stool as far as possible from the fire and sat down with a creaking sigh. She smiled at Fryth.

'I'm glad to see you're much better. God is good.'

'I have a great deal to thank Cwen and Bebba for. And you, my lady.'

'Everything we do is for the glory of God. He has chosen to preserve you. We must make you worthy of His choice.' She smiled again. Fryth cleared her throat and stared out of the window, saying nothing. After a pause she turned and looked at the Abbess. Heiu was sitting with her knees apart and Fryth's eye was caught by a strange box on her lap. It was wooden, like Osgar's travelling shrine, but smaller and flatter, and it seemed to be open on three sides. She could see what was in it – a pile of thin white skins. The box's lid was covered in soft red leather with a design in gold stamped into it. It was just the sort of thing that Wulf had delighted in, thought Fryth. Heiu lifted the lid of the box and Fryth saw that the skins were stuck together down one side.

'This is the Holy Gospel,' said Heiu, thumbing through the pile of skins. 'Can you read, Fryth?' Fryth was immediately wary. Did Heiu intend to make her betray her secrets? But her face was bland and smiling, and nothing seemed to lurk behind the smile. Fryth thought a moment, then took a deep breath.

'I . . . I am a rune mistress,' she said cautiously. It was the first time she had made any mention of her powers to these women. 'But it's not a thing I can talk about.' Heiu shifted on the stool and sniffed. Then she looked Fryth in the eye and, ignoring what had just been said, went on firmly,

'But can you read the written word? Look, here,' Heiu held out the box. She was pointing to one of the skins. It had thin black marks on it, as if a bird had walked across it. Fryth knitted her brows. They looked something like runes, but she recognized none of them. She felt a tingle of alarm and drew away, making a sign of protection. Heiu saw her agitation and laughed.

'I'm sorry, Fryth, I didn't mean to upset you, I knew you wouldn't know what a book was. *This*,' she brandished the red box, 'is a book. There's nothing to be afraid of. Look.' She held it in both hands and riffled through the pages. From where she stood Fryth could see flashes of colour: purple, red and even gold. Some of the skins were beautifully decorated. 'What's written in here are words,' Heiu went on, 'everyday words, words spoken by ordinary people. Well, perhaps not all people, they're written in the Latin tongue.' Fryth looked puzzled. Heiu sighed indulgently. 'You have a lot to learn, my child. Latin is the language of Rome, the language of the blessed saints. In this book, Fryth, is the story of our Lord. This,' she tapped the book, 'is how we know the story. It was written down, for people to read and understand throughout the world.' Fryth had drawn closer again. She ran her finger over the black marks.

'You mean,' she said slowly, 'these signs can talk. But Cwen and Bebba tell me over and over again that magic has no place here, that it is the devil's work. I don't understand at all.'

'This isn't magic, and writing doesn't talk. No, look. These signs signify words. Learn to recognize the signs and you can read the words.' She chose a page that had a brilliantly coloured design in one corner beside the thin black marks. Heiu began to follow the marks with her index finger, saying slowly, 'In principio erat verbum.' She wagged her finger in the air. 'There's no magic here; this is the work of man. Even little children understand its mystery once it has been explained to them. This book is Holy Writ, and the most precious of all, but we have others here, and will have more, containing all kinds of human knowledge.' Heiu held out the book to Fryth, who took it gingerly in her hands. She clutched the leather-bound covers and the skins flopped between them. She found she could not make them turn over one by one. Heiu took it back gently.

'A book needs careful handling. It is like a precious treasure, an heirloom, passed down from generation to generation.' Fryth smiled, this at least was something she could understand. 'But,' added Heiu, seeing her smile, 'not quite as you think. Some books of course are valuable in themselves, adorned with gold and silver or with precious jewels. But what is most important is what's inside. The blessed saints and scholars of the past wrote down their knowledge in these books, so that after their deaths their thoughts would live on to be read and understood by future generations.'

'Is knowledge in books so insubstantial that it would have been forgotten by their sons and daughters?' Fryth was scornful.

'Not at all Fryth. Rather, their knowledge was too deep and wide to be remembered word for word. In writing, everything can be preserved so that not one word or one idea can ever be forgotten. Besides, a book can be copied several times and spread about the world. Here, in this monastery we have a scriptorium where scribes are copying manuscripts all day long.' She paused, staring into the middle distance. 'One day we shall have a famous library here.' Heiu's eyes were shining, lost in a dream she looked at Fryth without seeing her. Then she recollected herself. She cleared her throat. 'Now, Fryth, I shall read a passage of scripture to you.'

Heiu patted the floor beside her and Fryth settled at her feet. Then Heiu crossed herself and closed her eyes. Opening them again, she turned the pages over until she found what she was looking for. Fryth was fascinated to see, on the page Heiu had chosen, a picture of a herd of pigs. Their ringed snouts, cloven hooves and gilded bristles were plain to see.

Heiu began to read. Fryth was mesmerised by the rise and fall of her slow, rich voice and the strange words she spoke. The *sounds* of the words were English but, try as she might. Fryth could make nothing of them. When she had finished reading, Heiu explained:

'As I told you, the Gospel is written in the Latin tongue, the speech of Rome, a city far away to the south across the sea. It is from Rome that the story of our Lord has spread, bringing the whole world to salvation. The passage I read tells of how our Lord Christ cast out devils from men who were possessed. It tells us that the devils leapt from the men into the herd of pigs and drove them squealing over a cliff. I pray daily, Fryth, that the devils who inhabit you will be cast out in the same way and that your soul will be saved for Christ.'

Fryth stiffened as Heiu placed her hand on the top of her head. Heiu had somehow slipped beneath her guard. She rose quickly to her feet.

'Thank you, my lady, for the story, and for showing me the book. As you say, it seems there are many things I do not know. Please forgive me if I am slow to understand. It's just that there's so much. . . .' She broke off with a helpless gesture, hoping to disarm Heiu and prevent any further reference to her devils.

'Of course, my child.' said Heiu kindly – the kindness of these people really did seem inexhaustible – 'I must remember not to go too fast. I'll leave you now. But we'll meet again soon.' Smiling, Heiu raised her hand in blessing and went out.

The fire had died right down. Fryth had not liked to attend to it with Heiu present. She had noticed that Heiu had done her best not to get any benefit from its warmth. Now she stoked it high and prepared for the evening's ritual, turning Heiu's visit over in her mind as she did so.

It was quite clear that Heiu had carefully planned her campaign to convert her; she had almost said as much – 'I must remember not to go too fast'. And yet, Fryth felt, she must have decided not to approach the matter directly. This was the first time that Fryth had openly alluded to her sorcery, but Heiu had said nothing when she had admitted to being a rune mistress. It was as if, by ignoring Fryth's powers, she was somehow belittling them, weakening Fryth's position, showing her that she was unafraid. It was obvious that she wanted Fryth to know that her god was the stronger.

It certainly was true that Fryth had more respect for the powers of the Christians now. What kind of magic was it that could trap the very words you spoke, even if they were not in mighty English, the language of brave warriors and hold them down on a piece of skin for a complete stranger to use, possibly even in a different land? This was sorcery she could not begin to approach, for all her knowledge. Yet Heiu had said that it was not magic at all, but the work of man. Nothing Fryth knew suggested that man was capable of such an achievement. She considered the story Heiu had read out to her from the book. It showed clearly that the Christian god controlled the world of spirits in a way she recognized; he had a way of dealing with possession that she herself might have chosen. Fryth thought it extraordinary that Heiu should accept the simple magic and deny the infinitely greater.

Fryth pondered on the strange interview long and hard. At one point, remembering once more Wulf's fateful words on the bridge before they parted for the last time, Fryth allowed herself a rueful smile. Her head ached with the effort of considering all the new ideas with which she was continually being confronted.

Fryth had not yet ventured outside. She had everything she needed to be comfortable in her little cell; there was even a narrow partition at one end of it through which a sluice ran. Bebba told Fryth that it was a Gaulish custom to bring water into the house. She explained its purpose, calling it a lavatorium; a Latin word. Fryth was disgusted at first but she soon got used to the arrangement, even coming to appreciate its advantages. The two nuns continued to bring her food and firewood and their company. They did not press her to leave the confines of her room, and she did not ask to be allowed to do so. Though she might be nearly restored to health she knew that she was not yet strong enough to face the outside world. Fryth recognized that she had yet another reason to be grateful to the sensitivity and kindness of her rescuer.

Heiu took to visiting Fryth every morning, She quickly established a routine. She would read a passage from the Gospel and then translate it carefully, scanning the rafters in the roof as she searched for the right word or the exact expression. She was good with words, and Fryth began to recognize a few words of the strange language captured in her books. As the readings progressed, Fryth built up a picture of the Christians' god-man. He was clearly a powerful magician who could heal the sick, and even raise the dead. He had a power over living things; Fryth listened with interest to the stories in which he blasted a fig tree, or made the fish move in the sea at his command. She heard his words of love and compassion, but also of punishment and endless torment. She was still at a loss to understand what special magic he had to influence the lives of people so far removed from his own world.

Fryth enjoyed the stories, but she would frequently rankle Heiu by interjecting her own thoughts and observations while Heiu was talking. Heiu translated the story of a man's immersion in the waters of a river.

'The same was done for me when I was born!' Fryth interrupted. Heiu's eyebrows shot up. 'My mother purified me, and introduced me to the spirits. This God-man knew what he was doing,' she added approvingly.

'The sacrament of baptism was ordained by Christ to purify the souls of those who are accepted into his Church,' said Heiu, in dignified reproof. 'It is a Christian ritual, not some pagan practice. Whatever it was your mother subjected you to, she could not have been doing other than committing you to the devil.'

Heiu and Fryth had many such exchanges. A great many of

the stories Heiu read out were concerned with things familiar to Fryth: healing, visions, wrestling with evil spirits, controlling the elements, transformation. These were things which she herself had studied long and hard to master, but every time she said as much to Heiu, Heiu contradicted her. She was always gentle, and sometimes, to Fryth's mind, almost offensively patient, but she held fast to the view that Fryth's magic was diabolical. How could it be otherwise? Only true believers could work for good in the world.

'How can you say that?' Fryth would cry out, driven to exasperation by Heiu's insistence that she was misguided. 'I cast out devils, I healed the sick, I made the earth fruitful.'

'How do you know that?'

'I don't understand your question.'

'How do you know that you made the earth fruitful, did you put it to the test?'

'Every year,' replied Fryth slowly, as if explaining to a child, 'my mother and I, after I had joined her in her work, would perform the field ceremonies. We would appease our Mother the earth and ask her blessing.' Heiu sighed.

'But did you put it to the test? Those ceremonies have long since been forbidden in Northumbria and yet the rain falls and the grain ripens.' Fryth thought of her own secret ceremonies.

'Someone, somewhere is still performing them, you can be sure of that. Our Mother hasn't been forgotten.'

'You are misguided, Fryth. You imagined what you were doing, and maybe what some misguided women still continue to do even here in Northumbria, was effectual, but you were wrong. The earth is simply earth, a stone a stone. They are dead things, no power of prayer can move them.' Fryth's jaw dropped. This assertion, flying as it did in the face of all observable facts was so absurd as to be breathtaking. Heiu ignored her amazement.

'It is the devil working in you who gives them life in your mind. He wishes to distract you from a knowledge of the one true God. But now the Devil's reign in this poor land is over,

Fryth. This is why it is so important for people like you who have never met the truth to be brought into its light.' She looked her directly in the eye. Fryth met her gaze.

'Is that why you are so patient with me, why you keep this poor benighted pagan by your side?'

'God sent you to me, my daughter. To win you for Him would be my greatest prize.'

'However long it takes?'

'However long.' Heiu stood up. The day's interview was over. Fryth caught her arm as she moved towards the door.

'My lady.' Heiu turned and looked down at her. 'It's not the story of your god that I find difficult to understand, it's why it must throw over mine.'

'Then you are half-way there,' was all Heiu said.

Fryth sighed. 'If I could, I would,' she said, 'I have no other way to repay your generosity.'

Heiu shook her head, and slowly left the room.

Heiu's Gospel reading eventually came to an end.

'I have read the whole story to you now, my daughter.' She had taken to calling Fryth 'daughter', something which caused Fryth more pain than pleasure. 'I think it would be best now for you to see the life of Christ in action. You have remained inside these four walls long enough.' She looked thoughtful. 'I haven't pressed you, as much for the community's sake as for your own, but you can't stay here indefinitely.' Fryth felt her heart beat fast. She had known this had to come eventually. Although her initial terror of the outside world had left her, she still felt that life in this place had nothing to offer her and she clung to the security of her room. Nevertheless, she had no real reason not to follow Heiu's advice.

'If you think so,' she said quietly.

'Good, I do think so,' Heiu smiled. 'What point would there have been in rescuing you if you remain a prisoner in this cell?' She clapped her hands on her broad knees decisively and stood up. 'I'll ask Cwen and Bebba to show you the monastery. Tomorrow would be a good day to begin.'

When Heiu had gone Fryth walked slowly to the window. She put her hands on the sill and breathed in, straightening her arms. She looked out at the familiar scene. It was deep winter now. The vegetable garden was bare. A thin young monk hurried past, his hands buried deep in his sleeves, his nose glowing red with the cold. He disappeared inside one of the two larger buildings at the end of the row of cells, opposite the shrine. Fryth realized that she knew nothing about the life of the monastery. She had seen the monks and nuns entering and leaving their shrine at intervals throughout the day, and waited eagerly to hear the lovely music that they made; she watched the gardeners digging the last root vegetables from the patch between the houses; she had talked a little to Cwen and Bebba about their lives; but mostly she had felt no curiosity. It was as if what went on outside her walls had been taking place in some different world, a world far removed from the other-world she knew of, but as remote. The daily meetings with Heiu provided her with more than enough new information. She had no desire to ask for more.

Fryth took another deep breath. Now her quiet existence, almost non-existence, was over. She considered what Heiu had said. It was true that she could not remain within these walls for ever. She was fit now, and the daily exchanges with the Abbess had sharpened her mind. She would soon become restless and look upon the life that she had led till now in the monastery as a living death. She had no option but to move on, to meet the future. It occurred to her that neither she nor Eangyth had seen beyond this point. A shiver tickled her spine. Her eyes narrowed. The shiver was excitement.

She turned back to the fire. The new hearth was already turning black, soot was settling in the rafters. At least she would have a familiar spirit to return to. She prayed for strength as she made her morning offering to its flames.

CHAPTER 13

Fryth was quite clear about her destination on the first day she ventured outside her room. She had become accustomed to the salty tang that filled the air, thickened her hair and sometimes tasted on her lips. She had watched the thin band on the horizon between the houses opposite change from palest blue to leaden grey as the weather changed. The sea fascinated her and she longed to stand beside it; the mighty whales' bath of the poetry of her childhood.

Cwen and Bebba accompanied her down the narrow path that covered the short distance between the monastery and the headland bluff. There, standing in a bitter wind that carried their voices away, she stood between her two nurses and gazed at the sea-shore for the first time. Her eyes widened. The sea was a huge, shapeless, jellied monster, caught in the bottom of a pit. Fryth watched spellbound as it heaved and flopped and struggled to escape its confines. Repeatedly it threw itself against the shore, desperate to be free, then, running out of energy, fell back with a despairing sigh. All the while, above its ceaseless motion, white birds wheeled and screamed in the open sky. Away on the right the headland ran down to a small harbour. Boats were moored there, bobbing in the waves.

Fryth turned an enraptured face to her companions.

'Please leave me,' she shouted above the wind, 'I would like to be alone.' Cwen and Bebba nodded smiling and turned back the way they had come. Fryth remained quite still, gazing out to sea.

Birds were gliding all around her, riding the currents of air at the cliff's edge. Others, further out, were fishing in the waves, plunging straight as spears into the water, sending up little plumes of spray. Watching them, Fryth knew at once why it had been one of these that woke her from her trance. Like her, they were wanderers. Their world was like the world in which she now found herself; unpredictable, pathless, lacking any signs to guide them on their way. She was filled with an almost peaceful sense of resignation as she watched the lonely creatures wheeling in the sky. She sat down on the stiff, short-cropped grass and allowed the rush and slap and sighing of the waves to fill every crevice of her mind.

After a while, she raised her eyes and shivered. Something was picking its way delicately along the shore-line far below. She screwed up her eyes. It was a fox. The small brown creature was sniffing among the rocks. Every now and then it turned a stone with a quick flick of its white paws, snatching hungrily at what lay beneath.

The fox worked its way slowly along the beach until it stood directly underneath where Fryth was sitting. Then, as she knew it would, it looked straight up at her, and she understood that she was not alone. Even in this alien place she had not been deserted by the spirits. Her messenger had come back to tell her that the way into their mysteries was still open to her.

The three runes the fox had shown her at their first meeting came into her mind. The evergreen yew, bright within like the knowledge she had acquired, poisonous without like the fate that had overtaken her; the hail caught in the hot blast of wind rising from her burning village, whipped away to fall here and melt and change; the sun a symbol of hope to seafarers, bringing them safe to harbour. Fryth looked down at the little haven, the first harbour she had ever seen. Then she stood up, squared her shoulders, and walked back to the monastery.

The monastery grounds were deserted as she entered the gates of the enclosure that surrounded it. Music was floating from the open doors of the shrine and, without stopping to think, Fryth slipped inside the high, white building. With hands clasped behind her, she pressed her back against the wall beside the door.

She stood stock-still. No one appeared to notice her. The shrine had been built for a greater number than it was holding now. The small community of monks and nuns were gathered at the far end, facing what looked like some kind of altar. Their heads were bowed. The altar stood in a pool of light that glowed in the surrounding gloom. As befitted the altar of a sky god, the light that illuminated it came from above. Three large lamps hung from chains attached to the roof beams. Fryth had never seen such lamps before. They were of burnished bronze set with round jewel-like discs. The light they shed twinkled from one lamp to another above the altar in a glittering display, and shed a soft glow over it and the people standing beneath. Fryth could see that the altar was draped in a bright cloth, richly embroidered in reds and purple and gold. The designs were difficult to distinguish in the dim light, but Fryth thought she could discern an eagle and a bull.

Behind the altar stood the priest. Fryth recognized him at once as being the little man who had accompanied Heiu on her very first visit to Fryth's room. She had forgotten about him and his penetrating stare until now. He wore a white robe, and an embroidered scarf hung round his neck. Small boys, also dressed in white, scurried about in front of him carrying bronze bowls and linen cloths. One curly-headed boy was wafting a smoking dish, filling the air with pungent fumes. A shiver ran down Fryth's spine as the light caught on his fair hair; he reminded her of Godwin, her brother who was lying dead somewhere in this foreign country.

Fryth looked on warily. This was the rite that Wulf had said was forbidden to all but initiated Christians. She knew she should not stay but could not bring herself to turn away. It was for the music that she had come, and she would have risked many things to feel the full impact of its power. What was happening at the far end bemused her, much of what she saw was familiar and as much was strange; but the music, now dipping, now soaring, now hanging in the air, note chasing note, deep voices weaving in and out of higher ones, this was what had drawn her in. She leaned back, entranced, against the smooth, plastered wall. She felt her spirit slipping from her. With no effort on her part it rose into the air and joined the world of light and ecstasy that the music was producing. It was a long time since she had felt such happiness.

She was so transported by the music that she neglected to slip out of the door when her spirit returned her. The ceremony ended abruptly, and by the time she had gathered her thoughts it was too late; the participants were making for the door. They spotted her at once and gathered in a little knot around her. Some frowned accusingly, all were making the sign of the cross in the air. Alarmed, Fryth looked round desperately for help. She saw Cwen in the throng and threw her a beseeching look. Cwen's face was anxious but not unfriendly, and she reached out a hand to Fryth. At that moment, however, Heiu appeared. She caught Fryth by the arm and began to pull her through the little crowd, which fell back, allowing the stately figure of their Abbess, with her slight captive, to pass through.

'Forgive me.' Fryth was genuinely remorseful. 'I meant no harm. I came to hear the music, not to defile your temple.'

'The house of God is called a chapel, Fryth, not a temple.' Heiu looked stern, but her voice was softening. 'It was wrong of you, but you've done no harm. God welcomes all who come to Him, even sinners. A few of the men and women here are disturbed by your presence, but I have told them that it is not for them to judge. God had a purpose in guiding me to save you and one day it will be revealed. In the meantine you are under my protection.'

Fryth felt a huge relief. Not until confronted by those hostile faces in the chapel had Fryth ever considered what a stir her arrival in the monastery must have caused. Now she saw that there was bound to be hostility from some of them. She was grateful to Heiu for her broadmindedness, whatever might be her motivation. Again she marvelled at the tolerance of these

Christians. If she had been interrupted in a hidden rite she would undoubtedly have laid a curse on the intruder simply to protect her secrets.

The experience had one effect on Fryth. From that day on she stopped performing the daily rituals in her room. That much at least she could do to repay Heiu for her protection. Instead she walked, morning and evening, a short way outside the monastery's enclosing wall. She found a little grove of oak trees in which she was well hidden from sight, and there, among the welcoming woodland spirits she built an altar of her own. Her ceremonies had more meaning to her there than in her sparse white room. Even so, she could not help acknowledging, as she walked back to her cell on that first dark, frosty evening, that Heiu and her god had won not only her respect, but a small victory too.

Somehow Heiu persuaded the community that Fryth was no threat, and Fryth began to make herself at home among them. She was given a long, brown, woollen robe to wear and was indistinguishable from the others, except on close inspection, which as a rule the monks and nuns were too preoccupied with work, or with their meditations, to make. However, some of them continued to draw away from her when they did recognize her, crossing themselves hastily after an encounter. These, she discovered, were the converted pagans, still conscious of a sorceress's power. Those who knew little of the old religion, who had been brought up in the Christian faith, were more open with her; Cwen and Bebba, and Heiu herself, among them. This confirmed Fryth in her belief that the Christian view of her religion was based on an ignorance of its strength.

Fryth derived a great deal of comfort from performing the daily rites in her little woodland grove. It was all the more important to contact the goddess and the spirits of the earth in this place where only the sky god was acknowledged. She began to use Wulf's cross in her magic. It was made of yew. The tree that held her knowledge in its core. She linked the yew's fire to the sun, whose image was the cross. She disliked working in a furtive way but she was certain that, however inadequately, she was benefiting her new companions by introducing their god to the gods of their ancestors, and this thought made her glad.

Sometimes, late in the night, crouched in her cell beside the ashes of her fire, she would revisit the spirit world, guided by the little shoreland fox. The world she entered was not inhabited by the spirits of her gentle midland country, but by sea creatures: whales and otters, sea eagles, seals and great, white, screaming birds. This world was harsh and inhospitable, and it was often with relief that she returned with the rising of the sun to her peaceful whitewashed cell.

No one suspected what Fryth was doing when she left the monastery each morning and evening. They accepted her explanation that she needed and enjoyed the exercise. She chose to go when the community was at prayer in the chapel; at those times she was unlikely to be discovered. On the whole, very little attention was paid to her. The monks and nuns at Heruteu were totally absorbed in their own devotions and in building up their newly-founded community. They had no time to concern themselves with other things. Besides, hospitality to the sick and indigent was part of their rule, and, as Cwen and Bebba explained to Fryth, if one particular guest was more unusual than the average traveller or beggar, it was not for them to question the decision of their Abbess, to whom they had vowed complete obedience.

Of all the members of the Christian community, only the priest, Hubert, remained openly suspicious and intolerant of Fryth. He was a local man who had been converted in his youth by the great Paulinus. He did not live in the monastery but in an outlying village. He was priest to all the neighbouring villages as well as to Heiu's community. He was overworked and his naturally sour temper was not improved by the rigours of his life.

There were few who liked or admired Hubert, but he was entirely necessary, since he was the only one among them who could perform the sacred rituals in the chapel. Heiu suffered him because she had to, priests were in short supply, but she had long since given up any attempt to soften his harsh manner and fanatical views. She explained to him that she was keeping Fryth with her in the hope that her pagan soul might be saved. She made Hubert accept her decision. She was the Abbess, it was she, and not the priest, however indispensable he might be, who had the final word.

It was obvious that Hubert felt uneasy in Fryth's company, although he frequently sought it. He had a patronising manner, quite unlike any of the others; where they at best ignored her or, at worst, treated her like an erring child, he could not disguise his contemptuous disgust. From their first encounter he was aggressively hostile.

'God has ordained me to save souls,' he announced, 'even the foulest and most evil of them.' He looked her up and down. 'Satan comes in all disguises, but there is no hiding place he prefers more than the body of a woman.' There was an unpleasant look in his eye. Fryth already knew about the strange customs of the monks and nuns. Bebba had explained to her that though men and women might live together in the monastery there was no sexual contact between them; indeed, she had been told, they had taken vows that bound them to a celibate life. She wondered as she endured his penetrating gaze, which disturbed Hubert more, her unreformed soul or her fully-formed body. She was alarmed by his intensity and wanted to show him that she could meet him on his own ground. She looked him steadily in the eye.

'I am a priest too,' she said, 'I know the secrets of my soul far better than you, and what possesses me.' Hubert's face contorted; he spat on the ground and crossed himself.

'Women are the Devil's priests.' He spat again. 'Their works are works of blood and darkness. You are an agent of the Devil, whose gospel is ignorance and superstition.'

'Is it ignorance to believe that your mother needs respect and care? Is it superstition to appease her and to try to win her favour? I do no more than that. I'm not ignorant of her needs, I've spent long years studying and attending to them.'

'You are deluded, and in the Devil's grip. He'll carry you to hell long before our Abbess can succeed in saving you.'

Hubert's unwelcome attentions gave Fryth food for thought. It was natural of course that a religion which only recognized a sky father would reject a woman priest. Women belonged to the goddess. Hubert knew that much. What she could not understand was the Christian's total rejection of the natural world. To them, everything in the world belonged to the Devil; to her, and her kind, the world was a mysterious place certainly, and dangerous frequently; but every natural thing: men, women, animals, water, rocks and trees were filled with the living power of Freya, the Mother of creation. This was a truth so obvious that to ignore it, as these Christians did, seemed merely wilful. Denying their sexual natures was just one more aspect of their peculiar view of life. It helped to fix their minds on their heavenly things no doubt, but Fryth knew that Freya would not be denied for long. The earth would be revenged on them eventually. Revenge was another law of nature they were unwise to ignore. Meanwhile Hubert's mind, composed as it seemed to be of fear, anger and sexual desire, disturbed and revolted her in turn.

Hubert continued to confront Fryth and they had many angry, bitter exchanges. He always returned to the same theme. Where Heiu tried to win her with promises of eternal bliss, Hubert had nothing to offer but damnation and eternal torment. He had a lurid imagination and seemed to take delight in detailing all the grisly tortures that were in store for Fryth. Once she turned on him in exasperation,

'Hubert, nothing you can say holds any terror for me. One day I'll tell you the story of my life. Not one of your foul torments could match the misery of that!'

There were tears in her eyes, and she spoke with such passion that for a fleeting moment Fryth thought she detected a slight wavering in Hubert's expression: but if there was, he quickly mastered it. In some ways Fryth pitied him. His one desire in life was to save souls. She could not help thinking that his main ambition would never be fulfilled.

Heiu had long since abandoned the direct struggle for Fryth's soul. She saw that Hubert's methods were having no effect and brought more subtle forces into play. She encouraged Fryth in her love of music and introduced her to Egfrith, master of the choir. Egfrith was a good-humoured, friendly man, with a broad, florid face, ginger hair and a bright red snubbed-nose. He looked more like a beer-hall drunkard than the artist that he was. It was when he sang that his gift revealed itself; he had a clear, bright, expressive baritone voice. He saw at once that Fryth had a gift for music and he was happy to instruct her in the mysteries of his art.

There were few meeting places in the monastery apart from the chapel, which Fryth had carefully avoided since that first day. The monks and nuns ate alone in their cells, and the only public buildings apart from the chapel were the Scriptorium, the Infirmary and the kitchen. The Scriptorium and the Infirmary were obviously unsuitable for music lessons, so Fryth and Egfrith took to meeting in the kitchen. It was set apart from the principal monastery buildings, merely a lean-to shed against the enclosure fence. But it was a cosy, smoky place, full of cheerful bustle and the smell of stew and new-baked bread. The kitchen was more like home than anything Fryth had found since coming to Northumbria, and she looked forward to the hour or two each day when she and Egfrith would settle down beside the sacks of meal and turnips in a corner, out of the way of the cooks.

Egfrith explained that James the Deacon had brought the art of chanting from Rome. In King Edwin's day it had been very widely practised in Northumbria; but now, since so many skilled musicians had been killed in the last wars, only a few places could boast a choir. Thanks to God's mercy Egfrith himself had been spared, and Heiu had invited him to join her here in Heruteu when she set up the monastery. He was very proud of what he had already achieved. None of the monks and nuns had any idea of the art of chanting when they first arrived, but they had learned fast. As yet there were not enough voices to set up an antiphonal choir. This was the most beautiful of all, he said, where the choir was divided into two and sang the responses alternately. He hoped to introduce the practice soon but, at present, he simply divided the voices according to their pitch. The weaving of voices like threads in the loom, separate, but all contributing to the whole, was called harmony. Fryth had a naturally fine ear, he said, to isolate the threads of music so expertly.

Egfrith brought a little pipe to their meetings and he taught Fryth the notes of the chants, showing her how to hold a line. The kitchen workers, glad of the diversion, would join in, and the sound of their voices raised in harmony would mingle with the noise of chopping knives and bubbling pots.

In the genial company of Egfrith, whose life was totally devoted to his art, Fryth found her own gift coming back to her. She confessed to him that she had once made up music of her own, and he asked her to sing to him. There, among the sacks and cooking pots, Fryth sang the song of the Wanderer, the last song she had sung to her tribe. Every sorrowful word had doubled in meaning for her since then, and, as she sang the cooks put down their spoons and Egfrith's head sank down in his hands. His eyes were full of tears when she came to the end. He put his arm around her and drew her to him.

'Both of us have been through terrible times,' he said. 'I on one side, you on the other. One thing your song makes clear to me; whatever you may be, wherever you have come from, you have the touch of God within you.' Fryth leant her head on his shoulder. Egfrith's words were like a blessing. He at least regarded one of her mysterious powers as benign. She saw in that moment how much Hubert's and, still more, Heiu's dismissal of her beliefs had wounded her, turning all her good to bad. Now this small acknowledgment was a reaffirmation of her life. She would remain Egfrith's friend for ever.

Her two daily visits to the woodland grove, and her occasional sessions with Egfrith were not enough to fill Fryth's day. She was used to an active life and found enforced idleness depressing. Additionally, she thought she ought to do something to earn her keep in the monastery. She had nowhere else to go and depended entirely on the community for survival. Heiu had said nothing to her, and she knew their rules of hospitality. But still, she felt she ought to repay the Abbess for supporting her. She asked Heiu if she could work on the little farm where the monastery grew its food. This consisted of a few fields outside the enclosure together with the vegetable garden inside. The farm land supported two or three milk cows and some plots of hay and wheat.

Heiu had other plans. Although Fryth was best suited by experience to helping on the farm, she was unwilling to give Fryth the opportunity to indulge her pagan practices. Anything connected with the land would clearly do that.

One evening after Mass she came to Fryth's cell with another nun. Fryth recognized the tall, slim figure of Hildigyth. She had never spoken to the woman but she knew that she was one of the chief workers in the scriptorium, and that she was a famous scholar. Hildigyth had always smiled pleasantly at Fryth when their paths had crossed, and she was smiling now.

'I expect you know Hildigyth by now,' Heiu was saying, 'and that she works at our great task.' Fryth raised a questioning eyebrow.

'Building up the library, Fryth,' Hildigyth explained. Her voice was soft and low. It lacked the rough edge that most Northumbrians seemed to have. 'Our Abbess is very proud of the work we do, as indeed we all are.'

Fryth bowed her head. 'I haven't had the pleasure of speaking with the Lady Hildigyth till now,' she said, 'but of course I know of her fame.' Hildigyth's smile broadened, increasing the fine lines at the corners of her mouth and eyes. She looked at Heiu.

'Our guest has excellent manners, I believe there is much nobility of heart among the Middle Angles.' She said this without a trace of flattery in her tone. Fryth was touched and warmed to her at once.

'Fryth,' Heiu went on, 'I would like you to join Hildigyth in the Scriptorium. She needs an assistant, the volume of work, praise God, is increasing, and there is a lot to do.'

'I have several monks and nuns working with me, but they're now completely taken up with copying and illuminating. I need someone who can prepare materials, and keep the scribes supplied.'

'I'm sure you'll be very well suited to the work.' Heiu turned to Hildigyth, 'I think you'll find her very quick.'

Fryth, still wary of books, was a little uneasy about the prospect of working with the scribes. Nevertheless, she was pleased to have a real occupation at last. She went early to the Scriptorium the next day. Hildigyth greeted her and gave her a small desk near the fire close to her own.

Fryth had never been inside the building before. She was delighted to see the high-piled hearth. The Scriptorium was warm even in the dead of winter; a fire blazed there all day to keep the blood flowing in the scribes' cramped fingers. The room was lofty and well lit. It echoed with the sound of scratching pens and the sniffs and coughs of the workers as they bent in silent concentration over their desks. Fryth was puzzled at first to see the shabby, chewed feathers in the workers' hands. She thought at once of her mother's eagle's feathers and wondered what magic powers were invoked in the process of writing. But Hildigyth soon explained the function of a pen. She gave Fryth a pile of uncut feathers, mostly gulls, and showed her how to cut a nib.

Time passed very quickly in the Scriptorium. The work proved to be easy and enjoyable and Hildigyth was a patient and undemanding teacher. Fryth learned to handle the soft pliable skins on which the scribes copied out their books; Hildigyth taught her how to smooth their surfaces with a block of walrus ivory, and to trim up their rough edges with a sharp knife. She learned to grind and mix the bright colours that went into the jewel-like inks. This was her favourite occupation as it gave her the opportunity to work closely with the scribes who drew and painted the glowing decorated pages. She discovered that the master of these workers was an Irishman. He had rich, black curly hair, a thick beard and glossy, red lips. His teeth were very white. He told Fryth that his home was an island across a wild sea. An island which was holy, magical, and loved by God. Unlike this barbarian place, he had added feelingly, Fryth looked offended and he had laughed at her discomfort. She found she often could not tell when he was joking. He said he had come to the monastery, like Egfrith, at Heiu's special invitation, and that he regretted it all the time. He called it his white martyrdom. His name was almost unpronounceable and he would laugh softly when Fryth tried to use it during their whispered conversations.

'Cruith . . . Cuth . . . Cruthneh . . . Cruithnech . . . !' her tongue would stumble. Cruithnechan would pretend not to recognize his name, forcing Fryth to struggle on until she attracted the attention of Hildigyth, who would frown a little at the disturbance she was creating.

To begin with, Fryth was a little in awe of Hildigyth. She knew very little about her but she noticed how all the workers in the Scriptorium deferred to her gentle discipline. She was often remote, even cool; giving directions in her quiet, musical voice that were immediately obeyed. There was no official leader in the Scriptorium, but Hildigyth's authority was undisputed. When she was not organizing the day's work, or giving advice, she worked at her own manuscripts. She had a large, clear hand and wrote steadily, with total absorption.

Fryth liked to watch Hildigyth at work. Unlike the other scribes, who fidgeted and scratched and shook the cramp out of their hands at intervals, she never moved or looked up from her page, except occasionally to refer to the sheaf of notes that was always by her left hand. She could work like this for hours at a stretch, and Fryth recognized in Hildigyth a true practitioner of a mystery. She knew that concentration as deep as that showed a trained and disciplined spirit.

Fryth had little opportunity to find out more about Hildigyth until one evening several weeks after she had started working in the Scriptorium. The other scribes had packed up and slipped out, one by one, to fetch their evening meal from the kitchen before the summons came to Mass. Fryth noticed that Hildigyth often went without food, preferring to work on at her desk, making the most of the daylight. Fryth had finished trimming a piece of parchment which Hildigyth had requested, and she decided to wait in case Hildigyth should need it that evening. She was hungry and wanted her supper before setting out to her secret grove, but she could not bring herself to interrupt. Instead she sat quietly at her desk, watching Hildigyth at work.

The empty workshop, the quiet concentration of its solitary occupant, reminded Fryth of another workshop, in another life. She sighed a deep sigh and rubbed a weary hand across her eyes. When she opened them again she saw that Hildigyth was looking at her. Hildigyth's large, near-sighted eyes were grey, her face was long and pale. It was a face that often smiled but seldom laughed. She had thrown back the hood of her gown, and Fryth saw that her fair, almost colourless, hair was drawn into a loose knot at the nape of her neck. Hildigyth put down her pen.

'What made you sigh like that, Fryth?' she asked.

Fryth was confused. 'I'm sorry. I shouldn't have disturbed you. I . . . it just slipped out.'

'A sigh like that should slip out more often. It seemed to come from some dark place that needs to see the light.' Fryth shrugged her shoulders.

'It is a dark place,' she said, 'the past.' Suddenly, and to her intense embarrassment, tears began to run down her cheeks. Powerless to stop them, she covered her face with her hands and wept as she had not wept since her first day in the monastery.

The tears went on flowing for a long time. At last they subsided into a series of sniffs as Fryth wiped the backs of her hands roughly over her cheeks. She felt a fool. Hildigyth was the last person to be sympathetic to such a display of weakness. She was always so controlled and calm.

'Forgive me. I'd better go.' Fryth stood up and clumsily pushed the parchment she had been preparing across her desk. 'I've got this ready for you. I'm sorry to have interrupted your work.' She started for the door, but Hildigyth had stood up too. Now she was blocking Fryth's path. Without quite knowing what she was doing, Fryth tried to dodge past her, making for the door, but Hildigyth gripped her arm.

'Sit down, Fryth.' Her voice was cool and quiet as ever. It was a voice to be obeyed, and Fryth falteringly went back to her desk. She gripped its edges as if to hold it as a shield between herself and Hildigyth's scorn. She raised her eyes nervously to Hildigyth's face and saw to her surprise that it was full of gentleness.

'I know nothing about you, Fryth,' she said. 'Indeed none of us do. We have so little time to spare from God and our work.'

'What little time is spent with me is spent trying to change me,' said Fryth bitterly. Then she bit her lip. 'Oh . . . excuse me. I know that I wouldn't be alive if it wasn't for your Abbess, and this place. It's just that. . . .'

'Just that what?'

'Oh, how can I explain? . . . It's all so *strange*.' Hildigyth's face was still as sympathetic, softer even than before, and Fryth felt something inside her give way.

'I didn't ask to come here. I wouldn't *be* here if it wasn't for my evil fate. I'm *not* a Christian, how could I be? I am Priestess of my people. I am a servant of Freya. My whole life has been spent in this work. I learned it from my mother who learned it from hers. And now everything I've lived for, my home, my people and my gods, has been taken from me. And, as if that wasn't enough, I'm constantly confronted with a new way of life, about which I know nothing, and which sets itself up as the enemy of my own.' Fryth had risen to her feet. 'It's hard, it's very hard to remember who I am.' She looked directly at Hildigyth, her face was still red with weeping but her eyes had cleared, they were bright again, even piercing. 'I am a Priestess, a leader of my people. And here you see me weeping, and in your power.'

'You are not in my power,' said Hildigyth slowly after a long pause. 'Don't forget, Fryth, that we are the strangers in this land. It's you, and people like you, who know and understand the land and its people. If Christianity is to survive it must win the hearts of men and women like you. We're the people who, if anything, are in your power. We want this land to find the true God. But that can't be done by force. It needs time and thoughtfulness and example.'

'Most people here are kind and thoughtful, but sometimes, like now. I feel as though I'm drowning.'

'You are a little like a shipwrecked sailor.' Hildigyth held out her hand as if to pull her from the water. 'Tell me about the ship that brought you here.'

Fryth smiled, her composure quite regained. Hildigyth's interest in her had restored a little of her dignity. She heard the crunch of feet on gravel. The monks and nuns were going into chapel. She looked at Hildigyth, who only smiled and nodded.

'Go on,' she said.

Fryth told Hildigyth her whole story. She kept nothing back, not Wulf, not her magic; she laid her entire life, like a hostage at her feet. It was a gift, she felt, a gift to this stranger who had reached out to her. Hildigyth listened with great attention, not moving or looking away until Fryth finally came to an end.

'. . . There was a seagull screaming, I awoke, and here I am.'

The two women sat in silence for a long time. The fire had died away and the building was in almost total darkness, only a few embers still glowed on the hearth. At last Hildigyth stretched and sighed. Still without speaking she stood up stiffly and threw a log onto the fire. Flames crept round it and reached into the air. She looked down at Fryth who sat quite motionless.

'Thank you for telling me,' was all she said. She stood, looking into the fire. Then she said,

'Would you like to see what I've been working on today?'

Fryth raised her head. This was not quite what she expected, but it was in keeping with Hildigyth's detached manner. She answered in a low voice, 'Of course. I'd be very pleased.'

Hildigyth spread the parchment out on Fryth's desk. Fryth had not looked closely at any of Hildigyth's work before. She loved the Irishman's work, the great painted pages like embroidered cloths, but writing held no interest for her. She disliked the spidery black signs, and mistrusted their meanings. She looked warily at the page Hildigyth was flattening out in front of her and saw with astonishment that the page was covered with tiny, exquisite drawings of plants. She recognized them all. Every detail was there, down to the hairs on the stem of a deadnettle. Beside each drawing were a few lines of Hildigyth's firm, black writing.

'They're beautiful!' Fryth's eyes shone. She ran her finger across the page. 'I can tell exactly what they are. Look. This is feverfew, and here,' she moved her finger down, 'this is horehound.'

'For the treatment of rough throats, sweats and night fevers.' Fryth turned her face in wonder to Hildigyth, who grinned. 'It's in Latin of course, but that's what it says.' Fryth shook her head in disbelief. 'And you thought all our books were Gospels and Holy Writ.'

'I had no idea that this was what you were doing!'

'Of course,' said Hildigyth gravely, 'most of our work is sacred.' She swept an arm round, indicating the shelves round all the walls that bulged with finished and unfinished parchments, and a few bound volumes. 'But I have a special interest in medicines and herbs. I've been working on this for many years. You could say it is my chief distraction.' She smiled. 'Not that there is anything sacrilegious in studying God's creation. We look for God's purpose everywhere, Fryth. If we do not believe the trees are gods, we see God in them.'

Fryth pushed her fingers through her hair. 'I had no idea that Christians valued knowledge of this sort. No one told me.'

'You've said nothing until now about what *you* know. There's a tendency among us, pagan and Christian alike, to assume ignorance in people with whom we disagree. I think you'd be surprised to know how much we have in common.'

'I have felt the spirit in a tree. The tree in my shrine was a guide and friend to me.'

'I have seen God's healing grace working in a flower.'

The two women looked at each other.

'Horehound's also useful where there's congestion in the ears,' said Fryth quietly. Hildigyth smiled. She picked up her pen, dipped it in red ink, and scratched something in the margin of the page. Fryth grinned.

'Will you teach me to read?' she said.

CHAPTER 14

Fryth had to admit that Heiu was right. Reading was an easy matter. Once she grasped the idea that each letter had a special sound of its own, she discovered that stringing them together to make words was not difficult at all. The only problem was that every written word available was in Latin. But Hildigyth devised a way of teaching her the sounds by applying them to English words. Vellum was far too valuable a material to waste on a project like this, so Hildigyth obtained some potter's clay.

'This is how I was taught to read,' she said, spreading the damp clay out in a thick slab on the hearth of the Scriptorium. 'If we keep it wet we can use it again and again.' She was crouched in the ashes, with Fryth beside her. There was a broad smile on her face, an almost childish glee. Fryth sat back on her heels and looked at her. Hildigyth's customary calmness had quite deserted her. It was obvious that she was taking enormous pleasure in this undertaking.

'Who taught you to read, Hildigyth?'

'My mother. My father and mother were converted in King Edwin's time. My mother learned reading from a priest at court. My father was a nobleman, he died in the wars, like your father, Fryth. I was brought up at court.'

'I've no idea what a king's court is like. I suppose it must be very different from this.' Fryth looked round her, and then down at the wooden plates of vegetable stew she had brought from the kitchen. It was the end of the day, and she and Hildigyth were working in the Scriptorium after the others had gone. Fryth's lessons took place during the hour set aside for supper. She had worried to begin with that Hildigyth would regret losing an hour of solitude and meditation, but Hildigyth assured her that as far as she was concerned all work was prayer. Remembering Hildigyth's complete stillness and concentration as she worked, Fryth realized that in her case this must be true. Even so, the way in which she was now scratching contentedly at the clay with a sharpened stick, setting out the letters of the alphabet, seemed more like a game than prayer.

Hildigyth finished what she was doing, then sat back as well. There was clay on her fingertips and she rubbed it between them into a little ball.

'The court *was* very different from this.' She dropped the pellet of clay onto the hearth and stared at it. Then, collecting herself, she said briskly, 'Now. Look here, this is an "F".' She was pointing to one of the marks she had drawn in the clay. Fryth's eyes followed hers. In a short while she had learned all the letters of her name. She was a little shocked at first to discover that writing was capable of trapping English words as well as foreign ones, but she soon overcame her initial suspicion. By the end of that first lesson on the red, sticky clay she had mastered half the alphabet.

Fryth's lessons continued every evening as winter gave way to spring. When the first buds were showing on the oak trees in her grove, and the first shoots poking above the cold earth in the vegetable garden, Fryth could read and write with reasonable confidence. Hildigyth had begun to teach her Latin. This was far more difficult than the simple procedure of remembering which sign represented a particular sound, but she was making progress.

They began to read texts together. To begin with each one was a battleground. Fryth wrestled with the meanings of the outlandish words as if they were a living enemy, but by degrees she conquered them. Hildigyth chose the subject matter carefully. They read through her own, unfinished, treatise on medicinal herbs soon after Fryth began to learn the language. Hildigyth's style was clear and direct, and Fryth was gratified by Hildigyth's eagerness to have her opinion on her work. She was complimentary; Hildigyth knew almost as much as she did.

Other pieces of writing were not so easy, but Hildigyth chose them for their content rather than their style. Fryth read painstakingly through a work on cosmography. It told her very little more than she already knew about the stars, but she enjoyed the vivid descriptions of the five zones of heaven: one, in the middle, glowing with the flashing sun, scorched eternally by his flames; two, at each end of the world, set fast in ice and black storms; and between, two more zones, of temperate winds and mild waters, which by the grace of God had been granted to the feeble race of men.

They avoided the scriptures. Hildigyth seemed to regard them as unsuitable for use as text books. Even Fryth could see that there might be something unpropitious in pulling apart the grammar of sacred writing. But there was a book about the Bible lands. Fryth had no very clear image of the country from which the Christian god had come, and she was not very much the wiser after reading vague descriptions of camels, lions and other monstrous and fearsome beasts. Certainly, she found it impossible to imagine a land where the sun was so fierce it turned the ground to sand and stone.

'How would they live? What crops would grow? Hildigyth, I do think a lot of this must be lies!' They were sitting in the doorway of the Scriptorium in the thin spring sunshine. The monastery was quiet. The wind was blowing softly from the sea, and Fryth thought she could just hear the waves breaking on the pebble shore.

Hildigyth laughed. Fryth had noticed how she laughed a good deal now, since these lessons had begun. She did not think it was always at her expense; Hildigyth seemed to enjoy the work as much as she did.

'No, it's all true.' She scraped her spoon round the bottom of her dish and finished the last mouthful of her supper. She wiped her mouth on her sleeve. 'My father met a man from Egypt once. He came to Edwin's court trading in cloth and lamps. His skin was black from the sun. Quite black. He said his country was all stone and sand. Why would he lie? It's hardly a thing to boast about!'

'Did you see him and his black skin?'

'No, I'm sure I should remember if I had.'

'What was Edwin's court like?' Fryth had rolled up the manuscript she had been studying. She leant back against the door jamb and closed her eyes, trying to conjure up the royal court in her mind. All she saw was the brightly coloured cloth that she had glimpsed on the altar in the monastery chapel. She gave up and opened them again. Hildigyth was thinking. She looked up at the sky.

'It was loud and fractious, always busy, always full of intrigue. There was no peace there.' She laughed again. 'And then my father invariably chose the wrong side, when sides were taken over some slight issue or another, which was nearly every other day. We were often in danger of being turned out in disgrace.' She paused. 'But Edwin liked my father; he may not have trusted him, but he did like him. So we always managed to keep our place.'

'But what did it look like? Was it very rich?'

'I suppose so.'

'How could you have exchanged that for this?' Fryth swept an arm encompassing the plain little buildings. 'To leave a king's hall for this! Even Cerdic's hall was rich in comparison.'

'But I didn't come straight from court. When my father was killed, my mother and my sister and I went to live on our estates. They aren't far from here. My father had a grand hall of his own, and many warriors. He was a great war-leader. He had a lot of property. My mother and sister still do. I brought my inheritance to the monastery when I joined. I own nothing now, at least nothing that the world would call riches. But of course I think differently.'

'What made you give it up? Why did you come here?'

'Do you really want to know?'

'Of course! I told you about me, more than I should. More than I will ever tell anyone else.'

Hildigyth smiled. 'There's nothing very exciting about my story. I was always studious. I enjoyed books and reading more than anything. I learned to read and write in Latin as a very small child. I was quite an object of interest at the court. Well, it was obviously a gift of God, and as I grew up I began to look for ways in which I could repay Him for the happiness and fulfilment His gift had brought me. How this was to be achieved I did not not then know. I spent long hours in prayer.' Fryth nodded. 'But that didn't seem enough. There were always distractions.'

'Did you ever consider marrying?' asked Fryth, thinking of her own distractions.

'No. I needed time for my books and for prayer. The distractions were in the form of my duties on the estate. My mother was growing old. Anyway, that problem was solved when she suddenly took a second husband. A much younger man. He had no marriage-gift to offer, but he was willing of course to help her to run her affairs; it was in his own interest. You can imagine the scandal. But my mother always knows what she wants!'

Fryth laughed. 'I suppose that was court behaviour!'

'Well, she is a woman of the court. I could only be pleased, since by then I'd seen an answer to my own needs. Aidan had set up his monastery on Lindisfarne.'

'What did your sister think? Who is Aidan?'

'My father left my sister well provided for. She has enough lands of her own. My hope is that one day she'll join me here. Aidan is a monk from Ireland, Oswald invited him to come soon after he became King. He founded the first monastery in Northumbria.'

'An Irishman. Like Cruth . . . Cuthic . . . Cruithec . . . ?'

'Well, an Irishman,' Hildigyth smiled. 'But not like Cruithne-chan. Anyway, I heard about the religious life that Aidan and his monks were living. How they were creating a world of scholarship and prayer. A new sort of life, quite unlike anything that had been tried in our land before, and I wanted to join it. I went to visit them, I went all the way to their Island. It can only be reached at low-tide, it wasn't an easy journey. I begged them to take me in, but they wouldn't accept me. They were a community of men. At that stage there were no nuns in Northumbria.'

'Heiu told me that this was the first monastery to accept women.'

'She was the very first to become a nun. She is a remarkable woman. She felt as strongly as I did, but she did something about it.'

'How?'

'She went, like me, to see Aidan, but she persuaded him to make her a nun. She told him she would set up her own community and accept women as well as men. He saw that God was calling her. And this is the result.' Hildigyth looked up. 'As soon as I heard what Heiu intended to do I asked to join. I took orders from Aidan and came here on the day it opened its gates.'

'Heiu told me that this was the first monastery to accept women. I didn't understand what it meant. I could see she was proud, but I didn't know then that women are not very highly regarded in your religion.' She glanced at Hildigyth, but saw she was not listening. She had risen to her feet. Men and women were hurrying into the chapel. Hildigyth put down her plate and followed them. Slowly, Fryth stacked the plates together and carried them to the kitchen. The choir was singing the opening of the evening service as Fryth passed the chapel on her way out of the monastery. She was going to her woodland grove.

Surrounded by bright new leaves, and the murmuring of birds preparing for the night, Fryth forgot the stony countries, the camels, and the strange ways of her hosts. Smoke spiralled upwards in a thin plume and the trees shook.

Fryth was kept very busy in the Scriptorium. Now that she

could read and write a little, her duties increased. Hildigyth put her in charge of the shelves. She would fetch and carry for the scribes, proud that she was able to find what they wanted among the jumble of vellums stacked round the walls. She even began to put them into some kind of order, subject by subject. Everyone was pleased with the results.

There was not the same intimacy between Fryth and Hildigyth during the working day as there was when the day ended. Hildigyth at work was as distant and absorbed as ever, and she still maintained the same quiet discipline. There were some days when she did not come to the Scriptorium. She would go out gathering plants to study for her herbal. From time to time she would go travelling with Heiu, acting as the Abbess's secretary, and although Fryth missed her calm presence on these days, there were compensations. The workers relaxed, they would chat among themselves in low voices, or even leave their desks to sit warming themselves at the fire.

On one such day Fryth was helping Cruithnechan, who was having difficulty with a nib. His page was blotched with a splash of ink. Fryth brought her sharp knife and began scraping at the skin. She looked closely at what he was drawing on the page. He had not yet begun to fill it in with colours, but the outline was there, pricked out in black ink, the ink he had just spilt. It was a drawing of an eagle. She knew she had seen something like it before. It was not unlike the images on her mother's brooches.

'Isn't this the same eagle as the one on the altar cloth in the chapel?' Cruithnechan peered at his work.

'Not at all, not at all,' he said firmly, 'this is a far nobler bird than that old hen!'

'But doesn't it mean the same thing?' Fryth persisted. 'It must work the same magic. What does it mean?'

'It is the eagle of John the Evangelist.' Fryth looked at the drawing. The eagle was in profile. She could see its sharp talons and its cruel beak. Cruithnechan had drawn its feathers one by one in graceful curves. In fact the whole creature was a swirl of curving lines, and yet the drawing managed to convey a strong feeling of the eagle's strength and swiftness.

'How did he use it in his work?'

'The Evangelist? He didn't *use* it. This bird is his emblem. It signifies his grace and majesty. An eagle can look at the sun, you know. And the blessed Saint John lay with his head in our Saviour's bosom. He was an eagle among men.'

'It must mean more than that.'

'And isn't that enough? Look.' He began sketching quickly on a scrap of vellum. Three more animals appeared beneath his pen. 'Each one of the Gospels has its beast. They are symbols of the truth that lies within.'

Fryth shook her head but she pressed him no further. She bent over his desk and scraped busily at the vellum until it was quite clean.

'It's as white as my martyrdom now,' said Cruithnechan leaning over it with a sigh of satisfaction. He picked up his pen.

'He's never far from that theme,' someone whispered.

'What's that?' Cruithnechan looked up. He turned to Fryth. 'How *could* I be far from it, when all the while I'm far from my beloved home. I get scant pity here, and yet I've given up my holy land to come and live among these barbarians.'

'I'm far from home too.'

'I know you are, my child, so you will know as only a wanderer can the pangs of my martyrdom. Of course, you will not suffer as much as I. After all these are your own folk, and this is your dreary land.'

'Northumbria is not my home.'

'No, well. But still your home is not a land of green hills, of sweet water, of high sunny skies. It's sinful how beautiful my homeland is. That is of course why we take the martyrdom. Not that it always works out as you might expect.' He scratched himself thoughtfully. 'I'll tell you a story.'

The whole room had been listening to this speech, though they had heard it a hundred times before, and at the mention of a story all pens were lowered, and all heads came up.

'It was long ago, when I was just a lad. I was new in the monastery. You should have seen the place, it had a remarkable beauty.'

'We know that,' came a chorus of voices, 'tell us the story.'

'Well,' continued Cruithnechan unasbashed, 'It was too beautiful and comfortable in the view of several of the brothers. Regretfully they decided that they must take the white martyrdom – that is to travel from home to spread the Gospel. They built themselves a boat. The largest that was ever seen, all made of leather, and they put out to sea. Let the wind and waves carry them where they would, they trusted in God to bring them safe to some foreign shore, where they could spread His Word among the heathen.

'Not so much as a day had passed on their journey before a terrible storm blew up. The wind tossed them to the waves and the waves tossed them to the wind. There was nothing they could do but cling to each other and pray to God. On the fourth day the wind abated. They were in sight of land. It was a barren and a rocky shore but they made for it with all the strength they had left.' Cruithnechan paused and looked round with gratification at the rapt expressions on the faces of his audience. 'At last they dragged their boat, all knocked to shreds, up the inhospitable strand. They had no food and water and were too weak to move. They kept themselves alive for several days by singing praises to their Creator and telling stories from the scriptures. With such nourishment they forgot their empty bellies, and their need for earthly food.

'At last, when all of them were on the point of translation to a happier land, a man leading a donkey cart came down onto the strand. He had seen them in their distress from the road that skirted the shore. They staggered to their feet and found . . . that they were gazing at the guest-master of their own monastery!' Cruithnechan's face creased with mirth, tears began to trickle down his cheeks. 'Their own guest-master, who was returning from a visit to his mother. They had been washed ashore *not ten miles from their cells!*' Cruithnechan was heaving with laughter and gasping for breath. He wheezed and stamped his foot. Then he looked up at his audience, and saw nothing but incomprehension or dismay in their faces. His laughter stopped. He rolled his eyes to the ceiling, clicked his teeth and let out a long sigh.

'The English!' he groaned. 'The English!' He turned back to his desk. He winked at Fryth. 'To be sure, martyrdom is a terrible thing, glory be to God,' he said. Then he added, as much to himself as to her, 'But . . , but . . , the white is preferable to the red. The white is preferable to the red.' Shaking his head sadly he picked up his pen.

The stock of vellum was getting very low. There had been an increase in the number of completed texts since Fryth had started work because the scribes could now spend all their time in writing. The monastery got its supplies from a sheep farm on the moors above Heruteu and Hildigyth suggested to Fryth that she might like to join her on a trip to fetch new skins. She found it sensible to go herself, she said, since only by doing so could she be certain of the quality.

They set out before sunrise. Two mares had been provided for them from the monastery farm. Fryth was glad not to have to make an issue out of refusing to ride a stallion. She thought perhaps Hildigyth had thought of the difficulty, but she did not ask. They rode in silence in the dim dawn light. The sun was slowly rising behind them. The ground had been gently sloping uphill all the way and Fryth turned in her saddle to look down to where it had lifted itself out of the sea. A lark was singing in the air above them, a tiny point of sound, and the rough grass of the coastal plain was giving way to the scrub and heather of the moorland. Fryth thought she had never seen anything as bleak and barren as this treeless landscape, or as beautiful. She tipped her head back and sang. It was a new song. Hildigyth murmured her approval.

'I haven't heard singing like that since my childhood. The

songs in my father's hall.' They were riding slowly, side by side, saddles creaking, stirrups occasionally bumping together.

'Egfrith's music is the most beautiful music in creation, but it isn't English music!' laughed Fryth. Then a shadow crossed her face. 'I miss English music.'

'You may hear some when we reach the farm. The overseer has a famous voice. It was my farm once, you know. I endowed the monastery with it when I joined. We used to come here often when I was a child. It was my father's favourite place.'

'You said your father owned estates?'

'Yes, he had farms everywhere.'

'In my country there were no big landowners. We all owned small plots of land. Even the chief. It meant that no one of us grew stronger than another.'

'It's strong landowners that make strong countries.'

'I learnt that,' said Fryth ruefully.

The landscape was growing wilder. They had passed through a few straggling villages as they climbed up onto the moors, but soon left all signs of human habitation far behind. They crossed a desolate moor and joined a river valley leading up into the low hills. The grass was greener here, and rowan trees, their berries already a bright orange, grew at intervals beside the rushing water. Fryth leant from the saddle and spat into the current, showing herself to the spirit of the river. It was an unfamiliar spirit, unlike the soft gurgling inhabitant of her midland stream. The spirit here was clear and bright and active, splashing over sharp black rocks, swirling in dark, moss-fringed pools, skirting lichen-covered boulders, and the mossy trunks of the rowans. Fryth sensed a cruelty in the stream, it scarcely recognized her, and felt nothing for the human race. She looked at Hildigyth, expecting to see the same unease that she felt in her companion's face. Hildigyth, lost in her own thoughts, was as serene as ever. Fryth had forgotten that a Christian would not be conscious of the spirits of a place. But Hildigyth did acknowledge Fryth's look. She turned and smiled.

'What were you thinking?'

'I was just thinking how strange it is that I should be a traveller here when I never travelled in my own country, never even left the boundaries of my village until the end.'

They reached the farm at nightfall. The sound of the horses' hooves on the road announced their arrival, and a tall, burly man came out of the house to greet them. He was carrying a smoking lantern, and by its flickering light Fryth could see that he had only one eye. A puckered scar slanted across his cheek and disappeared into his hair.

The house was warm and smoky. An enormous fire was blazing on the hearth, and a cauldron that matched the proportions of the fire swung from a tripod over it, steaming gently, wafting appetizing smells about the room. In a sudden painful moment Fryth was filled with memories of home, and a longing – so intense she thought that it might kill her – overpowered her. She buried her face in her hands, and stood quite still, shuddering. Hildigyth, seeing her acute discomfort quickly stepped to her side and put an arm round her shoulder, drawing her to the fire. Fryth sat down, and the moment passed.

'I'm sorry,' she said, 'I'm very tired.' They made her a bed in the corner of the wide, shadowy building. She was too tired to eat. She lay down, shutting her eyes tightly against the sight of hams and ropes and shovels and strings of onions hanging from the rafters. The last thing she heard before she drifted to sleep was the soft elegant voice of Hildigyth saying the evening office for the assembled household. Fryth realized that she had never heard the prayers before.

The following day was bright and windy. The farm was in a sheltered corner of the river valley; but, looking up, Fryth could see the wind flattening the stiff brown grass on the bare hillsides. Cedd, the overseer, brought a soft pile of lamb skins from the barn and spread them out in the yard in front of Hildigyth and Fryth. Both women had an expert eye, but Fryth was, if anything, more particular than Hildigyth. It was she, after all, who would have to do the final work on the vellums. The

218

selection went on for most of the morning. When it was done
Hildigyth complimented Cedd on his work.

'I think that's probably the best crop of skins you've yet
produced. It must have been a good year altogether.'

'It has, thank God; one of the best in a long time.'

Fryth lost interest as they began to talk about farming matters.
She got up and slipped away unnoticed. She wandered back into
the house. A baby was crying somewhere in its dark recesses.
She followed the sound and found a young girl bent over an
ancient wooden cradle. Fryth smiled at the girl and peered under
the hood of the cradle. The baby looked new-born. It was lying
on its side. Fryth blinked, and looked again. There on the pillow
beside the small pink head was, unmistakably, a rune stave. She
could read the rune quite easily, it was the rune of protection.

'Where did you get that?' she asked the girl, who looked up
in some alarm and pushed the rune out of sight beneath the
pillow.

'It . . . it means nothing,' she said falteringly, then added
desperately, 'You won't tell my husband . . . ?'

'It means protection,' said Fryth softly. 'I won't tell your
husband.'

She walked out of the house and began to follow the river
upstream. She was glad, but not at all surprised, to find that she
had been right. Of course there were women, even in Christian
households, who had not abandoned the old ways. She walked
on and up. Freya would not allow them to forget her, especially
in a place like this. She looked down at the rushing river. The
valley was closing in ahead of her. She could hear a distant
rumbling, a throbbing sound, such as she was used to hearing
in her shrine. She was approaching a gigantic waterfall. She
walked on up to where the river came tumbling in a long cascade
down the hillside from the moorland plateau, high above. It
dropped in three long, mist-hung falls from the high plateau to
pool to pool, and at last to the sloping valley floor, from where
the river coursed away. The fall of water had cut deep into the
hillside, exposing the living rock; small stunted trees overhung

the pools, and heather, dripping spray, clung to crevices in the boulders scattered in the falling water's path.

Fryth felt a stillness take possession of her. She watched the waterfall without moving for a long while. Then she began to climb. She pulled herself from tree to tree, from rock to rock until she reached the highest pool. There she found a ledge of moss-green grass beside the deep, black water. Her resting place was already occupied by a rowan and an alder tree, whose branches swept low over the pool. The thundering of the waterfall was all around her. She looked up, and there was pounding water. She looked down and there was more. It was the elemental energy of nature, grand and awesome, made palpable. Its terrific force swept through her, and, for the first time in many months, even for many years, she felt safe, protected and assured. Nothing in the mind or bodies of weak human beings would, or could, ever divert or change its endless flow.

She remained, perched between earth and sky, until darkness fell.

They had scarcely noticed her absence at the farm, although she felt a lifetime might have passed since she had set off up the valley. They made room for her by the fire. A bowl of meat was pressed into her hands. It was the first time she had tasted mutton for many months and she ate greedily. Mead was going round. There appeared to be several families living on the farm. She counted six faces, men and women, round the fire.

'Fryth would like to hear you sing, Cedd,' said Hildigyth. 'I told her you had a fine voice.' She leaned over and touched Fryth's hand, 'And so has she.' Someone fetched a harp. It was a large, clumsy instrument, but Cedd drew a mellow tone from its thick strings. He sang several songs, and then the harp was passed to Fryth, who sang several more. It was wonderful to her to feel the strings beneath her fingers once more and to find the words of her old songs coming so easily to her lips.

'These are songs from my own hearth,' she explained to her appreciative audience. 'For many years, since the wars, I haven't felt like singing them.' She smiled happily. 'I'm truly glad I've not forgotten them.'

'Where is your own hearth?' asked one of the women. 'From your voice, you are a stranger here.' Before Fryth had time to answer, Cedd cut in,

'We had a bad time during the last wars. I lost two of my sons' he rubbed his scarred cheek and sightless eye, 'and this. Mind, that was a great fight.' His mouth opened in a wide grin revealing crooked, broken teeth. 'When we beat that British bastard!'

Hildigyth shot Fryth a look. 'Fryth is from Middle Anglia,' she broke in hastily. Cedd's eyebrows went up.

'I *was* from Middle Anglia,' said Fryth quietly, she had clenched her fists and was staring at them intently. 'It's all Mercia now, though. Penda overran my country, long ago.'

'Well,' said Cedd. He strummed the harp noisily. 'I'm glad you haven't forgotten how to sing. Let's sing the last one again.' Fryth sang it through while Cedd accompanied her.

'I think I've learned it now,' he said when it was over.

Much later that night when all the songs were sung. Cedd moved to Fryth's side. He pressed the harp into her hands.

'It's not a good one,' he said. 'I was thinking of making myself another. Please take it. You should have an instrument,' he smiled modestly, 'however poor.'

Fryth shook her head. She could find no words. He nodded, frowning,

'Go on,' he said, 'take it!' Smiling her gratitude, still shaking her head, she took it from his large, rough hands.

'Thank you for bringing me,' she said to Hildigyth as they set off the next morning. The harp was firmly tied to Fryth's saddle-bow. 'It has done me a great deal of good to get out. More than you can know.'

Hildigyth smiled her calm smile. 'I'm glad,' she said, 'and I'm glad to have had your company.' The journey home was passed in companionable silence.

The days at Heruteu succeeded each other in tranquil succession. The week was punctuated by two fast days, Wednesday and Friday, and by Sunday, which was entirely set aside for worship and meditation. Heiu was very strict about its observance. No work was done on the farm, except the milking, and the whole community remained inside their cells, emerging only to spend long periods in the chapel.

There was a uniformity to life in the monastery which Fryth had found disquieting at first. The monks and nuns had taken a vow of poverty. They had no possesssions of any kind. Even the plain brown robes, worn alike by men and women, were common property. To begin with Fryth had missed seeing brightly coloured clothes and sparkling jewellery; she missed her own possessions, not only because they were essential to her magic, but because they afforded her status and dignity. These were qualities not much regarded in Heiu's monastery, where every natural feeling seemed to be turned on its head.

By degrees, however, she came to appreciate the slow rhythms of monastery life. She was proud that she had kept alive her old beliefs, as Eangyth had enjoined her all those years ago; but in some strange way that her mother would not have understood, she knew she had been enriched by her contact with the new religion. After the struggles and responsibilities of the past years in her village, the peacefulness and quiet contentment of the men and women with whom she lived was very comforting. The life they led, and which she now shared, gave her the time to consider her own beliefs as well as to begin to understand the appeal of theirs.

On Sundays, when the Scriptorium was deserted, she would stand for hours at her desk, reading and thinking. Whatever Heiu had taught her, she still regarded writing as a kind of magic. And now, as she stood poring over the words of a long dead philosopher, geographer or natural historian, she realized that part of its magic was the change it had brought about in her. She felt her consciousness spreading out beyond the monastery walls. The experience was a familiar one but it was at once both like and quite unlike her travels in the spirit world. On those she travelled inwards, into the recesses of her soul and the soul of the earth where thought was nothing and daily life forgotten. When reading she travelled in a world of light, busy with the clamour of ideas, responses and interpretations.

Her magic dealt with local things, the immediacies of life. It defined her and her people in relation to the place in which they found themselves, gave meaning to themselves and to the natural world. The books she read enlarged her mind. Where it had been reactive, submissive, propitiating, it had become active, questioning, pursuing. The Christian world denied the world of nature, dismissing it as tainted; but it offered a beguiling substitute, a world of factual knowledge and ideas.

The conflict between her own beliefs and those of her companions was constantly on Fryth's mind. One Sunday she had begun to read a passage from the scriptures that Hildigyth had recommended to her, but her mind had wandered. She found the passage difficult and the subject matter obscure. She looked up from the page and her eye fell on a page of vellum lying on an adjacent desk. One of the scribes had left it ready for the following day. His pens and brushes were laid out in a neat row. Fryth would have to prepare the inks for him tomorrow. She slipped from her stool and glanced at the half-filled page, wondering what colours he would want. The illustration had been sketched-in in a series of fine dots. Fryth's eyes lingered over the design; she traced with her finger the sinuous movement of the decoration. She picked up the vellum and carried it to her own desk. The design was not unlike the decorations on Gadd's jewellery, or Wulf's carving; patterns that she recognized and understood. She saw the coiled limbs of birds and beasts winding round the letters on the page, and through them she could see her mother's brooches in the firelight, and the sacred pillar in the forest grove.

She was looking at the manuscript with new eyes. Here on the page was evidence of what she had held to all along. The new religion never would entirely eliminate the old. Even here in the centre of the new world, she could reach out and touch the subterranean stream, running through the hearts and minds of men. If she could only draw it into the light and show it to them, not as something evil, dangerous and bad, but full of health and vigour, like clear water.

Fryth was leaning on her desk, lost in thought, when she felt a gentle tap on her shoulder. She started. It was Heiu, come to the Scriptorium in search of a commentary.

'I'm sorry. I was a long way away.' Much further than you know, she said to herself. Heiu told her what she was looking for and Fryth found it at once. Heiu thanked her and, tucking it under her arm, made to go. Then, as if on second thoughts, she put the book down on Fryth's desk, and stood looking at her with a calm, thoughtful gaze.

'What have you been reading, Fryth?' Fryth pushed the text that she had been studying for Hildigyth across the desk. 'You spend a great deal of time in here. Do you find it valuable?' Heiu picked up the manuscript and peered at it.

'Oh yes, it means a lot to me. It's taught me a great many things.'

'It would do that, of course. What do you think is the most important thing you've learned?' Heiu was looking at her over the top of the vellum sheet. Fryth would have liked to tell her what she had just been thinking, but instead she said,

'I've learned about the strengths of the Christian religion.'

'What strengths *does* a pagan find in the followers of Christ?' Fryth thought for a moment.

'Christianity needs so little. It's all in here,' she pointed to her heart, 'it's all ideas. The world's in confusion, the old ways are breaking down everywhere. My village was burned, my tribe destroyed, I'm separated from the land that gave me my power.

But you can't burn or destroy, or be separated from an idea. Your power is in the mind, or on the skins of dead animals.' She pointed to the vellum clutched in Heiu's large hand. 'My magic, and the magic of my mothers, depends on living things. We need the power of sacred places, the help of animal spirits, the movement of water and fire.'

'But you know we have our chapels, our holy flames, the water of baptism, the beasts of the evangelist.'

'But they are still ideas! They are not the living things. You could stay forever in this room and be a Christian. You need no family, no home, no kinsmen, no love of the body, no warmth even. Nothing can destroy you, there is nothing to destroy!' Heiu was silent for a moment, then she said,

'Do you understand what you have been reading here?' She was looking again at the manuscript in her hand.

'No, not really. Hildigyth suggested I look at it.'

Heiu began to read in her slow, deep voice: ' "This Melch-izedek, King of Salem, priest of God most high, met Abraham, returning from the rout of kings and blessed him, and Abraham gave him a tithe of everything as his portion. His name in the first place means 'King of Righteousness'; next he is 'King of Salem', that is, 'King of Peace'. He has no father, no mother, no lineage; his years have no beginning, his life no end. He is like the son of God, he remains priest for all time." '

'Who was Melchizedek?'

'He was a pagan priest, like you, and see what honour he's being given here, "He is like the son of God." '

Fryth sighed heavily, 'Then I was wrong to say that I under-stood anything.'

'No, Fryth, what is here is quite clear. The blessed Saint Paul is telling us that the old and new met when Melchizedek blessed Abraham and Abraham honoured the pagan. And he also says here that Christ is a priest "in the succession of Melchizedek". Not in his place, you see, but in his *succession*. Melchizedek is honoured because he represents the religious nature of man.'

'A subterranean stream?'

'A what? Yes, if you like, that's quite a good way of putting it. A stream of peace and righteousness, that has no beginning and no end. Why do you think I have kept you by me? You have shown so little willingness to accept what we have to offer.'

'I don't know,' said Fryth simply.

'Because I have hope for you. And because there is a lesson in you. Your resistance is so strong, it only proves how strong your faith is, stronger than many of ours. I hold you up as an example to my backsliding flock.'

'*Really?*' Fryth was astonished.

'I have no doubt that faith like yours, misguided though it may be now, will one day find its true object. So does Hildigyth. It must be why she gave you this to read. She has respect for you, I know.'

'I have more for her.'

Heiu smiled. 'You can tell her that you have grasped its meaning. She'll be pleased to have a further example of her success with you before she leaves for Gaul.'

'Leaves for Gaul?' Fryth felt a sensation in her stomach, like a blow. 'I didn't know . . . ?'

'I'm sending her to our mother monastery at Chelles. I told her of my decision this morning.'

'But . . . does she want to go? She loves it here.' Fryth was stammering. 'I . . . I had no idea.'

'I didn't mean to shock you, Fryth. Forgive me, I realize how attached you are to her. But in the monastic life we must have no attachment. There is a great deal she can learn at Chelles. It is a very old foundation. I want her to go.'

The interview was over. Heiu picked up the manuscript she had come in search of, raised her hand in blessing and went out, leaving Fryth staring after her in dismay and disbelief.

Fryth could scarcely concentrate in the Scriptorium on the following day. There was no change in Hildigyth's manner. She spent the whole day bent over her desk, hardly responding when Fryth slapped a pot of ink or a sharpened pen in front of her. Fryth's shock and sadness had given way to anger. The prospect of the impending loss of her friend had churned through her mind all night. By the time the dawn rose she had decided she had been very foolish to make friends with a Christian at all, however sympathetic she might be. All Christians were mad and unreliable. They set no store by any of the most important things in life, home, family, kinship. Why was Heiu sending her away? Wasn't Heruteu Hildigyth's home? Wasn't Heiu her mother? She always called her daughter. Obviously these words in Christian mouths meant different things. They were yet another foreign language. Well, she had misunderstood what they were saying all along. She bumped another pot of ink down on Hildigyth's desk. Hildigyth looked up in surprise. She stared with calm, grey eyes at Fryth a moment, and pursed her lips, frowning thoughtfully. Then, as calmly, she went on with what she was doing.

At last the scribes began to pack up their things. Cruithnechan called Hildigyth over to admire his nearly finished eagle. The page shone with brilliant colour, like enamel. She smiled approvingly. When Hildigyth finally came to her, Fryth was crouched on the floor grinding furiously at the colours that would go into making the Irishman's inks tomorrow. They were alone.

'Heiu told me she had given you the news. I should have preferred to tell you myself. Did she also tell you that I was not going for ever? Just a year perhaps, maybe two.'

'I won't be here in a year. I can't stay for ever, especially if you go. What is there to keep me here?'

'I thought you were beginning to be happy here.' Fryth continued to grind; the powder was smearing itself round the edges of the mortar. Hildigyth knelt on the floor and took it out of her hands.

'I want to go, Fryth. It's a great opportunity for me. Our library here is nothing.'

'Libraries!' exclaimed Fryth. For the second time in her friendship with Hildigyth she felt the tears running down her cheeks. She stood up, not heeding them, and went back to her desk.

'I'm not very wise,' she said. 'Whole libraries full of books would never teach me. I lost everything I loved once. Once is enough in a life. I should never have let myself get into the same position again. I should never have left my room.' Hildigyth was watching her carefully; understanding was dawning in her face.

'That's what it is!' she said. 'That's what you're afraid of!' She walked over to where Fryth was standing rigidly behind her desk. 'Listen, Fryth, you won't lose *me*. I'll come back. I couldn't leave here for ever. This is my home.' Fryth looked at her and her tears stopped. Her hands loosened their grip on the desk's edge and her shoulders relaxed. She almost smiled.

'I've never heard a Christian use that word before.'

'Do you believe *me* I *am* coming back.' Fryth nodded. She was pressing the back of her fist against her mouth. She took it away and breathed in deeply.

'Heiu told me about Chelles.'

'There's a great deal I can learn there, plenty of books to copy and,' she gave Fryth a pointed look, 'to bring back with me when I return. They have some works by old Roman scholars. I've always wanted to see them. You'd be interested.' Suddenly her face lit up. 'Fryth! Why don't you come with me? I'll need an assistant. I'm sure Heiu would agree. It would be a very good idea to have someone I had trained myself helping me. We could get so much done!' She was pacing up and down, knocking her clenched fists together in excitement at this new idea. She turned to Fryth, her eyes shining. 'What do you think?'

Fryth did not answer at once. She was pressing her hand to her mouth again. A distant look had come into her eyes.

'Fryth, what do you think?'

Fryth turned to Hildigyth and slowly shook her head. 'I don't think I want to.'

'Why not?' Hildigyth's face had fallen.

Fryth went on thoughtfully, 'Of course I'd like to see the library, and I'd like to see what Gaul is like.' Hildigyth smiled 'But . . .' Fryth paused, biting her lips, 'I think I should go home.'

Hildigyth shot her an astonished look. 'Home? But surely, Fryth, this is your home now? What do you mean, "go home"?'

Fryth spoke slowly. 'I should not have stayed away so long. You have beguiled me with your books and learning.' She paused, seeing the pained look on Hildigyth's face. 'Oh, don't misunderstand me. I don't regret it. I chose to be enchanted but now you're leaving what is there to keep me here? Heruteu *is* your home, but it isn't mine, it never will be. It can't be. It's true, thanks to your friendship, that I am happy here. As happy as I shall ever be again. But I can't lead the life I was meant to lead in this place.'

'How can you say that? You're good at your work. You'll be a very good scholar one day. You will be happier still.'

'But that's not what I was meant to be, a book scholar. I was born a priestess. A priestess's duty is to make the gods happy, not to expect happiness herself.' The distant look came back into her eyes. 'My mother taught me that.' Fryth sighed. 'I'm sure you're right, Hildigyth, I should be happy staying here for ever, reading books. Perhaps even writing.' She smiled. 'I expect I could.'

'I'm sure you could. You could write a better book than mine on medicine now!'

'But that's just it! I shouldn't write books about it. I should practise it! Yesterday Heiu asked me what I had learned about Christianity. I told her that, from what I understood, your religion is a religion of ideas. Mine has to be lived. I need my shrine, I need my spring, I need my . . .'

'People? . . . Oh, Fryth,' Hildigyth's voice was full of anxiety 'you know what you're going to find there, if you manage the journey; and even that won't be easy.'

'The land will welcome me. The river will be there.'

'But your people, where will they be?'

'You see,' Fryth hesitated, then she looked Hildigyth in the eyes, 'I believe that's the greatest difference between us; between my religion and yours. It is *such* a difference. I look about me and see the life in everything. You devote your lives to your own kind. Wulf once told me that my understanding was limited. He said my world was small, but he was wrong. You have the time to think, to have ideas, and write them down, because *your* world is limited and small. I think I would become like that if I stayed here.'

Hildigyth shook her head uncomprehendingly. 'But you value all you've learned here, I know you do!'

'Of course I do. You've given me so much. As well as all you've taught me, you've helped me to understand better what I already knew. But I have never forgotten what my real nature is.'

'I know you haven't, Fryth,' said Hildigyth quietly. They sat in silence for a moment. Fryth felt Hildigyth looking at her, and smiled. She stood up; dusk was falling, filling the room with shadows.

'Both of us have work to do,' she said.